Chapters

Prologue
Chapter 1..................X
Chapter 2..................Monsters in the Forest
Chapter 3..................Questions
Chapter 4..................Confused
Chapter 5..................The Counsel Archives
Chapter 6..................Some Secrets Revealed
Chapter 7..................Escaping from the Tunnels
Chapter 8..................Hansrai
Chapter 9..................The Jin Warriors
Chapter 10..................The Gallows
Chapter 11..................Ghosts in the Woods
Chapter 12..................Traitor
Chapter 13..................Drago Warriors
Chapter 14..................Strategies
Chapter 15..................The Hunt
Chapter 16..................The Assassin
Chapter 17..................Spotted
Chapter 18..................Attack
Chapter 19..................Wizard Caspar
Chapter 20........The Entrance to the Midnight Labyrinth
Chapter 21..................The End of the Traitor
Chapter 22..................Preparing to Escape
Chapter 23..................The Labyrinth
Chapter 24..................Leaving Home
Chapter 25..................Cave Trolls
Chapter 26..................Track of Thorns
Chapter 27........Left Turn at Destruction, Right Turn at Delusion
Chapter 28..................Clash of the Thief and Assassin
Chapter 29..................The End of the Splendor
Chapter 30..................The Cave Troll's Return
Chapter 31..................SoundHarbor
Chapter 32..................Heart of the Labyrinth in Sight

Chapter 33.…………The Face of Seuderak
Chapter 34.…………The End, or Just the Beginning?

**To Ethan, the first to listen to my stories. You're
an awesome brother!**

Prologue

The storm clouds swirled overhead, threatening to develop into a funnel cloud. Lightning seemed to reach down every few seconds, followed by the deep voice of thunder. Little critters and minor monsters scampered to take refuge in the ruins of a destroyed town, which rested in the Northeast part of Ardara.

Standing right outside of the once city limits, a young woman watched silently in awe as the elements seemed to battle each other in a vicious conflict. Her long, dark auburn hair whipped around her beautiful, fair face. Seemingly keeping in rhythm with the storm, her eyes changed color from sea green, to a stormy grey, then sky blue, and harvest gold. Adorning her slender frame was a white sleeveless dress made of an elegant silk. Staring up with her rare eyes, she muttered, "Come home, Guardians. Come home."

There was a loud crackling sound, before a streak of eerie green light shot across the surface of the clouds, almost invisible to anyone down below on the earth. At first it shot forth, taking the shape of a dove, before morphing into the form of a giant arrow. It cut across the bleak clouds and then vanished from sight.

"They are returning?" questioned a muffled, raspy voice.

The young woman tore her gaze from the sky and turned to the man who had appeared behind her. "Yes, my brother, they are."

Hacking miserably, the man's body shuddered. His hands trembling, the man removed his dark hood from his head. "It has been far too long since we have awaited this moment-" He stopped abruptly as he went into another coughing fit.

Grimacing slightly, the woman stepped closer to her brother and laid her delicate hand on his shoulder. "Hadyn, are you all right?" she whispered.

"Y-yes, I am fine," he answered, wiping a drip of blood from his lip with the back of his hand.

The woman sighed, brushing her brother's jet black hair out of his weary face. He looked old and frail, though he was quite young. She knew that if they couldn't find a cure soon, her brother would die. "Soon you will be well."

Her brother nodded slowly, coughing occasionally. "Yes, Kalama, but I am worried."

She frowned, afraid of what he would say next. "What do you mean? The Guardians are returning! All should be fine soon…"

Hadyn glanced at the sky, tears in his eyes. "Though our protectors are returning and I will have my health back-"

"Everything will go back to how it once was. We will be able to fight side by side with our relatives. Once again, Guardians and men will be together again."

Hadyn's face darkened. "Back then, when Guardians still were part of Ardara, times were not how you imagine them in your daydreams. Times were grave then, with wars continually being waged. Bringing back the Guardians also means bringing back the nightmares that once hunted our blood."

Kalama glanced at the sky, where the streak of light had been, and took her brother's hand. *Bringing back the nightmares that once hunted our blood…*

The deafening blast that followed the streak of

shooting light rang through the chilly air. The ground beneath began to tremble as the force of light started to descend to the earth, making way towards a tall white tower that stood on its own a hundred feet away, constructed upon a flat surface of ground. The arrow crafted of light struck the tower with such force, a circle of energy burst forth, spreading over the lands. The sea of long, waving grass twisted and bowed beneath the extreme force.

Along with the loud roar of the energy erupting from the shuddering tower, a low, raspy voice followed the power ring, whispering to the country of Ardara in a menacing tone.

"Now that I am unbound from the curse that you once ensnared me, I will have complete control once again…"

Chunks of stone began to break off from the tower, debris flying everywhere. Two walls started to form out of blue, purple, and red lights from both sides of the tower, stretching out farther than the eye could see.

A long crevice cut its way through the middle of the tower like a knife piercing its victim. Black fog seeped out rapidly, as if more than eager to escape its prison. At the top of the split blasted out a ray of pure white light. The light seemed to take the forms of angels, soaring above the gloomy fog that crept over the earth, spreading quickly.

One of these illuminate shapes took its full form, closing his eyes and breathing in the air. "Free at last."

"But so is Seuderak," a melodious voice of a woman said softly from behind him. Part of the glorious radiance morphed into a woman, with beautiful feathery wings. "We must warn Xanthias and the others."

The other angelic being scowled, his eyes lighting with a bright fire. "Why should we trust him?"

"Because he is the only one we can trust right now," the woman whispered, looking down at the dark mass below, which began turning to the shapes of many, many monsters. Some were large, while others quite small, but no matter what size the beasts were, they were all equally dangerous. The woman turned swiftly towards the other being. "It is our duty as Guardians to protect Ardara, or have you forgotten? We must warn the people, before the monsters devour them."

Chapter 1
X

Lying restlessly upon his hard bed, Chief Xanthias stirred. A voice of an enemy was haunting him in the darkest parts of his troubled dreams. It seemed as his nightmares were about to go to the extreme- as if a wizard of dark magic were interfering-when something startled him awake.

Sitting bolt upright, Xanthias's unusual eyes began glowing immediately. Unlike many of Ardara, Xanthias's eyes were more like small orbs of light, resting where his eyes should be. Though his eyes were only part of his startling appearance. The color of his skin was a midnight blue, almost black, and appeared to have no marks or scars. Other than that, he almost looked human.

Quickly stepping onto the cool stone floor of his chamber, Xanthias eyed his surroundings warily. To any human, or even many other creatures of Ardara, the room would seem pitch black. But to Xanthias, he didn't need light. His eyes were light. Anything living glowed brightly in his vision, while everything else, like any walls, or furniture, glowed faintly.

"Kiran, Kirrat?" he said in his deep voice. He searched again for the white blaze that should be in the place of the two young hunters, but he didn't find anything.

Without warning, the ground began trembling beneath him. Xanthias spun around and strained to look ahead, through the thick walls of his home. His eyes widened as his vision focused on a wall of power soaring towards the village.

Not wasting a moment more, Xanthias flew to the door and flung it open. Rushing through the hall and down the stairs, Xanthias felt his heart thudding against his ribcage. He hadn't seen a force like this since...

"Father!" a boy called from the second floor. "What is going on?"

Xanthias kept running for the front door, but called over his shoulder. "Just stay here! Go get your brother, Kiran, and go underground! If I'm not back in ten minutes, find the others." With his last words hanging in the air, he ripped open the front door and dashed outside.

The sky was lighting up with the vivid strikes of lightning-a strange, eerie green lightning. The air around him was picking up to an extraordinary speed. Some crates and light wagons were being tossed around, while loose doors and windows swung open and shut closed. Somewhere to his left glass shattered and someone screamed.

Then he saw it.

The force that was heading their way.

Xanthias took a deep breath and took a defense stance, placing his hands in front of him. He hadn't used the amount of magic it would take to destroy this energy in years. But it was either save his village and family, or let this power rage onward.

As soon as he had summoned enough power, something hard crashed into his back, before a terrible force struck him from the front. Crushed between both substances, Xanthias began to lose consciousness. Then he felt himself freed and tumbling to the ground, before he completely blacked out.

Akira Darksong stood at the window to the tallest tower of the Drago Castle. The power ring hadn't been able to reach them, because of the force field she had created around the castle. At first she feared that it wouldn't hold up against such energy, but thankfully it had.

"Akira, it is happening, isn't it?" a girl's voice gently called from down the hall. Akira tore her gaze from the scene of the dark citadel below and turned to face the teenager.

"Yes," she whispered, bowing her head. Her blood red hood of her cape hung low over her pale face, obscuring her features. Though one could just notice her quivering lips to know that she was terrified of something.

The young teen looked out the same window Akira had been standing by. "You speak of it often when you think no one is watching or listening..." Akira quickly glanced up as the girl spoke these words. The young Drago Warrior slowly looked back to Akira. "Who is Seuderak?"

Akira hesitated, before turning to leave.

The girl watched her walk off, before calling after her, "You can't keep everything secret from me forever!"

One of the younger guardians landed gently on the ground outside the silent village. At first she was just a ball of pure white light, but slowly she took the shape of a girl, though her form was wispy and almost transparent. Looking around the damaged village, the guardian's face went grim. Fires burned and thick smoke wafted through the stale air.

The guardian slowly stepped forward and walked cautiously onward, into the village. The smoke not harming her, the guardian searched through the rubble and debris.

Xanthias, where are you?

The sound of steal scraping against a sheath reached the guardians ears. Reacting quickly, the guardian spun around to face whoever was behind her. At first she saw no one, but then slowly-so slowly-a shadow appeared in the thick clouds of smoke. The tall man moved forward steadily, holding a claymore sword ahead of him, ready to strike.

"Xanthias," the guardian said softly.

The figure stopped short, before sheathing his sword. "Who is there?"

"Do you really not recognize me, Master Xanthias? Has your sight gone dull?"

Xanthias stepped forward, before stopping only a few feet in front of the guardian. "Harmony?"

The guardian smiled, before catching a glimpse of a boy to her right. She turned to see Kirrat, Xanthias's eldest son. "You have children?" she asked Xanthias, still gazing at the boy.

Xanthias ignored the question. "You escaped. How?"

Harmony looked at him with a grave face. "I do not know how, exactly, master, but I am not the only one that did." She turned in a slow circle as the villagers began to come out of their hiding places. Once she came back around to face Xanthias, she stopped. "When the door to our prison shattered, it let loose hundreds of minor monsters and minor guardians, such as myself. The greater ones cannot escape yet, and are in a heated battle as we speak. But once the doors finish collapsing, the rest will come forth, evil and good." Her form darkened. "And so will Seuderak, once he has gained enough power…"

The guardian's words faded out as Xanthias examined the destroyed village. For the last couple thousand years, he had feared that this day would come. Now, it was upon them. It was time to start using his power again.

Summoning rain from the storm clouds, Xanthias doused the fires that burned around him, and swept away the smoke. "Kirrat," Xanthias called. His son immediately ran to his side, keeping an eye on the guardian suspiciously.

"It is happening," the boy said.

"Yes, just as I feared," Xanthias answered. "Go find your brother."

The teenager nodded and bowed respectfully, before sprinting off.

"Xanthias," someone called from the crowd of villagers who had gathered around. A Nyx Fairy pushed her way towards Xanthias and the guardian, her leathery black and midnight blue wings fluttering slightly as she seemed to float along.

Nyx Fairies were fairies of night. They were the same size of the humans, with pointed ears and wings that were a dark beautiful blue, outlined with black and adorned with dark designs that were the shapes of moons, stars, and wolves. Their skin was pale, almost matching the color of the moon. Their eyes tended to be the shade of jet black or navy blue. Natural tattoos covered their body and face, with a small, delicate quarter moon on the right side of their right eye, then a star by the left eye. Crawling up their arms and legs were tattoo vines of blue and black, creating more shapes of moons, stars, and wild dogs. Their clothing seemed to be made of millions of black webs, connecting to make scenic clothing.

"Xanthias, the chosen," the Nyx Fairy said, inclining her head just slightly.

"Yes, Lilith, I know," Xanthias replied quickly. He looked to the elves, nixies, humans, and fairies of his home. "The time we have all been dreading has come. We must leave our beloved village immediately. Nyx Tribe..." he turned to Lilith and her kin. "Find the other seven. You know whom I speak of."

Lilith inclined her head farther. "Yes, Master Xanthias."

"Alvar, take some of your warriors and scout ahead for a safe passage to the haven-"

"Do you mean, havens, Xanthias?" Harmony interrupted.

"All the havens have fallen to ruin, except for one," Lilith said bitterly. "The farthest one from all the villages."

Harmony's form flickered as she backed away.

Xanthias continued giving orders. "The Siria Tribe, help the Baldhart Tribe and I look for the chosen by scouting ahead for them."

Another fairy stepped out and nodded. She

was very similar to the Nyx fairy, but her skin was a dark tan, her hair was fiery red, her wings were a bright orange with sun, bird, and fire symbols. These images also were formed in the orange tattoos on her arms, legs, and face. On one side of both eyes was the tattoo of a fiery sun. Her clothes were woven of orange and red.

A fairy of the day.

"Yes, sir," the Siria fairy answered.

"Everyone else, stay here and prepare to depart," Xanthias finished. He turned to Harmony. "I will search for the chosen. Where are the other guardians?"

"Xanthias, you must be careful," Harmony warned. "Though many of us are still faithful to you, there are some who have not forgiven you for what you did to us."

Xanthias bowed his head. "I know." He then turned to the villagers. "Hurry along with your jobs." Chief Xanthias then turned back to Harmony. "We must find the chosen."

Chapter 2
Monsters in the forest

Dried leaves crunched beneath Millie Tinsel's small boots as she slowly made her way through the dark forest. She held her bow, her golden eyes darting back and forth, searching for game. Most children of Aselda knew not to go into that part of the forest, but Millie continued onward, heading deeper into the dangerous woods. She knew that this was dangerous, because of the wolves and large, poisonous snakes, but she could take care of herself.

Something moved to her right. The young huntress slowly turned, though her eyes were on the alert. A blackberry bush rustled slightly, causing her heart rate to pick up as she held her breath and lifted her bow, reaching for an arrow.

Screeeech!! The young girl jumped in alarm, dropping the arrow. A streak of green raced toward her so swiftly, she hardly had time to reach for her knife. As the small but deadly creature lunged at her, Millie drove her knife into the roof of its mouth. She fell back, loosening her grip on the handle of the knife. The monster crashed through the brush and out of sight.

What was that thing? The thought swirled around in her mind. It was like something she had never seen before...

Another loud shriek rose up from a mile

away, answered by dozens more. Millie scrambled to stand, half running, half crawling to get away. She could hear the creatures rushing after her. Millie climbed over a fallen log, tumbling to the ground. With her heart hammering against her ribs, throbbing with panic, she quickly stood and began running again. The noise of the little nasty monsters grew louder, until it sounded as if there were a stampede. Up ahead Millie could distinguish a break in the trees. Her mind raced, trying to process what was going on.

The first little beast attacked, leaping at her legs. Millie dropped to the ground, screaming and kicking at the slimy green monster. The creature was a small, round creature with greasy olive green colored skin, big black eyes, a pink nose of a pig, large fangs, and stubby legs, with sharp claws at the end. It was an amazement that they could even run. The little devil howled and started scratching at her legs.

Millie stifled a scream, reaching for another knife-her last-and stabbed the Scroddlerack. It let out a painful squeal before letting go of Millie. To Millie's horror, the Scroddlerack began to melt. Its skin started to steam as it liquefied, goo running down Millie's leg, burning into her skin. She screamed, trying to wipe away the slime. As she struggled to wipe it away, she glanced over her shoulder and saw the hundreds of other little monster like creatures scurrying through the forest, heading straight for her. She groaned and stood, quickly limping forward.

Time seemed to slow as she rushed onward. The shrieks grew louder, almost deafeningly.

The beasts were only a few feet away, right in jumping range when Millie burst out of the forest, running a few feet before collapsing to the soft grass in exhaustion. The beasts howled in disappointment. She glanced over her shoulder to see one attempt to run out of the forest, but immediately as the sunlight hit its skin, it began smoking and then exploded in a slimy fountain of green guts.

"You don't like sunlight?" she muttered, pushing herself up slightly, using her elbows to boost herself up just slightly. A few more of the unusual creatures tried to scurry out of the shadows of the trees, but they only came to the same fate as the first.

Millie shuddered, letting her head fall to the ground. Her leg burned and her head hurt. She didn't know what to do now. If she couldn't find help, who knew what would happen. Was the goo on her leg poisonous? She didn't know anything about these…creatures.

"Monsters," she breathed. It was the only thing she could think of. Maybe they were like the little beasts that had once been the nightmares of the surrounding forests. Millie only knew of this from stories her grandmother had told her.

Zzzzziiiinnnggg!

Millie froze, her heart seeming to leap into her throat. She heard more arrows fly through the air, followed by the little monsters' terrifying shrieks. Millie tried to sit up, looking back to the way she had come. She blinked, narrowing her eyes. Through the forest ran a mysterious figure, shooting down the slimy beasts. A cloud of blue smoke rose up, billowing into the devil like creatures' faces. Panic spreading through the horde, the small monsters turned and fled from the warrior, soon vanishing out of sight.

"Wow," Millie whispered in awe. Then the figure turned and started heading towards the wounded girl. The color drained from Millie's face. Maybe this warrior was evil too. Alarmed, Millie began to try and scoot away as quickly as possible.

After a moment she heard someone behind her, before a hand gently rested on her shoulder. "Calm down. I am here to help you," an older girl said, kneeling at her side.

"Ah…" Millie stared at the peculiar person, trying to decide if she should be scared or not. The girl's features were obscured by a hood, but Millie imagined a smiling face and sparkling eyes. Her sister's face. She knew this warrior wasn't her sister, but that was the only face she could picture in her mind as the girl talked.

"Lean against me and I will take you to a stream not far from here. I have some medicine that will help with the injury." She didn't wait for Millie's answer, but stood, gently lifting Millie to her feet. She was careful not to let Millie fall as they warily made their route away from the forest.

"Who…who are you?" Millie whispered, her voice trembling.

"That does not matter," the stranger replied quickly.

Millie looked up and stared at the stranger, before noticing a silver symbol on a clasp of the girl's cape. It was almost an oval shape, except the top came to a slight point. Inscribed on the clasp were three claw-like marks over an eye, an eye that looked like a cat's eye.

Millie gasped.

"Is something wrong?" the stranger asked flatly.

Millie shook her head, though her expression said differently. There had been rumors that the Alley Cat-the most wanted thief in all of Aselda-wore a clasp with these symbols-

They started heading down a slope and Millie clung to the person so that she wouldn't fall. Her eyes lit up as she saw a small stream snaking around small knolls. Her rescuer lifted her with ease to carry her the rest of the way.

When reaching the stream, the girl set Millie down, placing her legs in the cool running water.

"It will sting a little at first," the mysterious girl forewarned, reaching into a pouch that hung on her belt.

"What were those things?" Millie asked.

The teenager remained quiet as she gently lifted Millie's leg out of the water and began rubbing a salve on the burn. After a moment, she muttered, "I do not know...but I'll find out." Her voice held some bitterness, but was also covered thickly with sadness.

Millie watched, wincing slightly. "Who are you?"

The outsider stood, staring up at the sky. "Go home. Find your family. Speak nothing of this."

"Wait!" Millie said, trying to stand. "Can you help me home-"

"Millie!" a voice drifted over the hills. A

dog barked, before the person called again. Millie looked in the direction where the voice was coming from, her heart racing for joy. "Papa," she whispered. "That's my papa!" She turned to look at the girl who had helped her, but she had vanished.

Arella quietly but quickly made her way back to the forest, watching for the strange creatures she had fought off. Never before had she seen anything like it...A monster, perhaps, but monsters had vanished hundreds-even thousands-of years before. What were monsters to the people anymore anyways? The word 'monster' was only spoken of in the bed time stories mothers told their children to lure them to do what they were told, or to take their medicine. Long forgotten myths and legends might have told about them, but no one hardly knew much of those fairy tales.

Determined that she knew where to find the answers, she began running southwest of the hills and stream, keeping along the edge of the forest, but out of sight from anyone outside the tree line.

She traveled for almost an hour, leaving the forest and soon running across grasslands until she could see Mt. Edavni rising up, the caves that carved into its side making a ghostly face that grinned down at the village that stretched below it.

Her cape flowing behind her, Arella entered the forest that surrounded the village, which carved in a crescent around the south side of the mountain. A stream snaked through this forest on the opposite side of the woods from where she ran, running from the west side of the village to the east, then up north, before bending to snake around the east base of Mt. Edavni. Somewhere in the midst of the beautiful woods, built between two tall, strong trees was a fort. Arella knew exactly where it was, and quickened her pace as she grew closer to the location.

Birds chirped with excitement and dove down to snatch prey from the forest floor. Squirrels and other woodland rodents scurried around. The golden daylight always poured down upon the charming woods of the Elganté forest.

Not seeming to notice the peace and beauty around her, Arella searched for any of the Royal Guard that might be patrolling this part of the woods. None appeared to be close by-and she didn't hear or sense anything, besides the little critters.

Pulling the dark brown hood back over her eyes, she quickened her pace.

Leaves fell upon the forest floor as Arella swung from a high branch, flying through a window to the fort, soaring inside and rolling to soften her landing.

Inside, a pallet of stolen bedspreads sat beneath one of the windows, then hanging in a corner was a hammock. The floor was blanketed by leaves and stolen goods. A painting of a man, woman, and two young children hung on one of the walls, slightly obscured by a hanging cloak, but Arella didn't even cast a glance in its direction.

Her brother, Jared, was no where to be seen, but she wasn't going to worry about it.

Arella shrugged, heading for the hammock. Her brother was thirteen, that was a good age to start going out on your own, trying to fight for your own life. Arella had gone out into the world at a much younger age, also having to watch her baby brother, and she hadn't turned out too bad. She froze in her tracks, a terrible memory scratching at the back of her mind. She *had* turned out pretty bad, no matter how much she lied to herself and her brother. She had made so many bad decisions, chosen to follow the wrong side. Now she felt lost, always running.

Do not think about it, she thought, shaking her head. She could make things right again…somehow. She would figure it out, but at that moment she wanted to rest. She had to think of other matters, like the strange monster like creatures she had discovered.

Arella crawled onto the hammock, but her mind hurt. She was thinking about everything that had happened in her life, not able to push it aside. Everything had gone wrong. The only thing that was good in her life was her brother, Jared. She rocked back and forth slowly in the hammock, before her eyes gradually began to close and she slipped into a troubled sleep.

Her dreams were as dreadful as ever, reflecting her past.

She saw herself at the age of seven, sitting beside her unconscious brother. Tears rushed over her grimy face. She sniveled, growing more and more upset as she thought about what she had done. "Jared…Oh, Jared, I am so sorry!" Arella wailed. Through the blurred veil of the tears, she looked down at the blood on her brother's tunic. "I should not have done it...but I did." She coughed, letting herself fall to her brother's side. "I did not want you to get hurt, that is why I did it..."

Arella lay there, weeping at the thought that her brother would die. She lost track of time, delving deeper into her grief. Soon she began to fall into darkness. She heard whispers around her, before strong arms gently lifted her off the ground. On the verge of unconsciousness, Arella could not make out what the man looked like, but only saw dark blue skin and kind eyes, before she let herself slip into a deep sleep.

She couldn't see anything, but she heard the voices of her rescuers around her.

"We cannot trust this one...Once she is well, she must leave," said a deep voice.

"But she is so young, and she has a brother who is here. We cannot separate them," another man objected, his tone sounding dangerous.

"Think about the safety of our people," the first man replied hastily. "I will send one of my warriors to fetch her when her brother is well."

"I won't let you do this-"

"Please, it is for your safety, for our peoples' safety...You know that she is too dangerous to have here for long..."

The voices faded away and then time seemed to speed up, until Arella saw herself at the age of thirteen, standing before another warrior. The other wore a cloak, its hood covering the man's face. They shouted at each other angrily. Though Arella could not hear their words, she knew what they were saying. The dream form of Arella started to reach for her sword-

BONG!

Arella let out a startled yelp as she fell to the floor, soaked in sweat. It seemed as either the world was spinning, or her head was. She felt nauseous as she crawled to one of the pallets and collapsed.

In her dream it had been as if she had just re-lived ten years of her life. The *worst* years of her miserable existence. Trembling, Arella rolled onto her back, looking up at the ceiling of their fort, a faraway look in her eyes. Those memories that haunted her-they were really like ghosts. Phantom images of her and those she had met in her past, always stalking her, never deserting her.

BONG!

Arella blinked, suddenly coming back to the present fully. She quickly sat up, listening to the melodic call of the castle's bell. After a moment, the bell stopped ringing. Arella stood abruptly, swaying slightly, but she ignored any pain. Pushing away her troubled thoughts, Arella rushed for the exit of their fort.

Chapter 3
Questions

Hiding in the branches of the trees beside the road, Jared eyed the warriors that rode past. One Royal guard sat upon the largest horse, which was in the lead, guiding the others over the uneven road.

The horses they rode upon were black and looked as if they were made from smoke. Red eyes, huge hooves, and being twice the size of a regular horse, these steeds looked terrifying as they marched east, toward the castle. Near the middle of the group two of these horses pulled a large cage. Sitting in the cage was a bulky figure with large black wings.

"What," he muttered, pushing back the hood of his cloak just slightly to try and see more clearly.

His dark purple eyes shone with interest as he watched the cage pass by. He started to lean forward, trying to have a better view, when he almost fell off his perch, but quickly steadied himself as he watched. Two of the Royal Guard abruptly looked in Jared's direction, before continuing to march onward.

Jared sighed in relief. By this time the cage with the large, mysterious figure was already farther down the road. Frowning, Jared quickly looked for any other suspicious monster like creatures they might have, but spotted none.

After the guard's were further down the road, he climbed down from his hiding spot. He had to find his sister and tell her of what he had seen. She might know what the thing was.

Quickly running through the forest, he began making his way east, but stayed far off from the road. Suddenly, in a streak of brown, someone rammed into Jared, covering his mouth with a hand as they rolled down a slope. When they reached the bottom, the attacker was sitting on top of Jared, holding a knife to his throat.

"Arella," Jared muttered, glancing down at the knife. "It's me." The attacker paused, before realizing her mistake. She quickly put her knife away and stood.

"Jared, I cannot let down my guard these days, with the Royal guard always patrolling this route." Arella offered him her hand. "They closed this road from the villagers, just so they can use it for their dirty work."

Jared nodded, taking her hand. "I understand, sister."

Arella pulled him to his feet, before turning to the direction of the road. "What news?"

Brushing the dirt off his pants, Jared looked up at his sister. "They have brought something…"

"What?" Arella questioned.

"I do not know. I did not obtain a good view of it. It was large, with black wings, and was black," her brother answered. "I thought maybe you would know what it is?"

There was a long pause, Arella bowed her head. "No, I don't know. I, too, ran into strange beasts this morning."

"Maybe the Royal guard and the king know about this and they are not telling anyone else about it?"

"Most likely. They are monsters themselves. I hate the Royal guard, the prince, and the adviser," Arella muttered, gripping her dagger.

"And I agree, sister," Jared said as he stepped beside her. "The King-"

"Prince," Arella hissed, gripping the handle of her dagger even tighter. "He's too young to be a king, he's just a prince."

"Uh, Oh-kay." Jared studied his sister's face for a long moment, before saying, "Should we do something about it?"

"Yes," his sister answered quickly. "We will find out for ourselves what is going on…We must go to the archives at the castle."

"You-you mean…Sneak into King Hansrai's palace?" Jared stuttered. "But his…his forces are too strong! His warehouses are heavily guarded and-"

Still seeming determined, Arella turned to

leave. "We have done it before, we will do it again. Besides, we are not going to the warehouses. Do you doubt me, brother?"

Quickly catching up with her, Jared swallowed. "N-no, sister," he said slowly, "but, well, it seems like an impossible job."

"We'll make it," Arella insisted. "The archives have never been well guarded. History no longer matters to anyone."

"Sister, for once, will you just listen to me!" Jared exclaimed, rushing forward and grabbing his sister's arm. He would not dare to look into her eyes as he spoke. "You're the only family I have left," he croaked. "I don't want to lose you. Do you wish to lose me, your only brother?"

His sister took in a deep breath, keeping herself from becoming too angry. "Let go of my arm," she whispered threateningly. Jared sighed, slowly loosening his grip. Arella continued. "We must do this. For our safety, for everyone's safety."

"You do know that that includes the Royal Guard, the k-prince, and the royal adviser," Jared commented. "Oh, and the whole of the capitol. The people that hate us."

"Can you really blame them?" Arella whispered. "I dislike most of them, yes, but I do not believe in unnecessary deaths." Her face turned pale as she started walking again.

"Anymore."

Arella froze in her tracks, before slowly looking over her shoulder. "What did you say?"

Jared sighed and bowed his head. "Nothing."

Chapter 4
Confused

The throne room seemed rather lonely and dull to the young king as he sprawled out upon his throne. He'd had to sit there for almost a year, every day, practically all day long, ever since his father had died. To him, the throne room was nothing much; just a long room, with pillars spaced every six feet apart. Then the black marble throne with the lion's fur spread across it. Carved on the walls were tales about the different kings. The newest additions: King Hansrai the II and King Hansrai the III. The king scowled at the carving of him. He hated everyone calling him Hansrai. He despised that he had a carving of him on the wall, staring back at him like a reflection. All the figures reminded him of his ancestors' failures and that he, new King of Aselda, had to make things right. However, he was too young and inexperienced to make a good king.

Hansrai sighed, his dark brown eyes full of sadness and confusion. An eighteen year old as king. He was sure he'd fail. His people looked to him with admiration and loyalty. On the outside, Hansrai appeared strong and brave, with a dark tan skin tone, medium brown hair that reached his shoulders, and a muscular frame. He was a tall and strapping young man, who most all the girls in the kingdom were *very* fond of. Too fond for Hansrai's liking. Whenever he went out, a mob of girls would surround him like a swarm of bees, their flirting and chatter being the beestings. Hansrai would feel as if he was being trampled on and all he wanted was to escape. If he had to live the rest of his life like this, he would go insane-

"King Hansrai?"

A jolt went through the young ruler, startling him. Floating in front of the throne was a young Shathrack. She had a ghostly look to her, the young girl's body being almost transparent and a light purple. Her face and the top of her appeared to be human, but from the waist down there was nothing but wisps of purple light. "My apologies for disturbing thee, my lord," she said, her voice as quiet and gentle as a whisper. "I have come to see how thee are doing, master."

King Hansrai sighed. "Calista...Um...I'm fine. Is that all you've come for?"

The girl's form flickered as she looked around nervously. "Well, my king, I was sent here by Abraxas. He says that his guards found a creature from the West. They are on their way here as we speak."

"Another?" King Hansrai looked worried. He quickly sat up, his leg swinging harmlessly through the Shathrack's body. "I don't like this." He stood, pacing in front of his throne. "I think it wrong to capture these creatures. They have yet to seem aggressive or dangerous. If the people of the west are really hiding them...I think it is for a reason. They are not dangerous."

Calista followed the king, once or twice the two passing through each other. She sighed as she shook her head. "I am sorry, my lord, but I am just a messenger. I cannot give thee advice."

"Why not?"

The Shathrack stared at him, slightly stunned. "It is not my place. Thee haveth an adviser. Shall I fetch him for thee?"

"No, no," the king said, waving his hand. "You are my friend, and I wish for you to tell me what you think of this."

The color slowly drained from Calista's face, until she went completely invisible. "B-but, my lord...I am just a minor Shathrack. I-I cannot give thee advice, or speak my mind. It is against our ways."

"All I am asking for is what you think about the creatures."

"I...Well," Calista gulped, slowly becoming visible again. "I do not think they are evil. Just big lumbering giants, or tiny cuddly critters. There, thee have an opinion from me, King Hansrai!" With that, she spun around and flew for the doors of the throne room.

Hansrai sighed and dropped back onto the throne. He knew he had just put Calista in danger. If Abraxas found out that she had talked with him about the matter, she would be punished. Hansrai growled, gripping the armrests to the throne, his knuckles turning white. He felt as if Abraxas was ruling over him, instead of Hansrai being the leader. Quickly standing, Hansrai decided it was time for a little talk with his royal adviser.

"Strike harder, Thomas!" commanded the yellow Shathrack as he floated to the side of the arena. He had a mighty large head and nose, with a ridiculous and almost squeaky voice. If no one knew who he was, they wouldn't be able to take him seriously, but the knights in training knew better. If he was angry at you for some reason, he would give a hard punishment.

"Is that a dance I see you doing, Thomas?" he shouted, glaring at the young trainee. "You wimpy, dim headed boy! You're supposed to attack, not ask your opponent out for a dance!"

"I'm n-not, sir!" the young lad yelled as he tried to block an attack.

Abraxas raised his hands and shook his head in exasperation. "If those weren't sticks you're fighting with, you'd be chopped into millions of bits for Scroddlerack food! Move, boy! Move!" He then muttered to himself, "Mere human fighters are nothing compared to the mighty Royal Guard."

Thomas's face went pale at the mention of

"Scroddlerack food". He had seen the slimy green creatures the Royal Guard had found. They were small, but vicious. Shuddering, the young knight tried to lunge at his challenger, but the older knight easily sidestepped and Thomas tumbled forward, falling to the ground.

"No time for a nap, you-you-"

"Abraxas!" Hansrai yelled as he walked down the steps of the stadium as he headed for the arena. Immediately all the knights and Royal Guard stood up respectfully, while the youngest trainees bowed in admiration. Hansrai passed three of the Royal Guard, trying not to twitch much as he walked by the massive warriors. He was tall, but when he stood near one of these fighters, he felt insignificant.

"My king!" Abraxas exclaimed, quickly flying up the steps towards Hansrai. He went straight through one of the trainee's chest, almost giving the teenager a heart attack. "You are here just in time! A couple of the Royal guards' squads are returning, and they have a creature from the West!"

Hansrai sighed. "Actually, that's what I want to talk to you about-"

"Of course, of course." Abraxas waved a hand in the air, beckoning for all the knights, Royal Guard, and trainees to leave. "Leave us and go out to greet our new prisoner!"

Hansrai slammed the door shut, gritting his teeth as he tried to decide how to talk to Abraxas, without letting the Shathrack interrupt him. He turned around and started to walk toward a black wooden desk that stood on the right side of the room, in front of a large rectangular window with long burgundy curtains. Along the two longer walls were tall bookshelves, stalked with old, worn books and scrolls. On the left side of the room was a large fireplace with a golden mantle and a painting of Hansrai's father hanging over it. In front of the fire place was a red and green carpet spread across the dark wood floor, sofas standing around it in a U shape. On the left wall was another window, but this one was smaller, with the same dark red curtains. Standing guard on either side of the window was a statue of a guard. Then lazily walking around the room were a dozen little black dogs. At first they appeared like cute little cuddly puppies, but when one of them looked up to see the king walking in, its eyes turned red and it suddenly grew fangs. Hansrai let out a strangled yelp as he jumped back.

"Why do we keep these things?!" he asked as he scooted past the dogs and quickly sat down in the high back chair that stood behind the desk. It had red velvet cushions, and clawed feet at the end of the legs of the chair.

Abraxas hovered next to him, glancing down at one of the dogs. "They make excellent guard dogs, sire."

"But not very great house pets," Hansrai grumbled. "I would rather have a mastiff."

"No, not a mastiff." Abraxas shook his head. "These dogs are the breed you must have, my lord."

"Can I not select the canine of which I want to have?"

The Shathrack shook his head again. "What you want is not what you need."

"And who decides that?" Hansrai shouted, quickly standing. The dogs in the room growled, the hair on the back of their necks standing on end. "I am the master of myself, I will choose what I shall do."

"Too young," Abraxas said quickly. "Much too young and foolish to make your own decisions. Now, on to other matters. About the beast from the West-"

"I will change the subject when I wish to!" Hansrai walked over to the large window, looking down at the village below. He could barely see that a train of horses were riding through the back streets, a wagon with a huge cage being drawn behind two horses, away from the villagers. "Do not harm the beast," he said through gritted teeth.

"But my lord, these monsters must be dealt with. The chief of the west is surely sending them. If our information is correct, this beast that we captured can speak, unlike the last few. We need answers Hansrai. Answers we could possibly obtain through *it*," Abraxas pressed.

"No! Fighting these beasts...it-it just doesn't feel right," Hansrai said, looking confused, as if he was surprised at himself.

Abraxas rolled his eyes. "My lord-"

"Enough!" Hansrai shouted. With a heavy sigh, he collapsed into his chair and covered his face with his hands. "I will be in my room...Have no one disturb me." After a pause, he glanced up. "And do not harm the beast."

Abraxas started to glare at his king, but

quickly controlled his rage. "Yes, my lord."

Chapter 5
The Counsel Archives

Jared looked around at the counsel archives, at the hundreds of bookshelves, up at the second floor, railings, and the once beautiful glass ceiling that stretched overhead. The glass ceiling was filthy, as if no one cared about it anymore, covered in grime and vines, unable to let in much light. The bookshelves were thick with dust and cobwebs. The floor seemed as if it had once been beautiful, with blue, gold, and silver tiles, but now...the color was faded and filthy. Between the arches were large spider webs, some inhabited by an arachnid that lazily lay on their webbing.

"What happened to this place?" Jared asked, turning in a slow circle. "No one is here and it looks like they haven't been for a very, very long time."

"No one has been here in over a hundred years," Arella said grimly. "This place, these books, our history...It's no longer taken care of. It's a funny thing, how fast important history can be forgotten."

"Why?"

"Well, our people have forgotten our real history," Arella said. "Why is that?" Arella stopped at a set of large, golden-red double doors. "About five hundred or so years ago, the counsel were the only ones aloud in here. They began changing history, as in re-writing it. Then, when the counsel were eliminated, no one was aloud in here. It will be a pleasant surprise if we'll actually be able to read any of this stuff."

"Then why did we come?" Jared asked, stopping beside his sister. He looked at her for a long moment, before looking up at the double doors.

"Because I know of a secret underground chamber..." Her voice trailed off as she walked away from the large doors. "Magic keeps what is inside this chamber safe. Some of that magic has leaked from it and preserves some of this." As she said those words, she ran a hand along a bookshelf.

"Magic?" Jared muttered. "How do you know all this stuff?"

Ignoring his last question, Arella started searching the books, carefully reading the fading titles. "This was built before magic was banned," she said, wincing slightly. "Thousands of years ago. Most of it has faded, but the magic that still lasts protects this place. All we have to do is find where the magic is leaking from."

"How are we going to do that-"

Before Jared could finish, Arella stopped. One of the books on the shelves looked fairly new, it's title very vivid and no dust settling over it. "Find what is still very well preserved," Arella whispered, before reaching for the book.

"Wait, Arella!" Jared exclaimed. "Are you sure it's safe?"

"No, but is anything I ever do safe?" Arella said, before removing the book from the shelf. Jared cringed, ready for the building to start collapsing, or a booby trap to go off, but nothing happened.

Carefully Arella set down the large book on the floor.

"Um...What now?" Jared muttered.

"We find the chamber."

"How?"

Arella stopped, before glancing at her brother. "Shh," she purred, lifting a finger to her lips.

Jared held his breath as he watched her

reach her arm through the space where the book had been. He heard a quiet *clink*, before the sound of stone scraping against stone. The floor beneath him began to tremble and dust blew off the shelves.

"What's going on?!" he shouted, gripping the bookshelf in front of him.

Arella quickly removed her hand and leapt back. "The entrance to the chamber was supposed to be opening, but something is wrong!" she answered, whipping her head around to look at him. There was a loud creaking sound, followed by a loud blast from beneath the floor.

"RUN!" Arella cried, stumbling away. Books started falling off of the shelves, falling in cascades of paper and binding to the floor. Jared's eyes went wide as one of the bookshelves started tipping over, before hitting the shelf in front of it. Soon all of the bookshelves started tilting, hitting others, and causing a domino effect.

"Stay away from the shelves!" Arella warned.

Jared ran after her, keeping hard at her heels. "What is going on?!"

"Some invisible force is-"

The sound of glass shattering cut her off. The siblings looked up as glass started raining down. Arella raised her arms to shield her eyes-or so Jared thought. He dove to his knees, covering his head with his arms.

BOOM! All around him thuds resounded from the bookshelves tipping over.

A jolt went through Jared's body. He cringed, before slowly looking up. All around him were the ruins of the Archives. Billowing clouds of dust drifted through the stale air.

"Arella?" he called, pushing himself up onto his knees.

A cool gust of wind blew through the ruins, the dust swirling. The dirt whirled around like a small cyclone six feet away, before vanishing from sight. Standing where the whirlwind had been was his sister. She stood still and calm, staring at the debris, then slowly looking down.

Jared followed his sisters gaze, before squinting his eyes. Swiftly realizing something, Jared stepped back and stared down at his feet. Around Arella and him were all the remains of the wrecked building, but a circle roughly about four feet in diameter surrounded them. Inside the circle no debris or shattered glass cluttered the floor.

"Some great force is at play here," Arella muttered. Jared looked up at her quizzically.

"What happened?" he asked, walking up to her.

She bowed her head. "I do not know."

"You know something," Jared insisted. "Who placed the…uh, protective circles around us?"

Arella remained silent. She sighed and knelt down. Gently touching the tiles, she whispered, "So much history here…"

"I'm confused, Arella," Jared complained. "What is going on?"

"I already answered that," his sister snapped. "But we are going to find out."

"I don't like it when you say that," Jared grumbled, though he smiled slightly. "Yet…it sounds like a good idea."

"Of course it is, it is my idea," Arella said, starting to make her way through the wreckage. *Though my ideas usually lead to disaster.* "We have to find out what did this."

"And what or who protected us," Jared added.

Arella stiffened slightly. "That is not as important."

"I think it is," Jared remarked.

The two siblings stood right outside of the Archives. Arella crossed her arms, scanning the area. On this side of the castle, no villagers were around to witness what had just occurred.

Everything outside of the Archives looked fine, as if nothing had happened. Arella frowned, scanning her surroundings, before looking up at the roof of the Archives. Thin smoke tendrils rose up leisurely, a thick smoldering smell wafting through the air.

A wizard... She squinted, staring hard at the smoke. The vapors began to morph into the shape of a head-

"Arella...What is that?" Jared called from the other side of the Archives.

Scowling, Arella tore her gaze from the smoke and rushed around to where her brother was standing. "Where...?" Her voice drifted off as she watched something big and black lumbering towards them, running on all four legs.

"A bear," Jared said, though he sounded unsure.

"No…"   Arella reached for her sword. "That is no bear."

"Then what-"

The earsplitting shriek that came from the beast rushing at them surely proved that it was definitely *not* a bear. Jared winced and covered his hands over his ears. As the beast advanced, Arella was able to see it more clearly. It seemed as if it were a mix of a unnaturally giant black bear and a mole. It's body was the body of a bear, but the legs were like those of a mole, the claws being able to tunnel underground, yet they were not too long so that it would not hinder its speed while running. The head was probably the most interesting of all. It was an odd shape, very oval-like, with white streaks. The eyes were completely milky white, and its nose was the nose of a mole.

"Whoa, that thing is ugly," Jared observed.

The mole-bear snarled and leapt into the air.

"I don't think he appreciated that," Arella muttered, before calmly flicking her hand. The monster was suddenly flung to the side, before crashing down.   Arella narrowed her eyes and started rushing at the fallen beast, leaving Jared quite stunned behind her.

The monster shrieked as Arella swung her sword at it. Arella twirled around, before slicing at it again. It quickly stood, spinning around to lash out at Arella. She leapt into the air, hardly avoiding its sharp claws.

"Arella!"

The young thief ducked another attack from the beast. She shot a fleeting glance to her left to see her brother rushing forward to help.

"No, Jared!" Arella hissed. "Stay-" She rolled, escaping another slice from the beast. The monster started to attack her again, when it hesitated. Moments later it turned to face Jared.

"Jared!" Arella yelled. She lifted herself to her hands and knees, moments before she thrust her right hand forward. The overgrown mole screeched as it plunged back down.

Instead of running like he maybe should have, Jared continued to advance, holding his sword out in front of him. Arella growled, standing quickly. Though the monster now lay motionless, she felt as if the battle wasn't over yet.

"Jared, stop-"

Just as the words were coming out of her mouth, the monsters head shot up. In the blink of an eye, Jared suddenly vanished. Arella's eyes widened as she came to a holt. The monster started digging at a rapid rate, quickly delving into the earth. Arella shook her head and growled. After sheathing her swords, she ran as fast as she could, before leaping onto the giant's back.

Arella gritted her teeth as she held on tightly to the thick fur of the monster. She kept her head pressed against its back, gritting her teeth. The monster continued to tunnel beneath the ground, moving quickly.

Finally, the monster broke through to an underground tunnel, falling to the hard floor with a loud thud, stunned. A faint glow from strange emeralds on the ceiling shed just enough light for Arella to be able to see. Not wasting a moment more, Arella took quick breaths, building adrenaline. She rolled off of the giant and drew her sword. The monster tried to stand, but before the large creature could do anything in defense, Arella swung her sword at the monster and severed its neck. Another blow and she cut its head clean off. With a mighty shudder, the headless body fell to the floor again.

"That was easy," Arella muttered, before tossing her sword to the side. She dropped to her knees beside the creatures abdomen and pulled a long knife from her belt. "Hang on, Jared," she whispered as she drove her dagger into the beasts chest and tore it through its stomach. Immediately a rotten stench filled her nostrils.

"Ugh," Arella groaned, covering her mouth and nose with her left arm. "Worst job I have ever had to do." She tried to take a deep breath, but almost vomited. "The things I do to protect you, Jared." Closing her eyes and trying hard to concentrate, Arella lifted her hands in front of the large gash she had created and then made a ripping motion.

Kazuto, one of the youngest of the Royal Guard, made a quick hundred-eighty-degree turn at the end of the tunnel. He took long strides forward, hardly paying any attention to his surroundings. Ever since his training had ended, he had been guarding the underground warehouses that burrowed beneath Mt. Edavni-and the castle.

The guard passed a fork in his path, not even

glancing down the other tunnel. He walked a little farther, until stopping at a thick wooden door, listened, and then continued on. Everything was as usual-quiet, dull, and musty. Nothing irregular happening.

Coming to a crate and barrel-which Kazuto used for a table and chair-the young guard sat on the large crate and closed his eyes.

THUNK!

Opening one eye, Kazuto glanced both ways down the tunnel. For a moment, nothing. Then he heard a noise that sounded like something struggling, before another dull thud. Sitting up, Kazuto narrowed his eyes. He sniffed the air, before his eyes turned bright red. Humans. There were humans in the tunnels.

Arella gasped as she watched the black and gold dust floating around her. The only other remains from the monster she had vaporized were three large gel like sacks that encased three humans-one being her brother. In the other two were a man and a little girl. The captives didn't look dead, but stunned, mouths and eyes wide open with fear. Their skin was almost completely white, and their eyes were the only part of them that seemed able to move, giving them a ghostly appearance.

Gripping her knife, Arella placed her other hand on the gel bag that encased her brother. She carefully tore her dagger through the bag, cautious not to harm her brother in the process. As soon as she was finished, the color began to come back to

Jared's skin as fresh air touched his flesh, though he still seemed frozen. His clothes were soaked from a bluish liquid that he was laying in.

Scowling, Arella dipped a finger in the cold fluid. Almost instantly her finger went numb. Arella winced and quickly pulled her finger out. This stuff was all over her brother, no wonder he couldn't move.

The distant sounds of boots slamming on the floor came from the hallway. Arella glanced over her shoulder, suddenly realizing where they were...

"Jared-" Arella stood quickly. "We're in the stockrooms," she said, bending over to swiftly snatch up her sword. After this, Arella examined the room. There were plenty of crates to use as cover, but by the sounds of things, there might be too many guards.

Looking back at Jared, Arella's heart started to feel heavy. Her brother stared at her pleadingly. Shaking her head, Arella turned and started to run out of the storage room.

Chapter 6
Some secrets revealed

The stillness was about to drive him insane. Of course, many things seemed to be driving him crazy after he had been crowned king. Sure, he wanted to be alone, but this-this was maddening.

The king lay on his royal bed, frustrated as he tapped a finger on his chest. His mind was spinning as he tried to decide what to do. He wanted to believe Nicanor, but Abraxas insisted on them making war with the West. Nicanor was relentless on saying that the monsters hadn't come from the West. Yet, when the Royal Guard had come back from invading the West, they had reported many beasts living there. However, the few that they had brought seemed peaceful, unlike the ones that had been spotted in the forests.

"Troubled, my lord?" said a deep voice. Hansrai sighed and turned his head just slightly to see the purple Shathrack floating near the bed.

"Nicanor, why are you here? I asked not to be disturbed."

The Shathrack nodded as he flew over to the window, giving a quick glance outside. "We do not have long my prince, but I must speak with you."

Hansrai sat up slowly. "What is it?"

"The chosen ones are near. You will be going on your quest soon," Nicanor said quietly, as if he was afraid someone unwelcome was listening.

*Not this again…*The king sighed. Nicanor

had been telling him for a while about some quest that he would soon be going on. "So?" Hansrai said, rubbing his head. "We find them, greet them, and then go. I'll make an announcement-"

"No!" the Shathrack exclaimed. "No, not that. It won't happen that way."

"Why not?" the king asked, becoming puzzled. Ever since Nicanor had mentioned this 'prophecy' and *The Midnight Labyrinth*, everything in his life began to become more perplexing than ever.

"I'm sorry my king," Nicanor said, a far away look in his eyes. "I wanted to tell you the prophecy, but I have run out of time. Forgive me."

"What-"

"Save them. Do whatever you have to, but don't let Abraxas kill them."

Hansrai frowned. "Why would he want to kill them if they are the chosen ones?"

Before the Shathrack could answer, the castle bells deep voice blasted through the air. "The alarm," Hansrai muttered, looking to Nicanor as if to demand for answers.

"I am sorry, my king, but I have not the time to explain." Nicanor's form flickered. "Go, quickly! Whatever you do, do not listen to Abraxas, he will try and stop you!"

"But-"

"Please, my king," Nicanor implored. "Do this for your people. It is time for you to begin making your own decisions."

His own decisions. That sounded good enough.

Hansrai jumped out of the bed, running for

the door. He glanced over his shoulder to the old Shathrack, but he was gone. The king sighed, not knowing exactly what to do. Swinging open the double doors, he rushed out of his chamber and into a long hall. Suddenly the idea of making his own decisions didn't sound so good. What if he made mistakes? And he didn't know if the other two "chosen" ones would listen to him. Did they know about it too? Also, were all the fairy tales Nicanor told him about true? Too many questions. Of course, he had been waiting for this for far too long. He was ready for adventure.

A dozen of the Royal Guard rushed towards one of the storage rooms, where the human scent was strongest. However, when they entered, their senses began to go erratic. A strange odor mixed with the human scent, drilling an awful aching into the Guards' heads. This other scent that merged with the humans' was foreign to them. The lead guard roared and rushed forward, losing concentration, before tripping over three strange, gel-like sacks.

The other guards behind him slowly walked forward, narrowing their eyes as they tried to look at what the other guard had tripped on. Their sight had gone fuzzy ever since catching a breath of the unfamiliar odor. Whatever it was, they didn't like it.

One of the Royal Guards bent over and sniffed one of the sacks, before snarling. "Monsters," he rasped to the others.

Another heaved a club over his shoulder.

"One of them must have got out."

The one who had sniffed at the gel sack shook his head. "No, this one is different from the others."

"There is something in the sacks," a fourth grunted, kicking at one of them.

"Possibly eggs with infant monsters," the first said, standing and brushing himself off. "Or the humans."

"Let's find out," the second one snarled, bending down and ripping part of the gel sack. What he found inside was something he hadn't expected. A smaller one of the Royal Guard lay inside, petrified.

The first guard scowled and leaned in for a closer look. "What-"

"Surprised?" a hooded form hissed from behind them.

The Royal Guards in the back caught her scent, but it was too late. Two of them fell to the floor, dead, before they could even unsheathe their weapons. In a quick motion, the figure twirled around, slicing her two swords through two more of the guards.

Four down, eight more to go. The warrioress charged at the guards fearlessly, wielding her swords with amazing skill. She stabbed one guard, before deflecting an attack with her other sword.

"Rrr!" another girl screamed from deeper in the underground storage room. Four of the guards stayed trained on the first woman, while the other three turned to attack the second. Something moved behind a stack of crates, before a small pouch was flung at them.

One of the guards caught it and barred his fangs. "What's this?" he asked, before squeezing the pouch. As the material broke, a cold liquid splattered over his hand. Instantly his hand began to throb, a split second before it went numb.

"Arrgghh!" the guard barked, doubling over and clutching his wrist. As he did this, he only made the strange liquid cover more of his body, including his chest and stomach. Moments later he was on the floor, frozen in place. The other two guards stepped away, not sure what to do next.

Suddenly a cry rang out to their left. They spun around to face the oncoming enemy, but as soon as one was cut by the girl's sword, he began to freeze like the other had. The third jumped back to avoid contact with the sword. The girl leapt at him, swinging her sword violently.

The guard grimaced as the sword passed inches away from his face, his senses going haywire again. The sword had the strange scent all over it, almost like the warrioress had rubbed the monsters blood on the blade. Whatever it was, the guard knew that he couldn't even be scratched by her weapon. Instead of fighting back, the guard retreated, staying far enough out of the girl's reach.

Growing irritated, the girl growled and thrust a fist at him. He was too far away for her to physically reach, but the Royal Guard felt a force knock into him, sending him reeling backwards. He tripped over a small crate and dropped to the floor. For a moment he was stunned, trying to collect his thoughts. When he finally seemed to think partially clearly, the girl was leaping at him, her sword slicing through the air, heading right at him.

The guard rolled, avoiding the sword-almost. He quickly moved to his feet and turned to face the girl, but she didn't rush at him. She just stood there, staring at him with icy blue eyes.

That's when the guard felt the stinging on his cheek, but it faded quickly after that. As the stinging faded, his tongue, cheek, and mouth went completely numb. The numbness spread rapidly, until he couldn't stand. With a muffled groan, the guard toppled over.

Smirking, Arella turned away from her defeated enemy. The other woman stood over one of the guards, roughly ten feet away from Arella. She brought her sword down for a deathly blow to her fallen enemy, driving her sword into the guard's chest.

Arella cocked her head to the side, watching suspiciously. She didn't know who this person was, but she had helped her. Possibly another thief.

For a few minutes, no one spoke. Arella looked around in amusement at the guards they had taken out as she cleaned her sword. The other warrioress began moving the either dead, or petrified bodies behind crates, careful not to let the liquid that was on some of the Royal Guard touch her skin.

"Who are you?" Arella finally said, glancing up at the stranger. She didn't answer, but looked out the doorway and both ways down the hall.

"Where is your brother?" the woman asked, sheathing her swords on the scabbards strapped to her back.

The young thief watched her carefully,

narrowing her eyes. "Master Cairo. Do you know that name?" Arella questioned, trying to look at the woman's face, but her features were obscured by her hood.

The warrioress hesitated. She was about to answer, when shouts came from the tunnels. "We should leave," the woman said. "Quick, get your brother."

Chapter 7
Escaping from the tunnels

One of the Royal Guard roared as he charged towards the monster that stood before him. When he was only feet away, though, a long tongue whisked out of the strange creatures mouth and whipped around him. The beasts tongue rolled back into its mouth and it quickly swallowed the guard.

The rest of the guards backed away, glaring at the large monster. Their senses were scattered, also causing their eyesight to go fuzzy. After a few of the guards had been consumed by the monster, the other guards had stayed back, far out of reach of the whipping tongue. In defense against the beast, they were firing crossbows, warding off the monster for only a moment.

With an enraged snarl, the beast rushed at the guards. The guards shouted at it, but stood their ground, showering arrows upon the creature. The monster bellowed as it crashed into the front defense lines, before collapsing onto more of the guards.

For a moment, no one moved. The guards stood or lay still, keeping all eyes on the beast.

After the long pause, one of the larger guards moved forward and prodded the beasts head with the butt of his spear.

"Dead."

The guards cheered, some jeering at the defeated beast.

A smaller guard lumbered over to the one who had checked the beast, staring at the dead monster. "A monster from the West?" he asked, holding the ghostly eyes of the creature in his gaze.

The leader bared his fangs. "No." He turned to the rest of the guards. "The time has come. Seuderak will rise again!" The Royal Guard raised his spear and snarled.

"Seuderak?" Arella muttered, hiding behind the crates with the warrioress, her brother, and the other two they had saved.

Jared grunted. "The wizard from the myths?"

"Yes."

Arella and Jared looked to the warrioress. She ignored their stares. "We must leave," she hissed, "before the guards senses fully come back."

Strange day, Jared thought. *More so than normal. First, we visit the Archives, then we're attacked by a monster-which isn't supposed to be real-and I'm swallowed by it. My sister used magic. Now Seuderak is real.*

The juvenile bandit shuddered and followed, watching the warrioress help the man and Arella guide the little girl that had been trapped inside the monster with him. "What is going on?" he muttered under his breath.

"Hurry," the warrioress purred. "Unless you wish to be killed. More of those monsters are bound to come back."

Jared didn't need to be told twice. He quickened his pace, wincing at his still slightly numb legs. Though he no longer had the cold slime on him, he could still imagine how it felt. If more of those beasts were coming, then he wanted out of there.

"Humans!" one of the guard's voices echoed down the tunnel. Arella and the warrioress exchanged glances.

"Run," the warrioress said urgently. When Jared slowed down, the woman glared at him. "Run, you foolish boy!"

Jared nodded and started running forward, almost tripping once or twice. "Do we know where we're going?!" he exclaimed.

"Yes, I know the way out," the warrioress answered, dragging the old man along behind her. "Hurry, sir, we have to move."

The man gasped and tried, but almost collapsed. If the warrioress hadn't been helping him, he would've fell.

"Grandpa!" the little girl cried, clinging to Arella. The thief bit her tongue to keep from scorning the girl.

"Don't stop!" she grumbled, trying to push the girl forward.

"But-"

"You won't help your grandfather if you-don't-move!" Arella groaned and quickly scooped her up.

"They're gaining on us!" the warrioress hissed, pulling the old man onto her back. "Run faster!"

Arella nodded and picked up her speed. Even with the burden of another person, Arella and the warrioress were quicker than Jared. Soon they were five, six…seven feet ahead. Jared gasped for air, growing weaker. Whatever that liquid was, it had drained the energy from him.

"A…Arella!" Jared hollered as Arella and the warrioress disappeared around the corner. He ran a few more steps, before dropping to the floor. His vision was distorted and his head throbbed. Where was his sister? How far behind were the guards? Jared groaned and struggled to crawl forward.

"There's one!" a guard shouted from behind him.

It's over.

Jared winced as he thought this, knowing that the guards would surely kill him only moments later.

"Jared!" Arella's voice seemed distant and unclear. He lifted his head to see a blurry streak rush past him and at the guards. He heard the guards' shouts and a loud cracking sound, before he felt someone picking him up.

"How many times do I have to save you?" his sister complained. "I thought I healed you already."

Jared grinned. "I guess I-"

"No time for chitchat," Arella clipped. Jared felt a shock go through his body and winced.

All the energy he lost seemed to come back. His sight became more clear, or at least, it seemed to…Jared shook his head and blinked, staring at a mass of unconscious guards.

"Did you…?"

"Jared, come on!" Arella yelled, grabbing his hand. "We have to get out of here!"

Hansrai saw Abraxas out of the corner of his eye. He quickly spun around, keeping his hand ready on the hilt of his sword. "Abraxas, I demand that you-" He stopped short when he looked down the empty hall. No one was there but him. The king frowned, positive that he had seen the Shathrack moments before. "Abraxas?"

No answer.

The alarm bell rang again. Before leaving, Hansrai gave one more thorough look down the hall, before turning around and heading for the east side of the castle again. He jogged down several more halls and ascended a set of stairs, before coming upon another hall.

He ran through the hall until he pushed open a pair of doors and rushed out onto a balcony on the east side of the castle. The terrace overlooked part of the village, the stream, and the entrance to the channels that tunneled beneath the mountain. Two hooded figures burst out of the entrance and ran for the stream, one of the Royal guards right behind them. The guard gripped the end of the cape that one of the thieves was wearing and yanked back on it. The thief screamed-a girl's scream. Hansrai's eyes grew wide as he watched while the Royal guard drew his massive sword.

"NO!" he yelled, gripping the railing to the balcony. But the girl quickly spun around and raised her hands. An invisible force knocked into the Royal guard and sent him flying backward, ripping the thief's cape. The girl swiftly turned and ran to the other bandit, as more guards poured out of the entrance.

"Magic," Hansrai murmured, watching as the two grew closer to the stream. He stumbled back, feeling even more lost. Only the master of dark magic, Seuderak, and his wizards used magic.

"Run! Quick, get to the stream, you know what to do next!" Arella screamed to her brother. When he hesitated, she shouted, "Go! I will hold them off!"

"What about you?" he called. Arella shook her head and then raised a hand at him. One moment his feet were planted safely on the ground, but the next, he was spinning through the air. He landed on a bush, on the other side of the stream. But his sister didn't follow. She turned to face a small, but lethal army of the Royal guard.

"Arella!" Jared exclaimed, starting to run toward her. She looked back at him for just a moment, slightly nodding as she said something. Probably, *go*. Jared swallowed hard, before turning and running for the forest. Behind him something exploded. He took the risk of looking over his shoulder and saw a wall of water from the stream shooting up into the air. "What..." He stopped and waited, hoping to see his sister.

No sign of her.

"Arella!" Jared hollered, trying to see through the wall of water. "Arella-"

A loud shriek came from the sky. A griffin and giant eagle flew through the air, searching for their prey. His eyes widening, Jared let out a startled yelp and backpedaled as quickly as he could. The griffin spotted him and dove down at a sharp angle, reaching out to catch him. Jared hollered and dove to the ground-but not quick enough. The griffin's sharp talons ripped through Jared's cape, before snatching him up.

Jared shouted and tried to wriggle out of the griffin's grip, but soon the large bird was soaring through the air again. "Whoa!" Jared hollered, feeling dizzy as the land flew by beneath him. He saw Arella fighting off the guards, not seeming to notice Jared was flying overhead.

The griffin circled over the battle, as if wanting Jared to watch. After a few minutes, the wall of water crashed down. The eagle that had accompanied the griffin swooped down and attacked Arella, chasing the thief into the forest beyond the stream.

Chapter 8
Hansrai

Jared yelled defiantly at the griffin as it flew toward the castle. Once or twice he glanced back to see if the eagle was following with his sister, but it had vanished from his sight. Maybe Arella had defeated it? He wished he had her strength and power, even if he didn't know where she acquired it from.

The griffin circled around the castle, making Jared feel sick to his stomach. Finally after what seemed like hours of flying around and around the black fortress, the griffin dropped Jared while soaring over a balcony on the east side. A young warrior stood on the terrace, almost as if he had been waiting for him. Though the knight looked strong and brave, he had a stunned and somewhat unintelligent look on his face.

"Who are you?" he asked.

Jared gritted his teeth as he stood. "First, who are you?"

The young man narrowed his eyes as he glared at him. "King Hansrai the III."

Jared glanced up at him, before quickly looking away, stuttering as he spoke. "You...You're King Hansrai?"

The knight stared back. "Yes. Now, who are you and where is the second one?"

"Second what?" Jared asked, trying to sound confused.

King Hansrai growled in frustration. "The other thief. Do not play games with me. I know there is one other...A girl. She goes by the name, Alley Cat."

"Well, technically, she doesn't. Everyone just calls her that-"

"Enough!" Hansrai grumbled. "Tell me, who are you?"

Jared went quiet, staring at his boots. When the griffin had dropped him, his hood had fallen over his face, thankfully. He hadn't risked the chance of looking up for long and now he didn't know what to do. From the northeast side of the castle more griffins were being set free from their cages. He had to do something, and he had to do it quick.

"I said, who are you," the king demanded.

Jared shook his head. "I'm never going to tell you, and I won't let you capture my sister-" He bit down on his tongue and clamped his mouth shut.

King Hansrai raised an eyebrow. "Sister?"

Jared swallowed hard. The king drew his

sword, and Jared knew he was dead. The sword tip felt cold against Jared's throat. He took in a deep breath and waited for death.

Arella stumbled down a slope, almost running into the base of a tree at the foot of the incline. The eagle was probably close behind, though she didn't hear it. Hopefully her brother was safe. Maybe he had made it back to their fort.

The sky suddenly turned dark, as the deafening noise of dozens of wings filled the air. Arella slowly looked up. The sky was full of griffins and eagles, all set loose to hunt her and her brother down, most likely. Her face turned pale while she watched one of the griffin's dive down, its talons ready to shred her to bits.

Arella drew her sword in a quick motion and swung it in an arch toward the eagle, slicing through the eagle's right wing. The eagle shrieked in pain as it crashed down to the ground, splintering wood flying in every direction while it tore through the trees.

Arella glanced from the wounded eagle, to the birds in the sky. They now knew where she was. Taking a deep breath, Arella dashed off to find a hiding place.

King Hansrai eyed the young lad that stood before him, guessing that he was about thirteen, fourteen years old. He slowly lifted his sword and used the tip to lift the hood off the thief's head. The bandit looked up. Dark chocolate brown hair that was just long enough to hang in front of his dark purple eyes, a small and faint scar on the left side of his face, near his ear, a determined and strong look- Hansrai stumbled back, his eyes growing wide. "Who-who are you?" he stuttered, his mind spinning.

The bandit wore a mental mask that hid any emotions. He stared at the king with those violet eyes, drilling through Hansrai, making him feel cold and confused. He had seen this thief before. He didn't know how, but he had. Something at the back of his mind told him that he had.

"Why does it matter? You don't care about your people. You don't care about what will happen if a war starts. What happened for your heart to turn so cold?" the thief said, his voice clear and strong as he stared king Hansrai in the eye. "So, tell me, what does it matter to know what my name is?"

Hansrai's throat felt dry. "I…it's not me," he managed to say.

The thief smirked. "Then who is it?"

"It's…" Hansrai frowned, feeling as if he had just been crushed.

"Just as I thought," the boy said. "You're a terrible ruler."

A scream rose up from the forest, followed by the angry shriek of a griffin. The young bandit rushed to the balcony railing, gripping it as he gazed at the woods. "Arella," he whispered, his heart racing.

"What?" King Hansrai asked, stepping

forward. "Please, I want to help you-"

"Yeah right." The bandit shook his head and leapt over the stone wall of the balcony.

"Wait, no!" Hansrai yelled, trying to grab him, but he couldn't. The thief fell, until he landed on the back of a griffin. Hansrai ran a hand through his hair, watching as the bandit fought with the giant bird. He shook his head and tried to think of what to do.

Jared growled, gritting his teeth as he tried to keep his grip on the griffin. The bird shrieked in fury, trying whatever it could to knock Jared off, but the young and agile boy somehow remained on its back.

It flew around wildly, not willing to let Jared stay on his back. It swooped down low, near where Arella was fighting off a swarm of the large birds. When the bird was only a few feet from the ground, Jared leapt off its back, landed, and rolled to soften his landing. He quickly stood and drew his sword, ready to help his sister, but unexpectedly the birds flew off as one, shrieking in terror.

Jared watched them in confusion, before spotting a billowing cloud of smoke. The color drained from his face as he watched fire streak through the atmosphere, at moments taking the form of a fiery red bird.

"A phoenix," Arella muttered, walking up to him. "Run."

"What?"

"RUN!" Arella screamed. Moments later

the fiery bird started to dive down. Arella grabbed Jared's arm and they both started running as fast as they could, but it was too late. The flaming bird dove down and scooped up the siblings, flames enveloping them.

Arella expected to feel the burning of the fire, but was surprised when the flames swirled harmlessly around her. She tried to look for Jared, but she couldn't see him through the blaze.

The bird let out a deafening screech and flew for the castle. It soared to the south side, where a giant gate was being opened. The phoenix flew inside, before dropping them to the cold floor and then shooting out. The gates were shut immediately and everything went dark.

"Arella!" Jared exclaimed, making his sister flinch in alarm. "Why? Why didn't you tell me? What else have you been keeping secret from me? What's next, I'm not even your brother?"

"No!" Something moved to Jared's side. "Do not think that way! I am your sister and you are my brother. I have not held anything from you that I should not have. It was for your own good. Now let us stop bickering and find a way out."

Jared swallowed, trying to let his eyes adjust to the dark. "I met someone when the griffin brought me here."

Arella was silent for a moment, before she shuffled her feet nervously. "Who?"

"The king," he answered, waiting for Arella's sharp response.

Instead, Arella hesitated. "And?"

"He wanted to know who I am," Jared answered slowly. "He...he wanted to know who you are. I accidentally said that I was your brother."

"I guess it doesn't matter now." Arella sighed. "Unless we can think of a way to escape, we're both dead. I am sure they will be happy to hang us for our crimes. And with that griffin out there…"

Was his sister giving up? Jared couldn't believe it. His sister was supposed to be sharp thinking, nimble, and keen. She couldn't just quit. Suddenly a sliver of light appeared ten feet away, until two large doors swung open. Jared grimaced and raised his hands to cover his eyes from the bright light.

"Gah, what's that light?" Jared complained.

"Whoa," Arella muttered in amazement.

"What? What is it?" Jared asked.

"Jared, l-look."

Slowly, Jared lowered his arms and stared toward the light. At first he couldn't make out anything, but then gradually his eyes adjusted to the light. Down a small flight of steps, in a room painted white, little people walked about, watching floating images of heroes and heroines from the past. Jared stumbled down the stairs as he gawked at the images. The short little individuals ignored Jared and Arella's presence, walking around them and not once glancing in their direction.

"What is this place?" Arella muttered under her breath, turning in slow circles as she looked around at the images.

"Maybe we're dead," Jared thought aloud.

"No, not dead." Arella reached out to touch a floating image, but the man in the picture scowled at her and drew his sword. Arella frowned at him and stepped back. "The images are alive."

"Creepy. Are you sure we aren't dead?" Jared asked, jumping to avoid a floating picture of a stern looking woman.

"Yeah…Let's get out of here," Arella muttered, looking around the room, which was rectangular. The walls, floor, and ceiling were painted white, with one window on the north wall. On the south side was the steps that they had gone down, then on the east wall was a door. "I think we should go through there."

"It is probably just a trap," Jared said, glancing down at two miniature women that walked by.

"Well, we can either stay here with these strange people and ghostly images, or try to find a way out." Not waiting for an answer, Arella headed for the door. Jared growled in frustration, but quickly followed.

Behind them two of the pictures slowly turned, until facing them. One picture was of a man with dark blue skin, the other of a woman wearing a black cloak. The two looked at each other, and the woman nodded.

Arella came to a quick halt, before looking over her shoulder. Two blank pictures hovered in the middle of the room, like two white eyes following them. Arella scowled, wondering why there would be two blank pictures here.

"Arella?" Jared called.

Shaking her head, Arella started walking again towards the door.

Chapter 9
The Jin Warriors

King Hansrai stood behind the desk, glaring at one of the little black dogs that stared back at him, sitting next to one of the couches. The dogs had gone surprisingly quiet, once the *Jin Warriors* had come in and made themselves comfortable on the sofas. Hansrai didn't trust either of the residents in the room. The Jin Warriors appeared human, but very…unusual. Their leader, a female, stood in front of the fireplace, the hood to her dark red cape concealing her face, except for her chin, which seemed almost ashen.

Leaning back in his chair, Hansrai tried not to pay much attention to the massive warriors that lounged in front of him. They all had dark tan skin, with black masks. The masks were the worst of all. They were in a strange shape to make hideous looking creatures. Hansrai shuddered and quickly looked away. He hoped the chosen ones would be transported to the room quickly. He glanced from the door, to the warriors, and then to a few scrolls on his desk. *I hate being king*, he thought.

"Do not think that way, young king," the female warrior hissed, never looking up from the fire.

Hansrai nearly jumped out of his royal skin. He had almost forgotten that the Jin Warrior was a mind reader. *Please don't do that. Stay out of my head.*

The woman laughed slightly, but her laugh was cold and evil sounding. "If you wish for me to."

Yeah, I really do.

The female warrior inclined her head slightly, before turning to look out the window on the west side of the room. Hansrai slumped in his chair, exhaling somewhat loudly as he tapped a hand on the table. If the chosen didn't show up in five minutes and he had to be stuck in that room with the Jin Warriors, then he didn't know what he would do.

There was a knock on the door, and Hansrai quickly sat up. "Come in!" he called.

The door opened and Calista floated inside, followed by the bandit Hansrai had spoken to earlier, and then a girl, who was a few years older than the boy. She had long dark brown hair that was tangled and dirty from her fight with the different kinds of birds that had attacked her. Bright blue eyes searched around the room, before coming to rest on the Jin Warriors, when they narrowed. The Jin Warriors, minus their leader, glared back. She didn't even flinch at the sight of their masks.

The boy stepped further into the room, towards the dogs. Hansrai was about to say something when one of the dogs leapt to its feet, snarling and barking at him. The bandit jumped back in shock, his face illustrating his surprise as he retreated a few steps back to his sister's side. The girl, however started to walk towards Hansrai, walking right through Calista as if she wasn't even there, which seemed to anger the Shathrack deeply. She walked past the dogs, who at first barked at her, but then cowered away. Finally, she came to the right side of the desk, where she rested her elbow on it and leaned forward toward King Hansrai. "You wanted to speak with us?"

Hansrai stared at her, not knowing what to say. She looked absolutely beautiful, with a perfect complexion, a deep lovely tan, and stunning blue eyes, yet she had a deadly look in her stare, as if she was warning him not to mess with her.

"Uh...Y-yes," Hansrai stuttered. He looked to the Jin Warriors. "Leave us."

The warriors stood and bowed before they left, along with Calista. The last to leave was the female warrior, who glanced in the girl's direction suspiciously. The Alley Cat glared back, her head moving to her side. With an amused smile, the Jin Warrioress lifted a finger to her lips, before walking out.

As soon as the door was closed, the girl rushed at Hansrai, quickly drawing a knife and putting it to his neck. "Now what do you want?" she hissed, staring hard into his eyes.

"Uh, it would be greatly appreciated if you removed the knife from my neck, so I will be able to speak more comfortably," Hansrai said, staring down at the knife, almost going cross-eyed. The Alley Cat narrowed her eyes as she looked Hansrai over. Slowly she backed away, quickly slipping her knife into her boot.

"I'm listening."

Hansrai sighed in relief, wiping some sweat from his brow. "H-have a seat, please."

The girl and boy looked to the dogs and then back to Hansrai.

"Oh..." Hansrai shrugged, glaring at the little demon dogs. "Well, I could stand, if you would like to have a seat, Lady...What is your name?"

The girl stared at him, but she slowly relaxed. "My name is Arella."

"Arella," Hansrai whispered, gazing at her. "I am-"

"I know who you are. Is it not obvious? Even if I did not know who you were, once I saw you in this room, with your royal clothes and hat-"

"It is a crown," Hansrai muttered.

"-I would know that you are King Hansrai the III," the girl finished, as if he had never interrupted her. She leaned back against the desk, looking at the floor as she waited for him to speak.

The boy snickered and walked over to stand at his sister's side. Hansrai glared at him. "You still have failed at telling me *your name*," Hansrai declared, jabbing a finger accusingly in the boy's direction.

The young thief looked amused. "Well, forgive me for not making you happy, my lord." He gave a cynical bow, a sneer spread across his face. "But after being chased by your birds and having the point of your sword at my throat, I was feeling unwelcome."

"How do you think I felt with your sister having a knife to my own throat?" Hansrai retorted.

The boy laughed, shaking his head. "Fine. Since my sister has given you her name, which means she must trust you a little, then I shall tell you mine." He gave another mocking bow. "My name is Stupidity the XXV."

Hansrai's face burned red with rage. "Something tells me that is not your real name."

Arella frowned, raising a hand. "Quiet down, majestic boy." Hansrai frowned at the name. Arella ignored him and continued on. "My brother's name is Jared. Now, what is it that you wanted to talk to us about?"

"I want to help you," Hansrai started.

The boy who's name was Jared-unless it was another trick, Hansrai thought-started laughing. "You. Help us? Oh, come on, you cannot fool us. Someone from the royal family-a king, helping thieves? That has *never* happened in all of the History of Aselda."

King Hansrai raised an eyebrow questioningly. "You have poured through scrolls and books that hold our history?"

Jared stopped, his face turning red from embarrassment. "Well, no...but know one has ever heard of something like that happening. Why would a king want to help minor villagers like us? I mean, my sister and I are criminals. What could you possibly receive from us?"

Hansrai sighed, massaging his temple as if all this was giving him a headache. "Because we three are supposedly chosen ones from a prophecy."

Jared sniggered and started to say something, but Arella slid across the desk until she was right in front of Hansrai, looking as if she was interested in what he had to say. Hansrai hesitated, before he stood slightly and scooted the chair back, farther away from Arella.

"Anyways, we are supposed to pull together and travel through the fabled *Midnight Labyrinth*," Hansrai finished.

Arella was quiet for a long moment, staring down at her boots and then up at the king. Finally she spoke. "Have you read the prophecy yourself?"

Hansrai shook his head. "No, but Nicanor, my father's adviser, told me about it. I do not know the exact words though, or what exactly it means."

"How do you expect us to believe you?"

Jared questioned.

Hansrai eyed him warily, wondering how he was going to convince them. "I will protect you, no matter what. I will make sure you will not be hung for your crimes. No one knows if Seuderak…" He wavered, wondering if he would sound foolish speaking of the evil wizard that was from the legends. "Uh…We, as in the majority of Aselda, do not know what to think about the myths we have all heard about the dark lord. If he is real, though, we have to find a way to destroy him. Apparently the only way is for the three chosen ones to come together and confront Seuderak."

Arella sighed, toeing at the carpet that lay beneath Hansrai's chair. "So what exactly do you propose we do?"

"First, we must find the labyrinth," Hansrai answered.

Jared shook his head, looking stunned. "Arella, we cannot trust him…We should just leave."

"Seuderak is real," she whispered, before she glanced at Jared. "We have to help in destroying him…Under one condition, King Hansrai," Arella said, looking back to the young king. "Do not make war with the West. If you agree to this, we will go with you to find the Midnight Labyrinth."

Hansrai looked relieved. "Yes, of course. I will make sure of it. The Royal guard will not assail them. When we return, I will try and find a way to make peace with the inhabitants there."

"*If* we return," Jared grumbled under his breath.

"Jared," Arella said in a low, threatening voice as she glanced his way. He sighed in disappointment. Arella turned her attention back to Hansrai. "Do you even know where we should go?"

Hansrai lowered his head. "No...but I can ask Nicanor." He grabbed a scroll from the desk and scanned over it. He gave a quick look at Jared. "Here," he said, holding out the scroll to him. "This is a document that speaks of your crimes. Burn it."

"Really?" Jared murmured, before taking it, gently holding it in his hands. He turned to the fire. "I...I can burn it?"

Hansrai gave the *okay*. Jared turned and walked toward the fire place, taking slow, shaky steps. On that thick piece of rolled up parchment were all of his and Arella's mistakes-and not all of them. Just the ones that the people of Aselda knew about. But he knew that, even if he burned this document, the villagers would never forget what they had done. Jared took in a deep breath and prepared to throw the scroll into the fire.

Suddenly the doors swung open and four of the Royal guard burst into the room, lead by Abraxas. "Arrest them!" he shouted, pointing to Arella and Jared.

The siblings drew their swords and rushed to each others side. Hansrai leapt to his feet and ordered the guards to stop. They came to an immediate halt, looking from Abraxas to their king. Hansrai glared at the intruders.

"This was a private meeting. Abraxas, you are in no place to be barging in like this."

Abraxas sneered at him, before floating over

to the desk. "I'm sorry, my lord, but these criminals are to be taken to the dungeons right away. At sundown, they are to be hung. I am disappointed in you for not sending them to the dungeons already."

"Hansrai, you promised to protect us," Arella said, rather calmly, though there was a hint of fear in her voice

The king grimaced as Abraxas laughed. "Ha! A king protecting lawbreakers? This is an outrageous idea. Guards, take them!"

"No!" Hansrai barked.

Abraxas shook his head and sighed in exasperation. "But my king, it is the law."

"And I am your king, so I command that they be set free," Hansrai demanded.

"Ah, but even you, *young* king, must follow rules." Abraxas floated over to one of the bookshelves, searching for a certain scroll. "Remember the one king who wanted to let a prisoner go? He was seduced by the woman. Everything went wrong after he did this, if I remember right. Do you want the same thing to happen again?"

"No and it won't."

Abraxas snorted in amusement as he turned to look at the young king. "So determined are you? Ha! Oh my. You entertain me, Hansrai. Even if you were to convince me to let these two scoundrels go, you would have to then persuade all of your guards and the villagers of Aselda. You could be hung yourself, little king. You must follow the laws of your home."

The table shook as Hansrai pounded his fist on the table, his face feverish from his fury. "How dare you speak to your king like that!"

Spreading his hands before him, Abraxas grinned coldly. "But my lord, I have been since you became king. Unless you can find a way to change these rules in less than two hours, your friends here will die. Oh, yes," he muttered, glaring daggers at Hansrai, "and if you risk the chance of trying to free them, without changing the laws in time, and challenge the people to follow a king who will go against the regulations, your people will turn against you."

Hansrai clenched his jaw. He looked in Arella and Jared's direction. Arella stared back, shaking her head, as if to say, *Don't listen to him. Keep your promise.*

Abraxas laughed. "Take them to the dungeons!" he commanded. The four Royal guard charged forward, but Arella pushed them back with one of her force fields. Two more of the Royal Guards dashed into the room next, heading straight for the two thieves. The little black dogs yelped and scattered.

Hansrai watched in horror as Arella started to raise her hands, but it was too late. The two massive warriors barreled into them, knocking them flat on the floor.

"Stop!" Hansrai shouted, rushing over to them.

The two warriors froze, their fists in midair from hammering down on Arella and Jared.

Hansrai took a shaky breath. "I…"

"Since the king cannot think of what to say, take them to the dungeons," Abraxas cut in. "If he can think of something that will show evidence that these two should not be hung before their execution, then they will be spared. Whatever the case, take them away!"

The two massive warriors hauled Arella and Jared out of the room. Soon only Hansrai and Abraxas were left. Even the dogs had somehow escaped without anyone noticing. Turning away from the door, Hansrai glowered at his adviser, seething.

"Oh, please, Hansrai," Abraxas purred. "Do not look at me so. I only did that for your own good."

"No!" Hansrai fumed. "You would not listen to me! You spoke to me as if I were just a child. As if you are the true ruler of Aselda. I am your superior and you *will* listen to me!"

"I was merely pointing out something that you apparently had forgotten." Abraxas drifted over to Hansrai's side. "Nicanor drilled into your head that those two bandits are some chosen ones, did he not?"

Hansrai looked away, clasping his hand on the hilt of his sword as he walked over to the large window of the room. The sun was only a couple of hours from setting. How could he find a way to save Arella and Jared?

"My king?"

Groaning, Hansrai turned to face Abraxas. "Please, leave me."

Abraxas frowned, hovering closer to him. "But we should speak, sire. I must help you. Nicanor must have poisoned your mind-"

"And how would you know if I have been speaking with Nicanor or not, unless you have been spying on me?" Hansrai stated, glaring at the royal adviser.

The Shathrack scowled at him, before bowing and immediately leaving. Hansrai heaved a sigh and sat down at his desk. He *had* to find a way to rescue the two other chosen ones. If the prophecy was true, he was responsible for keeping them alive so that the prophecy would be fulfilled. Yet, if it wasn't real, just a scam, his people would surely turn against him.

Chapter 10
The Gallows

Trumpet blasts tore through the air as the villagers of Aselda gathered at the gallows that stood on the west side of Mt. Edavni. The sun was ready to set in the west, casting beautiful shades of orange and pink into the atmosphere. A large gate was slowly raised, before two of the Royal guard shoved Arella and Jared out and through the crowds. The villagers jeered and yelled insults at the two thieves as they made their way to the gallows.

"Behold, the mighty Alley Cat!" someone hollered from the mass of people. Everyone laughed and started tossing things at Arella, who in return glared at them, as if daring them to keep it up. The majority of people shuffled backward, murmuring among themselves as they stared at her.

Acting as guard near the platform were the Jin Warriors. The villagers left a large space between themselves and the mysterious fighters. The lead Jin Warrior turned her head slightly when the thieves were being lead through the crowd. Arella glared back at her, even after the warrioress looked away.

Standing behind the platform where the two

criminals were to be hung, stood a row of young human soldiers. As the prisoners got closer to the gallows, they began pounding on their drums. Arella was the first to be forced up the steps, the beat of the drums throbbing in her ears. Behind her Jared was struggling against the guards, but was quickly thrown up onto the platform. He looked from his sister to the ropes that dangled from two poles, swinging lightly upon the soft breeze.

The two guards tromped up the steps and hauled the thieves below the swaying ropes. A short, pudgy little man adorned in green and gold robes wobbled up the steps and stood at the left corner. He cleared his throat to gain the spectators' attention. "Th-this is the Alley Cat and the B-Bandit," he stuttered, scratching his brown beard as he glanced in Arella and Jared's direction.

Jared raised an eyebrow as he gave a quick glimpse at his sister. "I didn't even know I had a criminal name," he muttered.

"The t-two of them are here-here by sentenced to death for their n-numerous c-crimes," the man stammered, starting to walk over to the steps, where a young lad stood, holding out a scroll. On his way over, the stubby chap tripped over his robes and fell face flat to the platform. Everyone laughed.

"Maybe this will buy Hansrai time so he can come and rescue us," Arella whispered to Jared.

Her brother shook his head. "I don't think he is coming, Arella."

"Grr...Er. H-help m-me," the little round man demanded. The boy who had been holding the scroll stopped laughing and ran up the steps to help.

After a moment, the plump man was back on his feet. He tore the scroll from the young man's grip and pushed him away. "N-now, th-this, this here is a v-very l-long list of the c-crimes of *The Alley Cat* and *The Bandit*."

"Hmm," Jared mused. "I actually like that title."

Lord roundship glared in his direction before he began to read what was written upon the scroll.

Arella sighed and looked at Jared. "I am not even sure that everything they are blaming us for we really did. That is a mighty long list."

Jared nodded slightly, only hearing bits and pieces of what the round man was saying. He had to find a way to escape. His sister was probably doing the same.

"…and for stealing Mr. Whitley's cattle…"

Arella's head shot up. "We never stole any livestock," she grumbled.

"My dear, someone did," Lord roundship declared, casting a phony look of pity at Arella. "If someone stole Mr. Whitley's cows, it was most likely you."

"Do you have any proof, fat boy?" she asked, narrowing her eyes.

"I-er-uh." The man's face turned red. "Where is a pen! Another crime shall be added to this list!"

Arella sighed and glanced over her shoulder to the castle. *If you're going to save us, this would be a good time, Hansrai*

The griffin scratched nervously at the floor while Hansrai strapped another bag to its back. "Are you sure those of the West will know where the entrance to the Midnight Labyrinth is?" asked the young king as he looked to Nicanor.

"Yes. That is probably the reason why Abraxas wanted to defeat them. Part of me suspects that he does not want you to find it," the Shathrack answered as he floated around anxiously. King Hansrai heaved a sigh and looked around the griffin stables. He finished fastening the packs to the griffin. "You must hurry, though. They are reading the documents already," Nicanor said tensely.

The king nodded, before he gave the griffin a quick scratch. "Go ahead, Summerday. Head west," he whispered to the bird. In response, the griffin tilted its head in a bow before walking out of its stall. Hansrai smiled slightly as he watched the magnificent bird stop at a large balcony. It glanced back at him before taking to the sky.

"Now for my part in the plan," Hansrai moaned.

Nicanor chuckled. "Yes, take your horse, Twilight, and go save the two thieves. I will send Fleet if you need any help."

Hansrai bowed deeply. "Thank you, Nicanor." He watched as a young griffin played with its parents. He sighed, looking back to his Shathrack friend. "Will I ever see you again?"

A shadow passed over Nicanor's face. "That, I cannot say....You need to go-*now.*"

Lord roundship rolled up the scroll and bowed to the people of Aselda who had gathered. "L-let the executions b-begin! We shall w-watch them swing!"

The crowd roared with delight as the two guards that stood behind Arella and Jared took the nooses of the ropes and slid them over the bandits' heads. These gallows had been built for larger criminals, so the guards had stood Arella and Jared on two barrels. The line of young men that stood behind the platform resumed their drum rhythm.

"Die! Die! Die!" the crowd chanted, stomping their feet with the beat of the drums. Arella stared out at the people, wondering what could have happened to them. They seemed hungry for death. Even her, being a thief, did not have that kind of thirst. She watched as a yellow Shathrack flew over, stopping in front of the platform.

"Today," Abraxas shouted, "these thieves shall be brought to justice!"

The villagers cheered wildly. The two Royal guards stepped forward to kick the barrels out from beneath Arella and Jared.

Arella started to holler something, but suddenly the barrel was no longer below her and she went swinging, dangling from the rope that wrapped around her neck. In a instant her life flashed before her eyes. She tried to breath, but she knew her life was about to end-unless some miracle could happen.

A few heartbeats later two arrows flew through the air, cutting through the ropes. Arella and Jared fell to the platform with two loud thumps. Villagers screamed and fled as Hansrai charged through the crowd, riding proudly upon a black stallion. A griffin spiraled downward from the sky, spreading terror and fear through the crowds as they scattered. The people screamed and ran in alarm, rushing for the village. Abraxas turned in bewildered circles, shrieking furiously as he glided past the frightened villagers. The Jin Warriors leapt into action-but instead of attacking the two thieves, they began fighting off the Royal Guard. The guards tried to attack the other warriors, but invisible forces sent them tumbling through the air.

The griffin swooped down low, citizens screeching bloody murder as they dove to the ground. The giant bird flew to the gallows, snatching up Jared, who started panicking like the villagers. Hansrai dashed up the steps, his steed trotting over to Arella's side. Hansrai cut the ropes that bound Arella's hands together and pulled her up behind him.

"Leave!" the Jin warrioress shouted to them as she drew her swords. "We'll hold them off."

Hansrai nodded and urged his horse forward. His mount immediately obeyed, leaping off the platform and then bolting for the forest. Arella looked over her shoulder at the warrioress, narrowing her eyes. Those twin blades...that was surely the warrioress who had helped them earlier that day, but with a different disguise.

At the woods edge a rank of the Royal guard formed, pointing their spears toward the king and escaping prisoner. Twilight came to a quick stop and reared, whinnying angrily at the guards.

"The village," Arella suggested.

Hansrai nodded, spurring Twilight. "Good

idea," he muttered. At once they raced past the crowds and guards, heading for the town, the guards near the forest running after them.

The people who had made it to the village had finally started to quiet down, but once Twilight broke into the city limits, everyone began to panic again. The horse's hoof beats vibrated across the cobblestone streets. Arella glanced over her shoulder for pursuers. Sure enough, a troop of the Royal Guard riding their large steeds were following close behind.

"They're right behind us," Arella warned.

"I kind of figured," Hansrai said through gritted teeth. Twilight galloped past a black smith's shop and then through the town square. "I think our best way out is to go into the forest," the king said as he looked around at the screaming civilians. "Maybe we can lose the guards there."

Arella thought for a moment before answering. "I guess it is the best we can-" An arrow zipped past Arella's ear. She growled and instantly put a force field around them. "Can you go any faster?"

"Twilight's going as fast as he can!" Hansrai answered, clearly irritated. The horse seemed to understand the situation and started racing even faster, past homes and more shops. Soon Arella could see the tree line. Twilight continued on, arrows bouncing off the force field that encircled them. Soon they left the city and dashed toward the woods.

"Oh," Arella groaned, laying her head against Hansrai's back.

"What's wrong?" Hansrai asked, trying to

look back at her.

"Watch where you are going, majestic boy," Arella said hoarsely.

Hansrai looked in front of him reluctantly. If she continued to tell him what to do for the entire quest, he would go mad before the end. Of course, he had felt like he would have gone insane while he was king, but now…he was a criminal to his own homeland. Who knew what could happen between Arella and the young king? They could either become dangerous enemies, or even become truly good friends. Though, how the tables were turning so far, Hansrai feared that they might turn out to be rivals before comrades.

"I…cannot hold up the shield much longer…" Arella gasped. "Are we almost to the forest?"

Hansrai shook his head, quickly breaking out of his thoughts. "Don't worry, we're almost there." Twilight galloped away, before entering into the forest; darting around the trees, leaping over logs and large roots that thrust out of the ground. Finally Arella let down the force field, leaning against Hansrai as she tried to keep from falling unconscious.

"Maybe if you would have been there earlier, we would already be far ahead of the guards," she muttered crossly.

Hansrai growled, ducking under a low branch. "Look, I'm all new at this. I did the best I could!" He glanced behind them. For a moment he thought they had lost the Royal guard, but then he caught a glimpse of three of the massive warriors. "At any rate, I saved your life. The least you can do is say thanks."

"Well, we're not out yet," Arella said, tightening her hold around Hansrai as Twilight leapt over a fallen tree.

The young king grinned slightly. *We'll make it.*

They rode on, the sun disappearing in the west until the woods grew dark, the woodland night creatures coming out of their dens or hiding places. An owl sat in its perch on a branch high up in a tree, watching as a horse as black as the night rushed beneath the limbs of the trees, two riders upon its sleek back.

After a while, it seemed as if they had lost their pursuers, though Hansrai thought he saw something moving out of the corner of his eye every once in a while. Perhaps the Jin Warriors that had saved them? Wanting to be careful, he asked Arella if she had seen anything, but she didn't seem worried.

Twilight slowed, until coming to a trot, tired from the long run. Hansrai loosened his grip on the reins and glanced around at their surroundings. "Do you think it is safe to stop?" he asked.

Arella thought for a long moment, before sighing. "Those mysterious warriors said that they would hold off the Royal Guard, but…they can't forever. It will be too dangerous to stop for long."

Hansrai brought Twilight to a halt. "We should get off," he told Arella. "Give Twilight a break."

Arella nodded and climbed off. "We also have to find my brother. Was that your griffin who flew off with him?"

"Yeah," Hansrai answered, sliding off of his mount.

"Do you know how to find it?" Arella questioned, turning to glare at Hansrai.

"*He* is going west," Hansrai grumbled.

Arella stiffened. "Why?"

"Because that is where the entrance to the Labyrinth is," Hansrai clipped. "Everything is under control. Your brother will be fine."

"I don't trust you or your bird," Arella stated, watching him carefully as he grabbed a canteen from the saddle.

Hansrai sighed. "Even after I just saved your life?"

Arella walked past him, heading west. "Hurry along, majestic boy."

The king gritted his teeth. "I hate you calling me that." He grabbed the reins and started following her.

Chapter 11
Ghosts in the Woods

A wood owl soared through the forest silently, hunting for prey. The cool, quiet night flew by, midnight swiftly approaching. A serene night in the woods.

Suddenly the peacefulness was interrupted as the owl swooped down low to snatch a small mouse. It quickly landed, hungry for its midnight snack. The mouse, which had been killed as soon as the owl's sharp talons had penetrated its skin, was quickly ripped to pieces and eaten by the owl.

Arella crouched behind a bush, watching the owl as it tore into its prey. She scowled, grumbling something under her breath. After the owl had flown away, Arella stood and turned to find Hansrai. She sprinted through the forest, leaping over logs and ducking under low branches. Soon she came to a steep incline and jumped.

Scanning the area around her as best she could, she frowned. Where was Hansrai? He should've been there already.

Standing straight, Arella narrowed her eyes. It was too dark to see much around her. The moon was full tonight, but dark storm clouds were veiling the moon. Hansrai could be lost out there. Not that she cared.

"Hansrai, where are you?" she muttered, slowly moving forward. She crept along, straining to see ahead of her, but it didn't take much to. Ever since discovering her "magical abilities", Arella had been able to see in the dark with little effort.

"Arella Zephyr," someone spoke softly from behind Arella. The young thief came to a halt, her hand coming to rest upon the hilt of her sword. She took a deep breath, before spinning around and drawing her sword in a swift motion. As she came to face her stalker, a bright flash of light shone in her eyes, causing her to be blinded for a moment.

When she could finally see, the Jin warrioress who had helped them escape from the gallows was standing before her, holding a strange orb of blue light in her right hand. In the warrioress's other hand she grasped a long knife. The bright light of the glowing sphere cast shadows across her face, giving her a ghostly appearance.

"Arella Zephyr," she repeated, her voice almost a haunting whisper. Her blood red hood hung over her eyes, but Arella was sure that the warrioress was staring hard at her. The Jin fighter's cape rustled on a gentle breeze, revealing knives and other sharp, but small, weapons on a belt.

"You are the Jin warrioress from Hansrai's chambers-and then the gallows," Arella stated, keeping her swords tip pointing at the mysterious warrior.

The warrioress hesitated, before bowing her head. "You have seen me more than that," she said, as she put her hand out and let the orb slowly roll off. Before hitting the ground, the orb froze in midair. With a wave over her face with her now free hand, the warrioress's hood gradually altered from the blood red, to black. The one sword strapped to her back morphed into two twin blades, and the weapon straps on her vanished.

Arella's jaw clenched as she stared at the warrioress. "The woman from the catacombs," she muttered. "Why have you been following us?"

"Someone needed to rescue you," the warrioress answered, stretching her hand out to the orb of light. Immediately it flew back to her hand. "Follow me, we must speak." She brushed past Arella, but the young thief didn't move.

The Jin warrioress paused and glanced over her shoulder. "We have your brother."

Arella's body stiffened at this. She slowly turned to face the Jin soldier, narrowing her eyes. "Where?"

With a hint of a smile, the warrioress turned her face away from Arella and began walking again. Arella glared after her, but sheathed her sword and followed cautiously. She made sure to stay roughly eight feet behind the mysterious warrior, keeping her hand on the hilt of her sword. The warrioress had saved her and her brother's lives twice, yet Arella was still skeptical about who the warrioress's alliances were to. Most certainly not with the Royal Guards and Abraxas, but there were others in Ardara that could be enemies with Arella. None of the cities had made contact in over a hundred years. Ever since the War of Ardara, the capitol of the country and the other cities became rivals and though they no longer fought each other, they were banned to have dealings together. The Jin Warriors were the first to make contact with the villagers of Aselda. Of course, no one really knew where they were from. They were almost like a group of mercenaries that would sometimes travel through Aselda.

Bounty hunters and other thieves from Aselda rarely got along with Arella. They were always trying to hunt her down. When these mercenaries came, they didn't really go after any thieves. The word "thieves" didn't seem to excite them at all. They mainly would "protect the people and ensure that any bandits would not enter the castle". The Royal Guard did not seem impressed with the Jin Warriors, but Abraxas was eager to learn any news that pertained to the outside world of Aselda. He had welcomed the Jin Warriors to Aselda and ordered for the people to treat the warriors with respect.

What Arella wanted to know was why and when the Jin Warriors decided to turn against Abraxas.

Suddenly the young thief came to a halt,

coming to realize that she had lost sight of the warrioress. One moment she had been there, the next, she had vanished. Arella couldn't even catch a glance of the glow from the light orb.

Moments passed and still no sign of her.

Arella drew her sword and started walking again, keeping an eye out for the warrioress. She remained as quiet as she possibly could, straining to hear the sounds around her.

Then she saw it. A small diamond shape of orange light floating near the top of one tree. After that a square of red light floated to her left, followed by a blue ball of light that morphed into different shapes as it drifted through the air. Soon many different sources of light were filling the forest, casting beautiful lights across the forest floor and trees.

The Jin warrioress appeared from behind a tree, holding her own orb of light. "This way. The king and your brother are waiting for you."

Arella narrowed her eyes. "The king, as in King Hansrai?"

The warrioress simply nodded, before motioning for Arella to follow. The thief hesitated, before following. Not long after, Arella began noticing more of the Jin Warriors watching them, some leaning against trees, others standing guard, and a few even in the trees.

Arella watched them carefully, gripping her sword. Something about these warriors seemed familiar. They called themselves "the Jin Warriors", but Arella had a feeling that that wasn't their real name. She searched her memories for something, anything that could help her figure out who these warriors really were.

Suddenly Arella knew. A chill went up her spine as she remembered. She had only seen these warriors once. It had been just a glimpse, but that had been enough to burn a memory in Arella's mind.

"You are Master Cairo's apprentices," Arella stated, glancing up at the mysterious warrioress. "I was right when we were back in the tunnels."

The Jin fighter stopped, before turning around to face Arella. "Yes. My name is Akira Darksong," she said, removing her hood. Long, wavy black and red streaked hair spilt over her shoulders and around her pale face.

Arella clenched her jaws. "Did Master Cairo send you?" she asked, her voice thick with bitterness.

Akira bowed her head. "No. Master Cairo is deceased."

"Then why are you here?"

"Because you are the chosen, and we are here to help you," Akira purred.

"How do you know if we are the chosen or not?" Arella pressed, glaring daggers at Akira. The warrioress glanced up at the thief.

"On Master Cairo's death bed, he told me that he had a vision," Akira explained, keeping a steady gaze on the Alley Cat. "Seuderak and all the monsters that once terrorized Aselda would escape and that three chosen would rise to defeat Seuderak. No one knew when the day would come. I thought perhaps we would have more time, but here we are, only two years after Master Cairo's death."

Arella took a step forward, raising her sword to point at Akira. "Tell me, how did you find us?"

"We have been watching over all of Aselda and beyond, for any signs of when Seuderak would rise again. Seuderak wants you dead before you can find him, so he has been sending out the monsters that have escaped to find and kill the chosen. He does not have the power to leave his prison, the Midnight Labyrinth," Akira answered.

There was a moment of silence, but then the warrioress bowed her head again. "Because of the conditions of magic being banned, we had to find a new identity. We no longer could be recognized for who we really are. So we became the Jin Warriors."

"Who are you then?" Arella questioned, glancing from Akira, to the other warriors in the forest surrounding them.

Nothing could have prepared Arella for the answer she was about to hear. When Akira spoke the words, Arella found herself staring at the warrioress. Everything that she had feared was coming true. Suddenly her already messed up life was being thrown into the deepest parts of hell.

Chapter 12
Traitor

Abraxas floated around anxiously, glaring at the burnt gallows, then at the dead bodies of Royal guards and Jin Warriors. He should have guessed that the Jin Warriors were working for Xanthias. But no matter, he would not let one defeat stop him.

Seuderak would win.

"Sir," said a gruff voice from behind him.

Abraxas turned to face a large group of the Royal Guard. He looked over them, before nodding. "Your job is to hunt down the chosen. Do whatever it takes to find them, even if you have to take all your soldiers!"

The guard grunted. "What about the people?"

"They are no longer any worry to us," Abraxas seethed. "They can die."

The guards raised their weapons and shouted, "Seuderak!"

Abraxas chuckled. "Yes, Seuderak will rise." He floated further away from them to another, but smaller group of guards, who stood before a large cage that was covered with a black tarp. Inside were slimy green monsters-Scroddleracks.

"The monsters will be able to find the humans," Abraxas said, motioning towards the cage. "Find the chosen quickly and kill them."

The lead guard snarled, a strange hungry glint in his eyes. "We will find them," he growled. "And kill them."

"Good," Abraxas chuckled, turning to leave. "Now there is one more thing I must take care of, before inspecting our new prisoners."

Nicanor drifted toward the top of the wall of books. He glided around in the large and round library, looking from one book to the other. The giant bookshelves reached from the floor to the ceiling, with a glass dome roof stretching over the library.

There was a large dark oak door, three steps that curved to make a half circle that lead up into the library, a cream and green colored carpet, and then in the middle of the room was a dark wooden desk. Scrolls were spread out across the large writing table, with a huge book open to a page with a beautiful picture painted upon the parchment. It depicted a girl and two boys riding through the woods on three magnificent stallions.

"Ah, Nicanor! I was just looking for you!" said a high, squeaky voice from below. Nicanor sighed, keeping his eyes trained upon the titles of the many books.

"Abraxas," he said in his deep voice. "What do you want?"

"Oh, I was just curious to know if you knew anything about where Hansrai and the two thieves will be going now, that they have escaped."

The Shathrack slowly turned to see Abraxas drifting around the desk. Nicanor did not answer, but sighed as he drifted down.

"Oh?" Abraxas smiled coldly. "No answer then?"

Nicanor heaved another sigh, glancing at Abraxas before he started to study the book that lay open upon the table. "They are about to do something that shall change all our lives forever." He suddenly looked up, his form flickering. "How long have you worked for Seuderak?" he demanded.

Abraxas laughed callously. "Oh, so you've figured me out, have you now?" The Shathrack shook his head, amused. "Years. Seuderak is my patron."

"Why? Why would you betray your

people?!" Nicanor shouted, his form flickering off and on. "No matter. Hansrai and those two 'criminals' will destroy Seuderak and everything will be in its right place."

"You are wrong. Even if they do make it to the labyrinth, Seuderak will slay them," Abraxas said, smiling coldly. "You have sent them to their demise.

The yellow Shathrack grinned viciously, hiding a dagger behind his back. A weapon that could only be held by a Shathrack and could only harm another Shathrack. "Hansrai and the two thieves will die, but first, you will!" Before Nicanor could do anything in his defense, Abraxas brought his knife around and stabbed Nicanor with it. Immediately Nicanor's form began to fade.

"You...How could you?" Nicanor groaned, glaring at the other Shathrack. "To your own people?"

Abraxas smiled coldly. "It 'tis a long story, but you do not have long enough to live to hear the tale." He drove the dagger in farther, until Nicanor completely vanished, his screams of pain filling the room. Then everything went silent.

The royal adviser chuckled, placing his dagger back into its place. "I have been waiting to do that for far too long, Nicanor."

Chapter 13
Drago Warriors

So they were real.

Just like Seuderak.

The myths were true.

He had been telling the truth.

Arella stiffened at the last thought. She had always had a feeling that all the legends were accurately correct, but part of her had also doubted. Now here was evidence that it was all true.

"Was Master Cairo a Drago Warrior?" Arella asked, glaring at Akira.

The Drago warrioress shook her head. "No, not a Drago Warrior. A Dragon Warrior. A true blood."

"If the labyrinth, Drago Warriors, Seuderak, and monsters are real..." Arella stared hard at Akira as she thought for a moment. "Xanthias lived thousands of years ago. If the stories are correct, the Guardians blessed him and the other mighty ones with long life. Yet, could he still be alive after all this time?"

The Drago warrioress smiled slightly. "He is still alive. You have met him."

Arella had a feeling she knew when she had met him. Her body stiffened at the thought. "You must know everything about me, then."

Akira hesitated. "Not everything, but most of it."

"Don't tell my brother," Arella said, her aura darkening.

"I won't. It is not my place...but yours." Akira stepped forward and laid her hand on Arella's shoulder. "You cannot keep your secrets from him forever. What has been done has been done."

"Yes, and it has made me who I am," Arella replied quickly, pulling away from Akira. "I am a thief...some call me a wizard of Seuderak. No one trusts me-and no one ever will."

"Your brother trusts you," Akira answered, stepping back.

"Only because I am his sister," Arella snapped. "If he knew…" She shook her head. "If he knew my secrets, he would no longer trust me."

"Then you should talk to him," Akira simply stated. "It will only make it worse if he discovers that you have been holding secrets from him." Her orb of light flickered. "You should tell him why your parents really died."

Arella glared at Akira, trembling with rage. "I have. I told him the truth! King Hansrai the II sent his guards to kill my family, because he mistook them for spies. He thought that they were working for King Abraden."

Akira shook her head. "You are smarter than that," she whispered. "You know it is much more than that. Though King Hansrai did not know the real plot."

"Are you saying that someone wanted my parents dead, so they tricked the King into thinking that my parents were spies?" Arella questioned.

"This is something you must figure out on your own." Akira started walking again. "I cannot interfere."

Arella didn't follow right away, but gazed up at the night sky. Why had someone wanted her parents dead? They had just been simple farmers living on the outskirts of Kyra. They hardly ever traveled away from home. And even if they ever did travel, they would just visit the city of Kyra to pick up supplies. They hadn't cared about what was happening in the rest of Ardara.

Why…The question drilled into Arella's mind. She wanted to ask Akira what she knew, but Akira had said that she could not interfere. She wouldn't answer any further question pertaining to the mystery behind her parents' death, so Arella wouldn't press her for any more answers.

Approximately 45 minutes prior…

Hansrai stared at the warrioress, unsure if he had heard her right.

"A Drago Warrior?" he asked, quite puzzled. Shaking his head, he muttered, "So the stories are true…"

Akira smirked. "Yes. Why do you seem so surprised? The tales of Seuderak were "just stories" and yet you helped the two thieves escape. Why would you do that unless you believed in the legends?"

"It was all a trap to kill us," Jared suggested, shrugging his shoulders. One of the warriors glared at him and he scooted farther down the log he sat on.

"How many times do I have to tell you," Hansrai growled, now staring hard at Jared, "my plan was not to kill you. If it was, you'd be a crumbled spot on the ground. Fleet would have killed you as soon as he snatched you up. Why would I save you from being hung just to try and kill you again?"

"To finish what your father had started."

Hansrai frowned, confused at Jared's statement. "What do you mean-"

"Can I just knock this one out?" one of the Drago Warriors grunted, motioning with his giant war hammer at Jared. "His blabbering is becoming quite tiring."

Akira sighed. "No, you cannot. Treat the chosen with more respect."

The teen warrior groaned. "Fine," he grumbled as he leaned against a tree.

Jared glared at him. "Yes, treat me with respect, though I don't mind what you do to Hansrai."

The king leapt to his feet. "Look, I saved your life-"

"So I have to suddenly trust you, blah, blah, blah." Jared waved a hand in the air. "It will take more than that."

Akira silently watched as they went into a loud, vocal quarrel. A king and two thieves, thrown into an adventure, expected to work together. Countless arguments were bound to happen along the way.

Scowling at the thought, Akira stood and walked away, heading off to find Arella Zephyr. As she quickly made her way through the forest, the thought of the three chosen made her think of her own warriors. Many of them were just teenagers. The majority of able bodied adult Drago Warriors had either died, or had been seriously wounded after the many battles they had fought to keep the tower from breaking. Now the tower was collapsing, monsters were breaking loose, it was only a matter of time before Seuderak would rise again, and Ardara's only hope were juveniles. Bickering ones at that.

The fate of Ardara seemed as if it would be lethal.

Chapter 14
Strategies

"Are you sure the people of Aselda will be safe?" Arella asked, her arms crossed and her eyes trained on Akira.

Hansrai frowned. "I thought you hated the villagers."

Stiffening, Arella scowled. "I do, but I do *not* believe in unnecessary deaths." She turned her attention back to the Drago warrioress. "How long will the monsters stay in Aselda?"

"By now, they are already gone," Akira answered, staring into the fire. "We do not have long. The monsters have most likely picked up on your trail. They will be upon us soon if we do not hurry."

"Why are the monsters after us?" Jared questioned.

Akira glanced up at him. "They work for Seuderak. Their job is to kill you before you reach the entrance to the Midnight Labyrinth. Our mission is to prevent them from completing their task. I, along with some of my warriors, will escort you to the west. The rest of my warriors will stay behind to hold the guards and beasts off."

"What about Adrian and the others?" one of the young warriors who stood guard asked.

The Drago leader hesitated, before bowing her head. "They will be all right. Adrian Raven Shadow knows what he is doing."

"Who is Adrian?" Jared inquired, leaning forward.

"We do not have time to discuss this," Akira said, waving her hand. "We have our plans, we must start moving out."

"Fly?" a scrawny warrior asked, pushing his overly large helmet up enough for him to be able to see his leader. Akira nodded.

"Wait," Hansrai said, standing. "What about my horse?"

"We don't have time to be worrying about animals," Arella grumbled.

"Arella is right," Akira agreed. "I'm sorry, Hansrai, but it would be quicker if we flew to the west."

Hansrai glanced over at Twilight, before shaking his head. "Sorry, boy." The stallion whinnied anxiously.

"We will use him as a decoy," Akira added, turning to one of her warriors, who nodded.

Hansrai eyed her carefully. "How?"

"Bring your horse to me," Akira said in a stern voice. Hansrai hesitated, before obeying.

"Watch and learn," Arella muttered as she appeared at his side. "The Drago Warriors are legendary when it comes to their powers."

"Powers as in magic?" Hansrai asked.

"Yes," Akira hissed. "But we prefer to call it powers…or abilities, since magic has been banned. We changed our names to the Jin Warriors because of the law."

"It was banned because of the wizards that serve Seuderak," Hansrai stated. "Magic was being used for evil-"

"Yes, I know," Akira said darkly, looking at him bleakly. "I should know better than any of you.

I know it all. When and where any magicians, wizards, and apprentices were hung. Your ancestors burnt any scrolls and books pertaining to wizardry. Fortunately for us, we were able to hide it out and when everything began to calm, we changed our disguise and were able to look after Ardara once again."

Hansrai started to ask more, but Akira raised her hand. "Mount your rides, we must depart from here immediately. Hansrai, you ride your griffin. Arella and Jared, find a Drago Warrior to be your ride. Here. These small pouches contain a buttery substance. Rub this on your arms, face, and any exposed skin. It will cover most of your scent."

"What about Fleet and Summerday scents-?"

"My warriors will take care of that. Now. Go." Akira motioned for her warriors to start heading out. The ground rumbled as the warriors started to change form, becoming larger as wings began to sprout from their backs. Jared stumbled back, hollering, as he stared up with a mixture of awe and horror.

Soon the air was full of red, black, and grey dragons, which quickly disappeared into the night sky. Two remained, waiting for Arella and Jared. The two quickly did what they were told, rubbing the strange matter on their skin. Before long they were on their mounts, flying high in the dark sky, the forest below soaring by.

Akira watched only for a moment, before turning to Twilight. "You served your master well." Twilight whinnied impatiently. Akira smiled slightly at the stallion as she raised her hands. A small stream of light shot forth, before slowly morphing into a larger shape. There was a bright flash, before it appeared that Hansrai and Arella were sitting on Twilight once again.

"Go, boy!" Hansrai shouted. Twilight raced away, bearing his master…Bearing his master for the last time. A master that was not real.

Akira glanced at the sky, at the bright stars that filled the broad atmosphere. She thought a silent prayer to the guardians, before reaching out to her light orb. It floated obediently towards her, spinning in slow circles.

Narrowing her eyes, Akira snatched the orb and then threw it after Twilight, a look of triumph on her face. The orb had been given to her, and now after a very long time of waiting, she had finally been able to use it. The longer Twilight could live, the longer the strong stallion would be able to lead the monsters away from the chosen.

Akira's keen ears picked up the faint sound of tiny little beasts running through the forest behind her. Turning towards the sound, Akira hissed and reached for her knife.

With a nasty howl, one of the Scroddleracks tore through the underbrush, barring its fangs. The scent of the humans were growing stronger. Food! Up ahead. The beast could sense it. It snarled as it came to a break in the trees, slowing slightly. No one…The Scroddlerack ran in a circle around a tree, smelling it and growling.

"They must have been here-recently," one of

the guards snarled, sniffing the air as he entered into the clearing.

Another guard followed, grunting. "What's wrong with that?" he asked, pointing at the erratic Scroddlerack.

"Don't pay attention to it," the first guard growled. "Alert the others." He sniffed the air. "I know where they went."

The second guard sneered. "Of course." He took a deep breath, before letting out a loud roar, his rough voice carrying off through the woods.

Harmony zipped through the clouds, far ahead of the others. She had already been through this part of Aselda, but had circled around and was scanning over it again. The young guardian lowered just slightly, right under the clouds as she searched the forest down below. She didn't need to be too close to the earth to be able to see what was on the ground. She was, after all, a guardian.

The chosen had to be close. She could feel it.

Then Harmony caught sight of a dark mass moving through the forest, some smaller bands moving ahead of them, patrolling the area.

Monsters!

Harmony shuddered at the thought. *We're not the only ones on the chosen ones' trail...*

Something from up ahead roared. The black mass surged forward at the cry, eager to bring their prey down. Somewhere from the back of the lines, it appeared as if some of the larger beasts began burrowing beneath the earth.

The guardian gasped. *Raebelom.* Harmony narrowed her eyes. She had thought that those monsters were still trapped…

Shaking her head, Harmony started following the group of monsters. She remained hidden, almost invisible to anyone who might glance up at the sky. Hopefully Harmony could catch up to the chosen before the monsters.

However, as Harmony floated along, she began to doubt that the chosen had gone down the trail she was following. The monsters were heading more southwest. The chosen *should* have been going west.

"What are they doing?" Harmony thought aloud. She looked ahead, searching for any sign of the chosen. The only thing she spotted was a trace of magic, rushing through the forest…

Harmony's eyes went wide. *Akira,* Harmony thought, looking towards the west. Without hesitating, Harmony quickly started heading westward, away from the monsters. She didn't know how long the decoy would divert the guards and monsters. They had to move quickly.

Chapter 15
The Hunt

Arella remained silent as they soared through the cool air, scowling as she tried to not be swept away- without having to really hold onto her ride. She would sooner travel on foot and fight off a thousand monsters, rather than ride a *dragon*. There was just something about dragons she really hated. Maybe because they had something to do with her miserable past…

The young thief glanced over her shoulder, to where her brother rode a small black dragon, that was just large enough for the teenager to ride. Jared was mesmerized by the scenery down below. Though it was dark and they were flying amongst the eerie clouds, it was an incredible view.

How long until we reach the West? Arella thought, looking ahead of them. *It won't be long before the monsters realize they're following the wrong trail.*

Not that Arella cared if they would have a battle against the monsters. She was angry and wanted to fight *someone* or *something*. The monsters and Royal Guard were the perfect targets.

Calm down, Akira's voice drifted into Arella's thoughts. *You're time will come.*

Arella scowled, though deep down inside, she knew that Akira was right. Her time to fight off the monsters would come. Her first duty, as a supposedly chosen one, was to defeat Seuderak.

That meant she had to figure out how to work with Hansrai.

Don't judge him.

The young thief frowned as she tried to push Akira out of her mind. *His father killed my parents! Now shut up and stop reading my mind, or I'll kill you.*

There was a moment of silence, before Arella was sure that Akira had left.

They were right ahead.

The chosen.

Akira and her Drago Warriors.

Harmony glanced over her shoulder. She didn't see any monsters behind her. Of course, the Raebelom could be burrowing underground, beyond her sight.

Hopefully, that wasn't the case.

If they continue on this path, then they'll surely meet up with Xanthias and the others at one point...Unless Xanthias decided to go another way. Harmony frowned as she quickened her speed. *Xanthias, please, please have stayed on course.*

Harmony figured that if the Siria Tribe, the Baldhart Tribe, The Drago Warriors, Akira, *and* Xanthias came together, they could most definitely escort the chosen to the entrance of the Midnight Labyrinth...Of course, that would become a large mass that would be easy to spot. They would move faster if they had a smaller group.

The young guardian frowned. She wasn't good with strategies. If they wanted a guardian for that, they needed Tactic. He was full of strategies, outrageous plans, and crazy ideas. Though, somehow, his methods always worked. Sadly, Tactic was one of the Guardians still gone, fighting off any monsters that were still trapped in the atmosphere prison.

Harmony sighed and paused for a moment. The chosen needed Xanthias. If anyone would know what to do, it would be him.

Harmony began humming softly as she flew through the dark sky, telling herself that everything would be fine. The chosen *would* make it to the labyrinth and Seuderak would finally be destroyed. The guardians would be set free, and everything would be well again.

The guardian's humming turned to song, and though her sweet voice didn't carry far, it was enough to keep her calm as she flew alone through the cold atmosphere.

"Darkness hath blanketed her lands,
Forced beneath the evil ones demands,
Lost and desperate forever and ever,
Oh, what a waste was her endeavor,
She has become a slave to the wicked master,
The young virgin has come to disaster,
She cries out though no one will come,
She struggles to fight and not succumb,

To that of which the evil persuades her,
Help this young virgin to transfer,
To somewhere safe, somewhere secure,
Give this young, depressed slave a cure,
Help her, the virgin, help her to shine,
Give the poor virgin girl a sign,
Help her troubles and dilemmas to unfurl,
From the wicked save this poor virgin girl..."

Harmony's voice drifted off as she scanned the area in front of her. She was sure that she should be catching up with Akira soon...

She caught sight of something up ahead. Just the power emanating from two flying beasts. Dragons. *Drago Warriors.*

Akira! Harmony thought as she started flying as fast as she could, zipping through the air. Akira and the chosen were close! Hopefully Xanthias was not far ahead. If he had stayed on track, then they should be meeting up soon after she caught up with Akira and her warriors.

The guardian glanced behind her shoulder. She still didn't see any monsters following. Hopefully that meant that the diversion was still working.

"I smell them," one of the guards snarled, gripping his spear. "They're not far ahead."

The lead guard narrowed his eyes as he looked ahead. "Send out the Raebelom," he commanded, turning his horse around. "Take a score of the Scroddleracks with you."

"Where are you going?"

"This could be a decoy," the lead guard barked, his eyes flashing.

With a grunt, the first guard shook his head. "How do you know if it is a decoy or not?"

The commander's horse whinnied impatiently as the leader brought him to a halt. "I am sure that the Jin Warriors found them. We cannot waste any time. I want you to find out if this is a decoy or not."

The lower guard barred his teeth. "Yes, of course."

The commander nodded. "Call our pets," he said with a sneer, before spurring his horse back the way he had come.

As the commander left, the lone Royal Guard let out a deafening roar up at the skies. Little woodland critters scurried away, retreating from the billowing war cry. They knew something was about to happen and they wanted to flee as quickly as possible. The ground began to tremble, causing some of the weaker trees to collapse as whatever was burrowing beneath the ground grew closer.

The guard's roar ended as the earth tore ten feet away, a large beast leaping out of the ground. It howled and swung its head back and forth, sniffing the air for the scent of human flesh. Behind it another one of the creatures leapt out of the hole, following the first ones lead.

"If you are hungry," the guard snarled, now standing before the Raebelom, "then go hunt down your prey."

The two beasts howled again, before diving

back down into their tunnels. The guard watched before turning to see a squad of the Royal Guard behind him, four of the soldiers pulling a large cage. They stood restlessly, waiting to be told to go after their victims. One of the guards gripped his spear and pointed it at the sky, roaring with sick excitement. The rest of the guards roared along with the first.

Twilight galloped through the woods, swiftly disappearing deeper into the trees. The decoy Hansrai and Arella rode heroically upon his back, as if they were the real things. Anyone who looked upon the decoys would, at first glance, think they were real. They would have to stare at them, before realizing that they were fake.

The earth beneath the galloping stallion began to quake, as if something immensely large was burrowing underground. Twilight whinnied anxiously as he sped up ahead, dashing swiftly between the thinning trees. He broke through the foliage and into an opening of the trees. The steed pranced around the edge of the clearing, bobbing his head up and down nervously.

"Whoa, boy," the decoy Hansrai said as he laid a hand on Twilight's neck. The ground had stopped trembling and everything had gone silent. Hansrai looked around for a sign of monsters or guards, but saw nothing.

"We should-"

Before he could finish, one of the large Raebelom tore out of the ground, only feet away from the riders and their mount. Twilight was thrown onto his side, the decoy Hansrai and Arella vaporizing almost instantly. The horse tried to get up, when suddenly the Raebelom beast was on top of him.

Chapter 16
The Assassin

Guardian Diamond Soulsong fought against the darkness that was following her as she fell. She tried to turn to her star form, but while she passed through the portal between the prison and Ardara, she could not access that power. Struggling against unconsciousness, Diamond glanced over her shoulder, where the assassin had been, but she had vanished.

Diamond narrowed her eyes as she searched through the swirling clouds. Nothing. No winged beast or rider. For a moment, it seemed as if the guardian was alone.

"Soulsong!" someone hissed.

The guardian shot a quick glimpse to her right, where the voice had come from.

"Give up your crown," purred the voice.

Diamond spun in midair, attempting to activate something-anything that could help her in fighting the assassin.

"Are you scared, little princess?"

The guardian gasped as she slowly stopped spinning. She closed her eyes, trying to regain her energy. When she opened her eyes again, fiery golden ones stared back. Diamond's eyes widened as the assassin reached for her throat. In a quick, fluid movement, the guardian had her knife out and nicked at the assassin's hand.

With an angry hiss, the assassin vanished again. Diamond felt her heart hammering away in her chest. She was trembling as her eyes darted back and forth in search of her enemy. If the assassin was able to leave the portal alive...

Something shrieked from above. Diamond twisted to see what it was, when iron hard claws with sharp talons gripped her body. Soulsong screamed and lost her grip on her only weapon.

She gasped for air as the creature who held her captive tightened its grasp.

"Pity, you had to die like this," the assassin purred. "Yet...I can take your miserable dead body to your friends, before I kill them."

"No," Diamond whispered hoarsely. She started to close her eyes, when she felt her body slam into a solid surface. She heard the creature shriek as it hit the same surface, letting go of her. Diamond's eyes opened wide as she struggled for breath.

She paused when she saw the winged beast and assassin floating above her. They looked as if they were in water…Diamond looked down at her robes and cape, which were floating around her. She was in water, yet…she could breath.

I'm almost there! she thought as she started swimming towards a bright light that took the form of a door below her. The doorway out of the portal. She was almost home.

As she swam up to the glowing gate, Diamond reached out to touch it. As soon as her fingers brushed up against the warm golden face of the doorway, everything around her began to glow, before it was too bright for her to see.

Next thing she knew, she was flying through the sky, the cool air rustling through her hair. Diamond blinked as she tried to adjust to the sudden darkness. It was night wherever she was…A beautiful night.

She began to drop, falling towards the earth. Smiling, Diamond took her star form moments before crashing down to the ground, creating a fiery crater.

Moments later, as the smoke started to clear, Diamond stood. "Home at last," she whispered. Lifting her hands up to the sky, Diamond exclaimed, "I made it father!"

The sky lit up with lightning, as if her father was cheering for her. She smiled, before looking for a way to climb out of the crater. Not finding an easy route, Diamond turned back to her star form and floated out of the crater with ease.

Standing near the edge of the bowl, Diamond searched through the haze, towards the tower. Her excitement of being home died as the tower began trembling. Loose chunks of the tower fell to the ground.

"Oh no..." she muttered, starting to run forward. *I cannot let Zara Cyan get through...*

She raised a hand and screamed something as half the tower collapsed. A large creature tore through the debris, roaring and whipping its tail around, hungry for its prey. It was a strange creature, its head, legs, and wings looked like a hawk. The neck, body, and tail was that of a snake. Diamond shuddered. She had fought this beast many times in the prison.

"Zara!" Diamond shouted, coming to a quick halt as she searched for the assassin, but the only living thing in the wreckage was the assassin's beast. Reaching out her hand, a long sword appeared in her grasp. She held it in front of her, slowly moving towards the tower.

The creature hissed as she approached, flapping its wings angrily, telling her to back off. Diamond narrowed her eyes and took another step forward. The beast knocked a chunk of the tower to the side, moving closer to the guardian. They circled each other, both adversaries staring the other in the eye.

"Where is your master?" Diamond asked as she raised her golden sword to point at the snake-like beasts chest.

That's when she felt the rock strike the back of her head. She groaned as she dropped her sword and collapsed onto the ground. Her vision going blurry, she saw a dark figure standing over her, the sword raised to pierce her throat.

Harmony gasped as something clasped her arms. She started to struggle against it, when she realized that what had captured her was a dragon…she recognized how the claws were built. Twisting in the dragon's grip, Harmony tried to see what color the dragon was.

When she did, her eyes widened. "Akira!"

The dragon curled its lips in an attempt for a smile. "Harmony, it has been a long time."

"Aye, a very long time," Harmony agreed, grinning. "I take it that you have the chosen nearby?"

"Yes, not far ahead," Akira answered. "Are you with any others?"

"I was traveling with Xanthias and some of his warriors," Harmony answered, "but I do not know where exactly he is now."

Akira hesitated, before nodding. "We will catch up with them soon, most likely. Unless Xanthias's sight has gone dull, he will find us shortly."

Harmony's smile widened. "With his help, do you think it will be easy to get the chosen to the West?"

"Nothing is easy," Akira said grimly. "But, yes, with his help, then it should not be as hard."

The guardian nodded. "Then I hope he finds us soon. The decoy that you created will not last forever."

Akira did not answer, but let go of Harmony to let her fly by her side.

The assassin hissed at Hadyn and Kalama as they stood in front of the unconscious guardian.

"You have no place here, assassin," Hadyn said, raising his staff.

Zara chuckled. "You can skip the speech," she purred. "I've heard it too many times."

Hadyn narrowed his eyes as he glared at her. "I thought that one of the guardian leaders had killed you."

"Sorry you are disappointed," she said, frowning under the dark hood that was draped over her eyes. "I am very much alive."

Kalama stepped forward. "Not for long."

The assassin shook her head as she smirked. "I'd love to stay and strangle you, but I have unfinished work." As she said this, her beast flew overhead, before swooping down and snatching her up. Hadyn spun around as the assassin and her winged monster flew over him.

"Unfinished business?" Kalama said, worried.

Hadyn watched as their enemy disappeared into the night sky. "The chosen," he whispered, before turning to his sister. "She was banished into the prison after her attempt at killing them."

Kalama's eyes widened with horror. "Do you think they will be safe?"

"We can only hope for now," he said, walking to Diamond. He gently started to lift her as he finished speaking. "If we are to find them, we must hurry."

Chapter 17
Spotted

Arella woke to the sun rising behind her. It took a minute for her to realize where she was, but when she noticed that she was riding a dragon, everything came back to her. She scowled and quickly sat up, shuddering at the thought that she had slept on a dragon.

Looking down at the ground below her, she noted that they were out of Aselda, most likely between the forest that surrounded the capitol and the lands of the West. Some of the dragons were starting to descend, while others were already on the ground. Arella looked around for the dragon that her brother had been riding on, but couldn't find him right away. If he was behind her, she wouldn't be able to spot him, with the sun being at her back.

Her dragon trembled beneath her, before making a quick dive towards the ground. Arella bit her tongue to keep from cussing as she closed her eyes and clung to the dragon's neck. At the last moment, the dragon spread its wings and hovered over the ground.

"What are you doing?!" Arella shouted, opening her eyes. "Land already, you-"

The dragon growled, made a hundred-eighty-degree turn, and soon landed near the other Drago Warriors. The moment the dragon touched ground, Arella leapt off of its back and landed neatly on her feet. Happy to be back on the solid ground, the young thief sighed and sat down cross-legged.

"Arella!" Jared exclaimed, limping over to his sister.

Looking up, she frowned. "What happened to you?"

Jared scowled. "I rode the dragon for too long."

"We all did, besides that pampered prince," Arella muttered, closing her eyes and trying to concentrate on something.

"I heard that," Hansrai said from somewhere to her left.

Arella shrugged.

"Chosen ones," Akira said as she walked up. Arella sighed and opened her eyes, to see a glowing figure standing beside Akira. Both of them stopped a few feet away. Glancing at the girl beside her, Akira said, "These are the chosen ones."

The radiant figure smiled and bowed. "My name is Harmony. It is an honor to meet you."

"I'm Arella and this is my brother, Jared," Arella said, pointing to herself, then her brother. She then looked to Akira. "How long are we stopping for? You know that we cannot stay in one place for long."

"Only for a few minutes. But I fear that we cannot fly for a while," Akira answered. "My warriors are young and cannot fly for long periods of time. They are already exhausted, but they know that they have to continue on."

"Maybe you should not have brought so many wimpy juveniles," Arella said. "How many Drago Warriors are here anyways?"

Akira stiffened when Arella insulted her warriors, but she controlled her anger. "A little over a dozen. I had more, but some were either killed or taken prisoner at the castle."

"Ah, I thought there were more," Arella murmured.

"No, there are only about fourteen," Akira answered sharply.

Harmony stepped between them. "Let's not fight," she said calmly, raising her hands. "We should be celebrating, if anything. We have found the chosen and are now on our way to the entrance-"

"Celebrate?!" Arella exclaimed, leaping to

her feet. "Why should I celebrate that I'm stuck with *him*." As she finished, she pointed at Hansrai, scowling.

Hansrai frowned and stepped forward. "Look, it's not fun for me either."

"Good. I wouldn't want it to be," Arella spat.

"At least you aren't having fun with it either," Hansrai shot back.

"Of course I wouldn't have fun with a spoiled, selfish-"

Harmony laughed nervously as she jumped between them. "This is *not* going to help. Your enemy is Seuderak, not each other."

Arella glared at Hansrai, before crossing her arms and nodding. "But I can't trust him. I never will."

She turned and walked away.

Hansrai grimaced. "Why does she hate me so? Have I done anything to her?"

"No," Akira answered him, watching as Arella left. "It is what your father did to someone very dear to her."

"And me," Jared added.

Akira glanced at the young thief, before turning to Hansrai. "Come with me."

As the two of them walked away, Jared glanced at Harmony. He scooted closer to her, smiling slightly. "So…what are you?"

Harmony laughed. "I'm a guardian. Have you not heard stories about guardians before?"

Jared nodded. "Oh, I have. I was just making sure you were what I thought you were…er…The stories were right."

Harmony cocked her head to the side. "Right about what?"

"Guardians are beautiful," he replied.

"Aw, well…thank you," Harmony said, blushing. "Do the stories really say that about us?"

Jared nodded. "Yes. They also say that guardians are very powerful."

"Well…" Harmony's voice trailed off. "Some guardians. Those are the more important ones who you heard about."

"So you do not have any powers?" Jared asked.

"Oh, I do have some powers," Harmony answered. "Nothing amazing."

"What are they?"

Harmony smiled. "I am the guardian of friendship and loyalty."

Jared thought for a moment, before nodding. "That is important too."

Harmony started to answer him, when her form flickered. "Jared, look," she whispered, pointing at the sky.

"A bird?" Jared guessed as he saw something dark disappear into the clouds.

"That," Harmony said quietly, "is a scout of Seuderak."

The color drained from his face. "Does that mean Seuderak is…out of the Labyrinth?"

"No, but it means that trouble is not far behind it," Harmony said, grabbing Jared's hand. "Hurry, we have to find Akira. We have to get out of here quickly!"

Xanthias rode upon the back of one from the Baldhart Tribe. The creature lumbered forward, hefting an enormous club over his shoulder. He was a massive giant, with black hairy limbs and body. He had large feet that left deep craters in the earth, long claws protruding from six of his large, slimy toes. He only wore black pants, which had rips at the rims. He had the head of a bat, black beady eyes staring down at the earth as he trudged onward, and long sensitive ears that came to a point. He had huge muscles covered with black fur, with black leathery wings sticking out of his back. The creature looked as if he was half enormous, oversized bat, and half giant human.

"Sir," the creature snarled. "I smell a spy."

Xanthias frowned as he looked to the skies. Sure enough, he spotted a large bird of prey soaring overhead, heading northwest. "Aye, that you do, my friend," Xanthias said grimly. He paused, before adding, "Keep heading southeast. Something tells me that the chosen is in this direction."

The creature nodded, before raising his club and shouting something to the others. The Siria fairies quickly circled around him, ready for their orders. The large bat-like beast pointed his club in the direction that Xanthias wanted them to go. Without hesitating, the fairies quickly started flying that way, eager to find the chosen.

"If the spy has spotted them," Xanthias said dismally, "then it won't be long before the monsters catch up to them."

"Unless they already have."

Xanthias grimaced. "Let us hope not."

Chapter 18
Attack

"Akira!" Harmony shouted, running as fast as she could towards Akira, Arella, and Hansrai.

"Seuderak spy!" Jared hollered, waving his hands in the air. "Whatever that is it can't be good and it was flying overhead!"

As soon as Jared had finished, they quickly looked up.

"Are you sure?" Akira questioned, still searching the clouds. She turned to Jared and grabbed his shoulders. "Are you sure you saw a spy of Seuderak?"

"*I* did," Harmony answered for him. "There is no doubt that it was a spy. We have to leave!"

Akira nodded. "Harmony, take the chosen and start moving westward. I will go gather my warriors. Hurry now."

Arella watched them carefully. "You know what comes after the spy?"

"Yes," Akira said darkly. "Pray that you do not meet it. Now go."

The young thief bowed her head and started running with Harmony and Jared. Hansrai called for his two griffins, before quickly following the others. After making sure they were doing as they were told, Akira rushed back to where she had left her warriors, only to find their enemies rushing towards them.

"Blimey," the scrawny Drago boy said as he slowly stood. "Look at 'em...There be at least a hundred."

Akira watched in horror as the mass of monsters flew over a large hill and began to spill into the valley below them.

"At least we are on higher ground," one of the young warriors said, holding his bow in one hand and reaching for an arrow with his other. He was the only archer there, but he was ready to start firing down upon the approaching monsters.

"No," Akira muttered, shaking her head. "That won't be enough." She looked at her warriors.

"It was nice knowing you all," the eldest of Akira's warriors said sadly, before changing into his dragon form and flying at the monsters head on.

"Arashi, don't!" Akira exclaimed, reaching her hand towards him, though she knew she wouldn't be able to catch him as he soared down the slope and into the valley. Akira and her warriors watched in alarm as the Drago Warrior crashed into the first line of monsters. He clawed at a giant, dark, bear-like creature, while whipping an overgrown lizard with his tail, but in moments monsters were swarming around him and the distressed Drago Warrior's cries reached Akira's ears.

Grimacing, Akira started running, before turning to her dragon form. She flew at the monsters, her eyes burning with an angry fire. The rest of her warriors roared as they followed, eager to help their fellow fighter.

Time seemed to slow as Akira and her warriors rushed at the monsters. A million of thoughts swirled around in her mind. The chosen.

Arashi. Seuderak arising...She had just leapt into battle, wishing to save her youngling, while completely forgetting about the chosen. Would Harmony be able to get them to the Labyrinth on her own?

Her eyes widened as she rammed into one of the larger creatures, roaring in pain as the monster growled and slashed at her cheek. Clawing at each other angrily, the dragon and monster plowed into the monsters behind them, crushing the monsters beneath them as they tumbled along. They fought violently with each other, before crashing down for the last time and started rolling over each other, biting, clawing, and doing anything to wound the other.

Out of the corner of her eye, Akira saw over half of the monsters continue on in the direction the chosen had gone, while the others stayed to fight the Drago Warriors. A ring of the nasty beasts swarmed around Akira and her opponent, snarling and barking. Strange, giant wolves, bears, lizards, spiders, snakes, and many other foul creatures.

The monster that was battling Akira managed to roll over once again, with the Drago Warrior on the ground-and it on top of its prey. It slashed at her face and neck, before opening its jaws wide and going in for her throat. As its razor sharp fangs came inches away from its target, a fiery hot blast exploded at its side. Roaring with pain, the large wolf-like creature was thrown off of its prey and tossed into a group of monsters behind it.

Taking the moment that the monsters were distracted, Akira quickly rolled over and leapt to her feet. She rushed at a monster to her right and gripping it with her front right claw, Akira pulled the startled monster towards her, before bringing down her dagger like fangs down deeply into the creature's thick neck. Wrestling with the writhing beast, Akira brought her sharp claws down and tore at the beasts exposed abdomen.

A monster from behind her leapt onto her back, biting into her neck. Roaring furiously, Akira released the monster she had pinned on the ground and tried to claw or bite at the one that was now attacking her. The monster that was on her back was a lizard-she could tell by its quick and slippery movements. It was able to avoid her, while still keeping its jaws clamped on her throat.

Akira struggled against it, before suddenly collapsing. Feeling confident that victory over its prey was close, the monster snarled and released Akira, raised its head high, and then started to come down for the kill.

"Whoa!" Jared exclaimed, jerking sideways as he looked over his shoulder. "Th-that wolf…it's ten feet tall and chasing us on its hind legs-"

"And getting closer," Arella said bitterly. "Jared, Hansrai-get on the griffins and start flying away from here. Guardian girl, help them to make sure they make it to the West."

"What about you?" Harmony asked, worried.

"I'll be right behind you."

She slowed her pace, before coming to a complete stop. Turning to face the large black humanoid wolf, Arella drew her sword.

"She's mad," Hansrai said as the griffins swooped down towards them.

"Yeah, she is," Jared agreed, before leaping onto the back of one of the large birds as it flew by. Hansrai did the same a few seconds later.

Harmony turned to her star form and followed as quickly as she could, moments before one of the large lizard monsters was only a few yards behind her. It quickened its speed, trying to catch her, but she was already too high up for it to catch.

Harmony looked over her shoulder at the lizard as it glared up at her. Her eyes drifted to Arella and the wolf, who were circling each other. The wolf barred its fangs, before pouncing. Arella swung her sword up at it as it leapt at her, slicing through its throat, killing it instantly.

The lizard who had first gone after Harmony spun around and rushed towards Arella. She raised her right hand-holding her sword in her left-and sent an invisible force into the giant lizard. She started to look up to search for her brother and Hansrai, when something hit her from behind. She was knocked flat onto the ground, a large creature jumping on top of her.

After letting out a painful cry, Arella tried to reach for her sword, which she had dropped when the monster had ran into her. The lizard snapped at her hand reaching for her weapon. Arella let out a strangled gasp as she fought against the large monster that was on her and the lizard that was now in front of her as the lizard now tried to nip at her head. She brought an invisible shield up right as its teeth was a few inches away from her hair.

Allowing the shield to spread over her body and under the dumb monster that was sitting on her legs, Arella tried to use the power to knock off the monster, while still keeping the lizard from biting off her head. Finally having the invisible force shielding her whole body, Arella lifted it just enough to be able to roll over onto her back. Gritting her teeth, Arella started lifting her hands, pressing them against her shield as she tried to lift the creature off of her.

The large bear-like creature looked puzzled as it was slowly lifted upward. The lizard started attacking the shield as it started to become visible. Cracks started appearing all around it, threatening to shatter at any moment.

Arella groaned as she gave one last effort to toss the monster to the side and off of her. The bear let out a startled roar as it crashed into the ground. Out of breath, Arella rolled back onto her stomach and gasped for air. She placed her hands on the ground to push herself up, when she felt a long, pointed tongue touch the tip of her head.

She stopped, trembling as the lizard stood over her. She didn't have her sword or the energy to send another blow at it. Shutting her eyes, Arella waited.

"Look out!" someone shouted from her right. A hot blast of air followed. Arella gritted her teeth and covered her head with her hands as the lizard let out a deafening shriek. When Arella opened her eyes again, a fairy with short, fiery red hair stood beside her, glaring at the lizard, which was now just a smoking heap.

"Hurry," the fairy said, as he reached out a

hand to help her up. Arella looked over him carefully as she took his hand and he lifted her to her feet. He had orange and black wings, intricate tattoos all over his body...

"A Nyx pixie?" Arella guessed, trying to remember the names of the many different creatures she had learned about.

"Siria fairy," he answered, glancing over his shoulder. "Come on!"

He started to fly upward, but Arella let go of his hands and fell back to the ground.

"What are you doing?!" he exclaimed as he landed beside her.

"I'm not flying with *you*!" she snapped.

Looking over his shoulder again, the fairy sighed. "You have no choice!"

Arella looked in the direction he was and her eyes widened. Fairies were flying overhead, the redhead ones pelting the monsters with searing hot arrows. Another kind of fairy was mixed in the fray. They were very similar to the Siria fairies, except with dark hair, blue wings, and-

"Hurry, they can't hold them off for long!" the fairy said, growing irritated as he grabbed Arella and lifted her up off the ground.

Arella allowed him to carry her off this time, peering over his shoulder at the battle raging on behind them. Something *very* large was lumbering through the mass of monsters, swinging a giant club around and knocking the monsters around like rag dolls. Arella watched it, trying to figure out what it was...

"One from the Baldhart Tribe," she whispered, her eyes widening yet again. "Those are

Baldhart and Nix fairies among your kind-"

Before she could finish, she felt a blazing hot gust of air blast into her, before she was flying through swirling orange and red lights. Fighting to keep conscious, Arella searched the tunnel like area they were now whizzing through. She searched her memory to figure out where she was.

"A fire portal," the fairy said, seeming to read her mind.

Arella gasped. A fire portal…of course. Siria fairies often used these portals in time of trouble. They used the rays of the sun to create one, if she remembered right.

Most humans could not excess one without receiving burns, or losing consciousness for days and becoming extremely sick. Arella shut her eyes and struggled to put up a shield around her. One started to form, before shattering.

"Keep your eyes closed," the fairy warned. "We're coming up to the exit of the portal."

Arella opened her eyes and glanced in front of them. A blazing wall of circulating fire awaited them, roaring with life. Arella grimaced and closed her eyes, before feeling the fire lick at her skin.

There was a bright flash, and then everything went dark as she lost consciousness.

Chapter 19
Wizard Caspar

Akira took in a shaky breath, finding it hard to breath.

Yet…she was able to breath.

She was alive.

Opening her eyes, she saw a blurry figure standing in front of her, fighting off monsters with a large sword…The warrior appeared to be using a claymore sword as his weapon, wielding it well. Fairies with fiery orange wings, and some with dark wings, fought alongside him, taking down any monsters who tried to go near the wounded Drago Warrior.

Rolling onto her side, Akira tried to see the warrior better, but her vision was to fuzzy. Akira tried to sit up, but felt a hand rest on her shoulder. Glancing at whoever was kneeling beside her, Akira gritted her teeth.

"Who…who are you?" she gasped.

"You know me," said a somewhat wild, but kind voice.

Akira groaned and started to fall over, when two strong arms grasped her. She could see a face hovering over her, complete with a grey and white beard and long hair that matched the whiskers. She tried to say something, but the person shook his head.

"Don't try to speak, Kira dear."

"What about…what about the chosen?"

"The Siria fairies have taken care of them, don't you worry," he answered, gently picking her up. "They will be fine as rain."

"Caspar, wh-where are the others?" Akira managed to ask as the wizard looked around for a way to move Akira to a safe place.

"Making sure that SoundHarbor is still standing. Since it is the last haven and all. Can't have it broken to pieces like the other-"

"Get her out of here!" someone shouted.

Akira tried to look for the warrior, suddenly realizing who it was. "Xanthias!"

"Go!" he barked, swinging his sword around at one of the monsters. "Quickly!"

Caspar nodded as he held Akira with one arm, and raised his staff with the other. It was made of thick, sturdy, white wood, the top end carved to look like a dragon's head, while the bottom end appeared to look like a lightning bolt.

There was a thunderous crack, a bright flash, and then the wizard and Drago warrioress had vanished. On the ground, where Caspar had been standing, was a mark imprinted on the ground like a dragon riding a lightning bolt. Quite a strange mark, but it was the mark of the brilliant, but slightly mad wizard, Caspar.

Seeing that Akira and his comrade wizard had been able to escape, Xanthias fell back to where they had been standing, and tried to reach out to the fairies with his mind.

It is time to leave. Set your portals for the West. The chosen await us to lead them to the Labyrinth.

The fairies started vanishing, some disappearing in a flash of light, while others departed after turning into black vapors. Some fairies quickly helped their wounded comrades, before quickly leaving. Two male Nyx fairies grabbed the Baldhart bat and helped him into their own portal. In minutes, the only one that remained was Xanthias and the dead.

There was a moment of silence, before the monsters turned on Xanthias. They hesitated, unsure if they should attack him or not. Was he real, or just something that would explode?

A large bear-like creature lumbered forward, circling the wizard.

Xanthias slowly turned, keeping his eyes on the monster, holding his sword in front of him, pointing it at the beast. *Caspar...*

The bear charged suddenly, heading straight for him. Xanthias swung his sword at it, before it could even reach him, sending a bright streak of light at it. The bear roared in pain as the searing hot light slashed through it.

Caspar!

The rest of the monsters glanced at the dying monster, and then to Xanthias. As one, the mass moved forward, stampeding towards Xanthias.

CASPAR!!

There was a bright flash and the wizard was standing beside him, trying to straighten his cloak. "What did I miss?" he asked, not seeming to notice the creatures rushing at him and his friend.

"CASPAR!" Xanthias hollered.

The younger wizard glanced up slowly, still trying to fix his sleeves. His eyes widened when he saw the creatures. "Wow, that is a lot of ugly hides," he muttered as he tapped Xanthias's arm with his staff. "I think it best that we leave now."

There was another flash of light and the two wizards vanished from sight.

Moments before the monsters would have been in range of attacking.

And upon the earth was a blazing image burning itself into the ground. An image of a dragon riding a lightning bolt.

Xanthias and Caspar appeared right in the middle of Xanthias's village, Caspar's hair singed and Xanthias's robes smoking.

"You were cutting that a little close," Xanthias breathed, giving a sideways glance at his friend.

"Well, you know I don't like my ham too thick," said the wizard as he reached into his sleeve. He frowned. "I've seemed to have lost my marbles again."

Xanthias just looked at his friend, who seemed completely unfazed by what had almost happened.

"Father!" Xanthias's boys called as they ran up. Kiran stopped beside his father, looking up with his dark eyes. "What was the battle like?" he asked, seeming quite excited.

Xanthias gave another glance at Caspar. "A risky battle."

"Caspar was asking if he could have some bacon, when Lilith started yelling at him to go back and get you," Kirrat said, grinning.

Xanthias chuckled as he ruffled Kiran's ebony hair.

"Where are they?" Caspar was muttering to himself, not seeming to notice the two boys.

Kirrat glanced at his father questioningly, before he cleared his throat. "What are you looking for, sir?"

Not looking up, Caspar said, "My marbles."

The two boys looked at each other.

"Marbles, sir?" Kiran asked, curious.

"Yes, yes," Caspar answered. "Oh bother, I *have* lost them…"

"Why do you need marbles, sir?" Kirrat questioned, watching as Caspar peered into a large pocket on the left side of his cloak.

"Every wizard has something to keep his sanity in," Caspar said matter-of-factly, as if *everyone* knew that. "And I've lost mine again."

Kiran started to laugh, but when his father pinched his arm, he started coughing.

"You think it funny, boy, that I lost my marbles?" Caspar asked as he finally looked up. He stared hard at Kiran, who bowed his head.

"N-no, sir," he said.

"Good." Caspar nodded and then turned to Kirrat. "Have you seen my marbles?"

Kirrat stifled a laugh. "No, sir."

Caspar shrugged and went back to looking for his lost marbles.

"Father, do you have marbles that keep your sanity?" Kiran asked Xanthias, looking up at him.

"No," his father grunted, crossing his arms. "I keep my sanity somewhere safe."

"*Father*?" Caspar gasped, dropping something furry that he had pulled from one of his pockets. The rat squeaked, before scurrying off. "Come back here, you rodent!" Caspar shouted, running after it. Once he had managed to snatch it up and place it back in his pocket, he straightened and turned to Xanthias. "You have *children*?" Narrowing his eyes, he looked them over. "But they look nothing like you. You have, well…blue skin and their skin is tan. You have no hair and they have hair-"

"Do you expect us to be bald?" Kiran said, frowning. "I'm only ten."

"-and their eyes…" Caspar shook his head, ignoring Kiran. "Far from a spitting image of you."

"They take after their mother," Xanthias said as he grabbed Kirrat's arm and pulled him closer. He placed a hand on each of the boy's shoulders. "One thing they have from me is my youthful stubbornness-"

"You mean your stubbornness, Xanthias, don't you?" Caspar chuckled. "You haven't outgrown it."

"Nor have you outgrown your foolishness from last we met," Xanthias said under his breath.

"No, I haven't grown up at all!" Caspar exclaimed happily, tapping his staff against his leg and almost falling over.

"That's for sure," a woman hissed.

Caspar slowly turned to see the Nyx fairy standing behind him with her arms crossed. Lilith stared hard at him. "Leastwise you have not grown up in maturity level. As in physically…"

"I'm in splendid shape," Caspar said, lifting

his thin, bony arms. "Why, my hair still has some black in it…"

Lilith rolled her eyes and looked at Xanthias. "I think it wise to send the chosen into the labyrinth before more monsters come."

Xanthias nodded. "Yes. Where are they?"

"In your home," Lilith answered, nodding towards his house. "All three of them lost consciousness while going through the portals."

"The girl woke up and yelled at me," Kiran said, shuddering. "She said to find whatever idiotic fairy had put her through the portal and to tell him to jump into a lake."

"A lake?" Kirrat asked, suppressing another laugh.

"It was a Siria fairy who had helped her in escaping," Lilith explained, sending a dangerous look in Kirrat's direction. "Siria fairies hate the water."

Kirrat tried to act serious. "Oh," was all he said.

Xanthias sighed as he closed his eyes. "They are very…"

"Snappy," Kiran grumbled.

"Hot tempered," Kirrat added.

Lilith raised an eyebrow at the boys. "You are most likely speaking of the girl primarily, aren't you?"

The brothers nodded. "The others weren't awake when we were in there," Kiran answered.

Lilith glanced at Xanthias as she spoke, "I suppose it is about time they wake up. They have to be in the labyrinth soon, before the tower collapses."

"Have there been any reports on the condition of the tower yet?" Xanthias questioned the fairy, looking worried.

The fairy looked at him grimly, but didn't speak. Instead, a familiar voice answered from behind Xanthias.

"Aye. It won't be long before the tower comes crashing down. But that's not the worse part. Zara Cyan is out. If she is out, then her brother can't be far behind her."

Chapter 20
The Entrance to the Midnight Labyrinth

Arella sat on the edge of the bed, staring down at her right hand. It had been seriously burned. During the trip through the portal or not, she did not know. She just remembered waking up to her hand burning…and this tattoo like mark had been there, when it hadn't been there before the battle and her strange portal experience.

After she reached for a bandage that was laying on the pillow, Arella quickly wrapped the binding around her hand-covering the glowing marks. She didn't want to study the markings anymore, having a dreadful feeling that they had something to do with her being a chosen one. She hadn't been able to tell what exactly the designs were supposed to be. Because they were glowing, it was making it hard to distinguish what the symbols were, and Arella was getting a headache from trying to figure it all out.

"Arella," Jared moaned from the bed to her

right. The poor boy tossed around in his bed, sweat beads running down his forehead.

Sighing, Arella slowly stood and walked over to the side of the bed. She watched her brother silently for a moment, watching him toss and turn restlessly. At one point, his arm was dangling over the side of the bed, and Arella saw something glowing in the palm of his hand.

He started to turn back over onto his left side, but Arella stopped him by grabbing his hand. He had glowing symbols emblazoned on his right hand, just like she did. Except, the symbols on his hand weren't glowing as brightly as the ones on her hand. She was able to make out what the symbols were...The head of a griffin, enclosed by two circles. Between the two circles were strange symbols that Arella could not read.

Staring hard at the mark, Arella lifted her right hand, glanced at it, then looked back at Jared's hand.

I wonder what would happen if I put our hands together...

Finding herself very interested in it now, Arella placed her hand on his.

Nothing.

Scowling, Arella let go of his hand and crouched down by the bed, holding her right hand up and staring at it. Maybe if she took off the bandage...Arella shook her head. She was being ridiculous. Childish.

"Come on, Jared, wake up," she said as she stood. "We have a lot to do."

Jared groaned and buried his face in the soft pillow.

"Yeah, I know you don't feel good. Blame the fairy that helped you," Arella muttered, grabbing one end of the bed. "That is, I'm guessing that a fairy is the one who brought you here. Ask one of the Siria fairies to make you a cup of their tea. It will help you feel better," she finished, right before pulling as hard as she could on the corner of the bed she was holding onto.

Jared let out a yelp as he tumbled to the floor, along with the mattress. After hitting the floor, he rolled over onto his side and groaned. "Really, Arella…"

"Yeah, I really am sorry and all that, but something tells me that we will be entering the labyrinth soon."

There was a moment of silence, before Arella heard the soft snoring of her brother. Rolling her eyes, Arella tapped his side with her foot. "Trust me, if you get up and go to a Siria fairy and drink some of their tea, you will feel better. They have heeling powers."

No answer.

Arella sighed and knelt beside him. "Jared, come on."

The door swung open and a tall man walked in, followed by two young boys and an old man with a long beard. What Arella found odd was that the first man had dark blue skin, and his eyes looked like stars. As she stared up into his peculiar eyes, she felt as if he could see right through her. Like he could see into her past…her thoughts, her fears, her hopes, her crushed dreams.

"Arella Zephyr," the warrior said gruffly.

"Yes?" she said bluntly, tearing her gaze

away from his stare.

"The labyrinth's entrance will open soon," he said, watching her carefully. "At midnight, precisely. I suggest that you, your brother, and the king prepare for your departure."

Arella nodded as she stood, kicking her brother gently. "We'll be ready soon."

Xanthias raised an eyebrow at her. Turning to Kiran, he said, "Go tell one of the Siria fairies to get the boy a cup of tea."

His son nodded and ran out of the room, followed by his older brother.

"Arashi is dead."

Akira bowed her head and sighed. One after the other, her warriors were being killed. Slaughtered. And no matter how much she tried to warn them against doing anything foolish, they would go ahead and do it anyway. Though, she couldn't blame them. Especially Arashi.

"Do you have his body?" the Drago warrioress asked Lilith.

"No. I tried to retrieve it, but could not."

"All right," she said grimly as she gave a small nod. "I need to get ready. I suspect Xanthias is almost ready to lead the chosen to the labyrinth."

"Yes," Lilith said, inclining her head. She watched as Akira slowly stood and walked over to a table. Akira picked up a small mug and drank from it, looking sullen.

"Siria tea," she muttered, holding up the cup. "It is said to have healing powers. I believe it…"

Lilith narrowed her eyes and laid her hand on the hilt of her sword.

Akira shook her head and set down the cup. "It does not heal the mental wounds though." She knocked the mug off of the table with the back of her hand, before turning to face Lilith. "You said a survivor is here, from the attack on the capitol? Who is it?"

"He says his name is Jack. Do you know him?"

A look of relief crossed Akira's face. "Yes. Is an Adrian Raven Shadow with him?"

Lilith scowled as she let her hand slip off of the hilt. "No one knows where Adrian is. The survivor says he ran off during the battle."

Akira nodded and sat down at the table bench. "Bring him in here."

The Nyx fairy turned and walked out, leaving the door to Akira's room slightly open. A few moments later a young boy peeked inside. He had a wild brown mop of hair on his head, some of which was singed, and cuts all over his face. As soon as he saw Akira, he stepped inside and bowed his head.

"Akira," he said, having a little bit of trouble talking due to a swollen lip.

"Jack." Akira quickly stood and walked over to him. "Is something wrong-"

"They have my sister," the young teen sobbed. "They took her and I couldn't stop them. The Royal Guards…they…they took Dakota, Cole, Ocean, Violet…"

"Are they dead?" Akira asked, grasping his

shoulders.

"I-I don't think so." Jack shook his head. "Not yet at least."

Akira released her grip on his shoulders and turned around, looking towards her bed, where her sword lay. "Then we have to rescue them before that sick minded Abraxas kills them."

"Do we leave now?" Jack asked, sounding hopeful.

"No, not quite yet," Akira answered as she was grabbing her sword. "I have to help Xanthias with something first. While you are waiting for me, gather the others and prepare for the battle that will surely happen. Now, go."

"What if we don't make it in time?" Jack pressed.

Akira glanced over her shoulder at him. "We will. Abraxas is most likely busy with sending off monsters and guards to catch the chosen, that he will be too occupied to deal with them."

"You don't sound confident," Jack murmured.

Akira stiffened, then quickly turned to face him. Though she glared down at him, she had a look of worry.

Hansrai, Arella, and Jared followed carefully behind Xanthias, as the chief lead them through the dark tunnels. A small ball of light floated before them, hardly shedding enough light for them to see what was in their path. Arella had slipped off the hood to her cloak, her braid draped over her right shoulder as she walked onward.

"I still say this is a bad idea," Jared murmured.

His sister glanced his way, before giving a quick look down at her right hand. "But we are the chosen."

Jared growled, pulling the hood farther down his face. "I can't believe you *believe* it." Turning to the warrior who was leading them, he asked, "Xanthias, what is the labyrinth like?"

Xanthias continued on, never looking over his shoulder as he spoke. "I cannot remember."

Jared stopped walking for a moment, deep in thought. "Why, has it been a long time since you've been there?"

"I could not enter the labyrinth," Xanthias said slowly, seeming slightly irritated. "Once the tower was erected, the portal of the prison closed, and the monsters locked away, the entrance to the labyrinth was also sealed off."

"Because it is the prison which Seuderak is confined," someone said from up ahead.

A figure walked out of one of the side tunnels and strolled towards them, clad in a dark cape, almost blending in with the shadows. "Hansrai, Arella, Jared," Akira said, nodding to each one as she said their name. She then turned to Xanthias and bowed. "Chief Xanthias. We are ready. The portal to the labyrinth is almost open."

"Portal?" Jared's voice echoed off the underground passage. They continued onward, no one answering him.

Xanthias and Akira lead them into an underground cavern. Glowing stalactites hung from the cave ceiling, shining crystals were embedded in the walls, and vicious fang like rocks jutted out from the cave floor. At the back was a large door, that seemed to be carved out of the rock. Inscribed into the enormous door in three circular formations were strange symbols, some of which appeared as if they were animals.

"Is this the entrance?" Jared asked.

"No, the entrance is inside," Xanthias responded, walking towards the great door. He pushed one of the symbols, which looked like an eye in a diamond. The inscriptions on the doors began to glow. Slowly they swung open with a loud groan, opening up into a long passageway, lit by torches. Along the walls of the channel were paintings of warriors and strange creatures. Dragons, eagles, griffins, and other flying beasts were pictured upon the ceiling.

"We must hasten our speed," Xanthias said. "The labyrinth can only be accessed at midnight, as I said before."

"Is that the reason for it having the name 'The Midnight Labyrinth'?" Jared inquired, looking at the murals as they walked along down the passage.

"More reasons than that," Xanthias answered. "When you enter into the labyrinth, it will always seem as if it is midnight. There will be no day, but always night."

"Oh…that is…nice." Jared shrugged. "Of course, the labyrinth is underground, so, yeah, it would seem like midnight."

Xanthias shook his head. "No, not in that way. You will see. I am sorry that your griffins cannot go with you. They might have come in handy."

Hansrai finally spoke, "You will take care of Summerday and Fleet, won't you?"

The chief looked his way, his eyes shining even brighter underground. "Yes, my sons will. They are quite fascinated with those birds."

The king nodded, hoping he could trust Xanthias and his two boys with the griffins. After losing Twilight, Summerday and Fleet were his only animals that had been given to him by his father and Nicanor. His father was dead and for all he knew, Nicanor was also.

For the next few minutes, they walked in silence. Finally Xanthias stopped, turning to look at the three chosen. "Inside this next cave is the entrance to the labyrinth." He turned a corner, entering into a large cave, a dark inky black lake inside. Reflections of the stalactites and crystals on the ceiling glimmered over the surface of the water.

"There are three pedestals, upon which statues used to stand, surrounding the lake," Xanthias said. "Inscribed upon the tops of the pedestals are the symbols that are on your hands. Find yours and place your hand upon it."

"How will we get into the labyrinth doing that?" Jared mused, glancing down at his hand. "And how did you know I-"

"He probably saw it," Hansrai offered.

"Once you entered into the area outside of the borders of the West-which is where this entrance rests-those symbols burned into your hands," Xanthias explained. "I know more about you than you know."

"Ah, weird," Jared muttered, glancing at Arella. His sister shrugged and the two siblings slowly walked away from each other, searching the perimeter of the lake. Arella found hers on the right side of the water, upon which she rested her hand. Immediately the symbol on her hand began to glow. The pedestal lowered a few inches, before a flat rock slowly rose out from the water. Cautiously Arella stepped onto the rock, which lowered an inch, its edge right above the water. She looked around, wondering if her brother and Hansrai had found theirs.

Jared leisurely went to the left side, half-heartedly searching for his pedestal. When he found it, he followed the same procedures of which his sister did. He felt a little nervous as the rock of which he stepped onto lowered.

Hansrai hadn't moved yet, but looked to Akira and Xanthias, a little confused. He took a deep breath and walked forward, towards where the last pedestal stood. When he placed his hand on the top, he expected a rock to come up for him to step on, like with the others, but nothing happened....at first. Suddenly one of the diamonds on the ceiling began glowing, a light beam shooting forth from it and hitting another diamond, until it spread to every gem. The end of the light beam hit one crystal, before coming down to touch the middle of the lake. Immediately the water started to swirl, creating a whirlpool.

The water rushed over Jared's feet and in

moments he slipped and was desperately reaching out for something to hold onto. He clung to the rocks, closing his eyes and muttering as the water seemed to try to pull him under. "Help!" he called, his grip loosening. He gritted his teeth, before calling out, "Arella!" Then the water took him, his head disappearing under the dark water.

"Jared!" Arella screamed. She searched frantically for her brother, until she saw him coming her way. She reached out with one hand, grabbing Jared. He only pulled her under as well, both vanishing from sight.

"Arella, Jared!" Hansrai shouted, rushing over to jump into the water. A strong hand held him back. He spun around to see Xanthias standing behind him.

"Do not fear, they are safe," the chief said. He looked at the water, as a rock rose up for Hansrai. "But before you leave, I must say something to you."

Hansrai pulled his arm from Xanthias's grip and stared hard at him.

"In this quest, you will have to play the role of the leader. There will be many hardships, struggles, and pain you must go through, but in the end, you must prevail."

The young king listened to his words carefully, staring out at the swirling black water. Play the role of a leader? Hardships, struggles, pain? *Must* prevail. The anguish stuff was for certain, but victory…well, it would all depend on how the chosen would work together.

"Stay strong, young warrior," Xanthias said.

The king nodded and stepped onto the rock.

He waited for it to lower, but it didn't budge. Frowning, Hansrai looked back, but before Hansrai could ask anything, the stone upon which he stood went under, and Hansrai was pulled into the icy water. He was dragged down, down, down...for what seemed like forever.

Chapter 21
The End of the Traitor

"My lord."

Abraxas spun around to see Calista floating behind him, looking as if he was on edge. He sighed when he saw her, as if he had been expecting someone else to be standing behind him. "What do you want?"

Calista's form flickered. "Captain Rajan has returned...and with news, my lord."

Abraxas floated nervously around the

thrown room. "Do you know if it is good news?"

"No, but by his behavior, my lord, I would guess it is grave news."

With a nod, Abraxas pointed to the doors as his face turned dark orange. "Leave me...NOW! And tell Captain Rajan to come in."

Calista's eyes widened and she quickly flew out of the room, leaving Abraxas alone again. The Shathrack growled and floated over to the murals of the many kings that had ruled Aselda. He stopped in front of the one of the young King Hansrai the III and glared.

Were the chosen in the labyrinth? If they were, then Seuderak would certainly kill him. His job had been to kill the chosen, but they had slipped out of his grasp. Of course, they had help from the Jin Warriors.

Drago Warriors.

Letting out an angry cry, Abraxas spun around to see the largest Royal Guard standing about ten feet away, watching the royal adviser quietly.

"Captain Rajan," Abraxas said, his voice trembling with rage. "What news do you bring?"

"As the tower collapses, the magical wall that surrounds Ardara falls also," the warrior grunted. "Creatures from the surrounding countries are now able to enter into our kingdom."

"What kind of creatures?" Abraxas asked. He had known that this would happen, but if certain creatures came about...

"Saber Killers."

"Good," Abraxas muttered, turning around and floating towards the throne. "Seuderak wished for them to come. They will wipe out everyone, just as our master wishes."

"If the borders break in the East, we will have to deal with sirens or mermaids, or possibly both," the Royal Guard said, barring his fangs. There was a moment of silence, before he finished, "The mermaids will fight for the people."

"But the sirens will most likely go ramped and attack anyone, just like the Saber Killers," Abraxas said.

Captain Rajan stiffened. "What are your orders now, Abraxas?"

The Shathrack stared at the throne triumphantly. "Prepare for departure...We must leave before the Saber Killers come and do their job."

The guard snarled and started walking away.

"Oh, and one more thing," Abraxas started to say.

"What?" Captain Rajan grunted.

"Leave no defenses up. We want everyone here to die," Abraxas chuckled coldly. "Ah! And kill a pig."

Captain Rajan seemed confused. "Pig?"

"Yes," Abraxas answered. "Make a trail of the blood leading to the prison, where the Drago Warriors are. That will be the Saber Killer's dessert."

Abraxas took a deep breath as he entered into his room.

Captain Rajan's news had been good, but

what Abraxas really needed to know was if the chosen were dead yet. If they were still alive, the guards had better deal with them quickly. If the chosen had been able to enter the labyrinth, then Abraxas had only one thing he could do: run. If Seuderak discovered that the chosen had entered the labyrinth-

The Shathrack shook his head. There were hundreds of monsters and guards hunting for them. Seuderak had said that he would send any monsters that had escaped the prisons to hunt down the chosen. There was no way the chosen could make it to the labyrinth.

Unless Xanthias and his friends find them, he thought. He closed his eyes and tried to push away the thought. *No, their supposed to be dead. Or...most of them.*

"Is something the matter, Abraxas?" asked a raspy voice. The yellow Shathrack flinched, covering his ears with his hands to block out the terrible noise. Slowly he turned to see an image of Seuderak himself, standing before him. The evil wizard wore a black cloak, that had burn holes and rips, the rims of the tears stained in blood of previous enemies, of which he had slain. Though his hood covered his face entirely, Abraxas could see a ball of white electricity sparking to life inside, looking as if there were a star in the place of the wizard's head. The sorcerer reached out a hand, which was claw like, and also stained in the sickly red.

"L-lord, S-Seuderak," Abraxas stammered, bowing his head. "What brings you here?"

The sorcerer did not say anything, but

instead delved deeply into Abraxas's mind, giving his message there.

Abraxas trembled, gritting his teeth and shaking his head violently. "N-noo!! STOP!" Abraxas howled. "It...it's too painful!"

The chosen have entered the labyrinth! You failed me! Seuderak's angry voice rang in Abraxas's ears. *YOU LET THEM ESCAPE!*

"M-my l-lord," Abraxas stammered, bowing his head. "They...they had h-help from the Jin W-warriors, which were actually the D-Drago-"

How could you have been so blind! The image of Seuderak flickered. *I would have pleasure in killing you myself, but I am not quite strong enough to leave my prison. My sister will take care of you for me.* The image of Seuderak vanished in a pillar of smoke, right as a sharp pain went through the Shathrack.

Abraxas fell to the ground, hitting his head on the stone floor. He lay there, half conscious. A few moments passed, until he finally started to come around. He brushed his hand across the floor-then his eyes widened. He had flesh on his hands...Quickly standing, Abraxas looked over his now human body. "Wh-what...?! No! Seuderak!!"

"Do you not like your new body?" someone hissed from behind him.

Abraxas turned just in time to see cold golden eyes staring at him. He heard the sound of two swords being drawn from their scabbards, and caught the sight of the assassin's wicked grin, before he felt the assassin's sharp blades press against his throat. The assassin hesitated just a moment, as if taunting him, before bringing her swords together, like closing giant shears.

Thunk.

The assassin straightened and turned towards a bed in the room. She scowled, unsure why a Shathrack would need a bed. Not really caring though, the assassin walked over to the bed and rubbed her twin blades on its bedspread.

She sheathed her swords and with not even a glance at the dead adviser, kicked open the door and walked into the hall outside. There was a loud thud from the crashing door, then everything went silent. The assassin narrowed her eyes and then quickly turned to her right, reaching for her blades once again.

One of the Royal Guards leaned against the wall, his arms crossed as he watched her. By his armor, she figured he was Captain Rajan.

For a minute, no one spoke or moved.

The assassin kept her eyes trained on the guard, listening for anyone else who might be stalking in the dark passageway. She waited, seeing if the guard would make his move. Finally, the guard started to move forward, but before he could finish taking one step, the assassin reached for a shuriken and threw it at him. The guard deflected it, but when he turned his attention back to the assassin, a dart hit him in the neck.

He groaned and fell to the floor with a dull thump. The assassin stood, watching the body of the guard carefully, examining him to see if he was still alive. If he was, the poison which she had smeared on the darts would kill him after a few minutes.

Suddenly the silence was broken as someone else in the corridor stepped out of the shadows, clapping softly. It was one of the Royal Guards-Captain Rajan. The assassin glared at him, before glancing down at the body that lay to her right. She walked over to it and kicked the helmet off of the head, staring hard at the dead figure's face.

Smirking slightly, the assassin glanced back up at the large guard, who was still quietly clapping.

"Impressive," the guard snarled as he finished clapping.

The assassin reached into her cape, but the Royal Guard raised his hand. "You wouldn't want to kill me."

There was a slight moment of hesitation, before the assassin threw three of the shurikens at the guard. Captain Rajan unsheathed his sword and brought it up just in time to deflect the sharp weapons, then turned to face the assassin, who was rushing at him. He brought his sword up to try and block the attack, but it was too late. He felt one of her swords pierce his chest, while the other one was driven into his stomach.

"My brother no longer has any need for you," the assassin hissed as she jerked the weapons from his body. The guard glared at her with wide eyes, then collapsed.

The assassin chuckled as she wiped her swords on his back and sheathed them. "I'm ready," she muttered.

A portal opened in front of her and she leapt through.

Chapter 22
Preparing to Escape

"I hope they succeed," Akira said as she stared at

the stilling water. "They bicker and do not know what the meaning of teamwork is."

"Were we any different?" Xanthias asked as he glanced at her.

She looked away grimly and didn't say anything in response to him.

The wizard nodded and turned to leave. "Come, we must hurry."

"Yes, my lord," Akira said, quickly following. "I will be leaving with my warriors soon to free-"

"No, you will not," Xanthias cut her sentence short. "We will all be leaving for the haven. On the way, we will find any villages that we can evacuate. The monsters will be crawling all over Ardara in a matter of days. We cannot wait any longer to head to SoundHarbor."

"What about my warriors?" Akira pressed.

"You will be able to save them once we reach Aselda, if they are still alive," Xanthias replied.

Akira bit her tongue to keep from talking back. Most of the time, she was used to giving the orders and being in charge. Everyone usually listened to her, but when she was around Xanthias or the other wizards, she was no longer anyone of great importance.

"Princess Amara-"

"Don't you dare call me that," Akira hissed dangerously as she reached for her knife.

Xanthias stopped walking and raised his hands in defense. "I am sorry...*Akira*."

Akira nodded and after sheathing her sword, she started walking again.

Xanthias shook his head as he watched her. *Her...and the chosen girl, Arella. They both have the same problem, but yet in different forms. Akira thinks she can change her name and act like she is not who she is, but when it comes down to it, she's ready to say she is who she is. Arella won't tell anyone about her dark past and tries to hide it, even from her own brother; who should have the right to know.*

He shook his head and started walking again.

"Father! Father!" Kiran called as he ran up to Xanthias. "Master Caspar says we may travel with him."

Xanthias looked slightly worried. "Do you *want* to go with him?"

"Yeah, with a guy who's lost his marbles?" Kirrat asked as he walked up behind Kiran. He looked at the huts that stood around them. "He almost blew this place up while you were gone, father."

"That sounds like Caspar," Xanthias muttered. "Where is he now?"

"Eating bacon by the campfire. Everyone is working but him," Kirrat answered. "Though he sometimes raises his staff to use his magic to lift a heavy crate."

"Have you helped?" Xanthias asked his sons, looking them both in the eyes. "Everyone needs to help. We don't have much time."

"Yes, father," the two boys answered,

nodding proudly.

"Good. Now go make sure your things are ready. Pack lightly," Xanthias told them, drawing them close. "All right?"

"Of course father..." Kiran hesitated, before venturing to ask, "May I bring a picture of mother?"

Xanthias sighed, his appearance seeming forlorn. "Yes...of course. You *should* take it."

The boys nodded grimly, before running towards their hut. Xanthias watched them sadly, thinking about his beloved Ayla. He missed her dearly, and so did the boys. They hadn't really known their mother, since she had died when Kiran was just a baby. Ever since she had been taken, something seemed to have been missing from their family. Part of their hearts had been chipped away, leaving an everlasting ache in them.

"You miss her."

Xanthias turned to see Lilith standing beside him. "Yes, I do," the wizard answered.

Lilith nodded, glancing over to a group of fairies that were helping an elderly couple with packing the last of their supplies. "We have all been through hard times. Many of us have lost loved ones...but we cannot let that hinder our job."

Xanthias smiled slightly at her, before walking away to make his rounds in the village. He had to make sure everyone knew what was happening. He estimated that they had about an hour before they would be ambushed by Seuderak's monsters. Not from reports, but from how the atmosphere around him felt. He could sense them.

"Are they almost ready?" Xanthias asked Akira as they stood right outside the village. The wizard was looking up at the night sky, as if reading the stars. The Drago Warrior, on the other hand, stood motionless, her hood obscuring her face.

"Yes, my lord," she answered softly, though her voice had an edge to it.

Xanthias gave a nod and after another moment of watching the stars, he turned to Akira. "Do you have any family in the Drago Territory? Children, perhaps-"

"I am not married and I have not been at any time," Akira clipped. "Consequently I have *no* children. My family are the Drago Warriors."

Xanthias was somewhat surprised, though he did not show it. After all these years, and she had never married? There had certainly been many warriors after her hand in marriage, considering who she was. On the other hand, Akira had never been the sort of person to flirt when she was younger and never seemed interested in a relationship with a man. She had been somewhat close to her master and the warriors, though she only bonded with them through training. Nothing else. While Xanthias had been distracted-

He stopped himself right there.

"Are your only children Kiran and Kirrat?" Akira asked, though she seemed despondent on talking about the matter.

"No, I have three older boys and a daughter, but they were captured at a young age," Xanthias answered bitterly. "If they are still alive, they should be young adults now."

"You waited a *very* long time before having children," Akira muttered, even though she didn't really care at that point. "I am sorry that they were taken away from you. Did any of them...resemble you? Your two boys, Kiran and Kirrat, look nothing like you."

"My two eldest sons," Xanthias replied.

"And the rest of the children take after...Ayla?"

Xanthias looked pained. "Yes."

Akira went silent, feeling remorseful.

Xanthias noticed that she had stiffened and stared at her, seeing right through to her heart. There was some guilt there. Narrowing his eyes, Xanthias questioned, "Akira, do you know something about what happened to Ayla?"

The Drago warrioress shook her head. "No...no, I don't." She turned to leave. "I will go check on the portal. Lilith and Seraphina should almost be finished with it."

"Akira, if you know anything about my wife's death, it would be best to tell me, instead of keeping it secret," Xanthias warned. "Or I will have to find out for myself."

Akira stopped for a moment. "Trust me, I know *nothing*," she hissed, before quickly walking away.

"Hello, Kira dear," Caspar's jolly voice said as he passed by her. She ignored him, brushing past him and quickly making her way towards the village. Caspar watched her as his eyebrows knitted together in confusion. "Humph. What is wrong with her? She can be quite friendly sometimes."

He quickly turned to Xanthias. "Yet, when we were younger she always seemed to become sensitive while around you. Now she seems to hate being around you even more so. Though, sometimes she hides it better than other times." He almost spit out something that was in his mouth and raised a hand. He quickly chewed and swallowed, before grabbing a handful of his favorite meat from his pocket. "Bacon?"

"No, Caspar," Xanthias replied sharply. His friend lowered his hand and looked somewhat hurt by his friend's tone of voice. The other wizard shook his head and looked away. "I thought by now we all would have outgrown this," Xanthias muttered, crossing his arms. "You haven't changed…Akira has, but she has only become more cold. From what I can sense, she has lived a dark life since we were all together."

"Haven't we all," Caspar said, surprisingly serious.

Xanthias glanced at him. "We thought life would be better after Seuderak was imprisoned and the protective walls went up. For a while times were not as dark, but then there was the civil war. The country split. Look at us now."

"And soon the terror that we locked away will rise," Caspar said, his voice just a whisper for a moment. "You cannot sweep your problems under the rug and expect them to never come back, Xanthias. Now you are having three younglings go to destroy *your* problem. Your problem that you should have dealt with long ago."

For a minute his voice changed and his eyes started glowing. "You were claimed a hero, when all you did was lock away your enemies, hoping they would stay locked up forever. While you should have been watching over your people, you were distracted and acting immature. Your people were wiped out during the civil war. You are now the last of your kind."

Xanthias narrowed his eyes at his friend. It took him a moment, but then he finally figured out what was happening. He tried to ignore what his friend had just said and asked, "Who released them?"

Turning to Xanthias, Caspar's eyes glowed brighter. "The-"

Before he could finish his eyes stopped glowing and he collapsed, as if another force had intervened. Instead of catching his friend, Xanthias looked up, to see black clouds moving in over the village. One of the clouds started to morph into the shape of a head. Seuderak's head.

"He's becoming stronger," Xanthias growled. He then turned to his friend. "Caspar, quickly, get up."

"Bacon," Caspar groaned.

"Caspar!"

"B-bacon…" Caspar stirred slightly as he muttered the word, drool oozing from the corner of his mouth.

Xanthias glanced back in the direction of the village as he started hearing screams. He could go after them, or try to wake his friend.

"B-b-bacon…h-ham," his friend mumbled.

Xanthias knelt down and reached for some bacon that his friend had dropped. He quickly waved it by Caspar's nostrils, glancing up and looking towards the village. He saw a bright flash of orange and purple, and he knew that the portal was finished and that the villagers were starting to make it through.

The sound of someone munching told him that his friend was conscious. He grabbed Caspar's shoulders and hauled him to his feet. "The village is being attacked," Xanthias said, starting to run towards his home.

Caspar licked his fingers and started to reach for another piece of bacon, then he stopped when a shrill cry tore through the air. He jumped, suddenly coming to reality. He followed Xanthias, running as fast as he could, while digging in his pockets for something that might come in handy.

Kirrat and Kiran saw their father and Caspar rushing towards them, struggling to move past the mass of panicking villagers. The boys started hollering to them, waving their hands wildly in the air as they tried to get their attention. Kiran looked up at the sky and then tugged at Kirrat's shirt.

"Th-that cloud…"

"Be quiet, Kiran, I'm trying to hear what father is saying," Kirrat snapped irritably.

"But look!" Kiran cried, pointing upwards.

Kirrat sighed and gave a quick look to where his brother was pointing. His eyes widened as he watched a giant hand created by the dark clouds reach down. Everyone screamed and moved out of the way, while still rushing for the portal. Everyone but Kiran and Kirrat. The two boys were frozen in place, watching the giant hand in horror.

"KIRAN!" Xanthias shouted, pushing past a fairy and elf. "KIRRAT!"

The two boys started crying out for help as the hand came crashing down, before its spiny fingers wrapped around them. "*Father!*" they hollered, struggling to wriggle out of the giants grasp. Two fairies flew towards them and tried to help, but another hand knocked them aside.

"Finally, at last," a raspy voice boomed.

The large cloud figure started to tighten its grip, which seemed impossible since it was created from storm clouds. But of course, they were created by Seuderak himself.

"AIIH!" the boys cried beating on the fist wildly. "Father help us!"

The cloud monster started to laugh, when there was a bright flash of lightning and the clouds started to evaporate.

"What is going on?!" Caspar asked, startled.

"Something is interfering with his connection to the world outside his prison, drawing him back in," Xanthias answered, staring up. "Where is Lilith?! We need someone to catch the boys when they start to fall-"

He glanced at his friend, who was running off. "*Caspar!*" he yelled after him, feeling himself becoming extremely angry. "CASPAR YOU-"

"Father!"

Xanthias quickly looked up to see the dark clouds quickly fading-and his children plummeting towards the ground.

Chapter 23
The Labyrinth

The caves trembled and the glowing crystals flickered as a thunderous roar blew down the underground tunnels, followed by a deafening crash that echoed down one of the smaller channels. The echo continued down the thousands of other passageways, startling several creatures that dwelt there.

A distressed rat rushed away to get out of the tunnel the crash had come from, scurrying over a pair of boots. Before it could scamper off of the object, the person to whom the boots belonged to kicked upward. The rat let out a terrified squeak as it was flung into the air and disappeared into the surrounding darkness.

"What did you do?" a voice resonated down the tunnel as a figure walked up behind the first. A third followed, coughing from the dust that had followed after the crash.

"I pulled on a stalagmite," Arella answered matter-of-factly, "that was like a lever."

"Are you sure you should have done-" Jared started coughing again.

"Something tells me whatever you did sealed us off from the outside world," Hansrai said, sounding stressed. When Arella seemed unfazed as she examined the tunnel, the young king shook his head. "Don't you get it? I think you closed the entrance to the labyrinth-We won't be able to-"

"I know," Arella cut in, scowling as she raised a hand to silence him. "Something is telling me that was the best thing to do."

"*Best thing to do*?!" Hansrai stared at her, shocked. "How will we get out?"

Arella did not answer right away, but started walking forward, down the tunnel. She stopped for a moment, tapped her fist against the cave wall to her left, listened, and frowned when the wall sounded hollow. She drew her sword, and after a moment of studying the wall, she brought the blade around and hit the rock surface.

There was the sound of her sword scraping against the hard, sturdy rock, before she let go of her sword and it clattered to the cave floor. "Huh," she muttered, bending over to retrieve her weapon. "That's odd."

"Even if it was hollow on the other side," Hansrai said, pointing at the wall and looking aggravated, "I don't think a sword would cut through it."

"My sword is enchanted," Arella hissed at him dangerously, shooting a venomous glare in his direction.

Hansrai stared back angrily, but didn't say anything else.

Arella watched the king, before striking at the wall again. This time, instead of the sound of her sword scratching the rock surface, a low, moaning cry whistled down the tunnel. Jared jumped, reaching for his sword immediately after his astonishment turned to fear. Hansrai already had his sword drawn, his eyes narrowed as he searched the tunnel ahead.

"When I sealed us from the outside world, I was trapping something else as well," Arella said, looking up at the ceiling as if something should be crawling across it. "Or *someone*. Seuderak."

Hansrai and Jared shuddered. They knew he was in there…They knew he was trapped in the same place where they were doomed to stay until they had killed him. But being reminded that as long as they were free to leave, so was *he*.

"It won't last forever," Arella muttered, sheathing her sword. "It will just delay him. He will have to become stronger before he is able to break free."

"What about that…that…" Jared couldn't finish, his face turning an ashen color. "That was *him*, wasn't it?"

Arella nodded grimly. "I believe it was."

"But…Did he really feel it?" Hansrai asked, shaking his head. "I mean, when you hit the wall. Did *he* feel the strike?"

Arella nodded again. "If what Akira told me was true, then Seuderak is imprisoned within the heart of the labyrinth…I think he somehow attached himself to the life source of the labyrinth to gain energy. That explains how he is gaining power so quickly."

"Attached himself to the labyrinth…" Hansrai thought for a long moment, looking worried. "Could that mean that maybe…possibly, he could use the labyrinth against us? Could he control it?"

"Yes," Arella answered darkly. "That means he will also know where we are at. Possibly the whole way." She started walking. "We have to hurry, before he gains absolute control over the labyrinth!"

Hansrai and Jared quickly followed, walking at a fast pace.

"This is a labyrinth," Hansrai thought aloud. "A maze...a puzzle, right? We have to try to find our way through here and find Seuderak. What if he messes with the maze? If he can control it at all, then he might be able to move parts of the maze."

"That could be a possibility," Arella said as they exited the cave and came to a small chamber, where at least six other channels split from.

"Oh great," Hansrai groaned. "Which one?"

"One will probably lead outside of this underground part," Arella said, turning in circles as she examined each of the tunnels. "If we are underground..."

"Then find the one that goes up," Hansrai guessed. "Which would mean..." He turned to one on his left. "That one appears to slope upward."

"Wouldn't that be a little *too* easy?" Jared asked, crossing his arms. "Plus, just because the tunnel appears to be going up, does not mean it is like that the whole way. It could just be like a hill or something."

"Then do we choose the one that slopes downward?" Hansrai questioned.

"No, that might really slope down," Arella put in, shaking her head.

"Which one do we use?" Jared hollered, his voice echoing down the tunnels. Arella was at his side in moments, her hand over his mouth.

"Shh," she hissed in his ear. "Do not be so loud."

Her brother stared at her with wide eyes and then slowly nodded. Arella waited a moment, before removing her hand from his mouth. She wiped her hand on her pants and sighed. "We could split up. Jared with me. Hansrai, you go down whatever tunnel you choose."

"That sounds more like you are trying to get rid of me," Hansrai grumbled. "Besides, I do not think it safe for us to split up. We should stick together.

"Say for instance we decide to split," Hansrai said, kneeling down and drawing a picture in the dirt on the floor. "Before separating, we decide that we go down one tunnel a ways and then come back here to meet up. Seuderak moves the labyrinth around, messing it up. Then what are we going to do? He will do anything in his power to keep us apart. As the chosen, we are supposed to work together in destroying him. That might be the only way."

Arella stared at him for a moment before shrugging. "You're smarter than I thought you were. All right. We will not be splitting up then."

Hansrai smiled slightly, feeling good about making a good choice. Of course, he had just made it and they hadn't felt the consequences from it yet, but he had a hunch that that was the best decision. It made sense. If they stayed together, then they could work things out together and wouldn't worry about getting lost-on their own.

"Let us try the tunnel that leads upward,"

Hansrai said, pointing his sword toward the channel of which he spoke of.

"I'm not so sure about this," Jared grumbled as he and his sister followed Hansrai.

"We have to try something," Hansrai said as he entered the tunnel. "We have to find Seuderak before it is too late."

Jared and Arella entered the tunnel and looked around carefully, making sure nothing was lurking in the shadows. "It looks like this tunnel becomes darker. The glowing crystals and gems are thinning out," Jared observed. "Do you think it best to travel this way?"

Hansrai glanced at Arella. "Could you take care of the lighting?"

"No," she answered slowly, "but Akira might have packed something that will work."

"All right. We'll go back for our packs," Hansrai said, starting to walk back the way they had come. "If there is nothing that will help with us traveling through the dark, we'll pick a different path."

They quickly made it back to the chamber, but when they did, Arella and Hansrai froze.

"What is it?" Jared asked.

"Which tunnel did we come through?" Hansrai asked, looking at the many other passage ways. "They all look the same now…"

Arella walked around, studying each of the tunnels. "Each channel is *exactly* the same. Even how the glowing rocks are embedded in the cave walls."

Hansrai spun around to face the tunnel they had just walked through, when his face went white.

"Now *all* of them look the same. Even the one we just went through."

"What are we going to do now?" Jared whimpered.

"Stop moping," Arella snapped as she pushed past him. She went to one of the tunnels and used her sword to scratch at the ceiling. "Look," she said as the blade went right through one of the crystals. "It is like an illusion."

"Does that help us?" Hansrai asked, stroking his chin. "We need to find those packs."

"This tunnel," Arella said as she walked up to the one behind Hansrai. "I'll be right back."

"Wait, what happened to not splitting up?" Hansrai asked as he grabbed her arm.

Arella glared at him. "Not splitting up, checking," she said, pulling away from his grip. "You and Jared will stay right here. I will go fetch our packs and be right back." Without waiting for an answer, she walked towards the tunnel. As soon as she entered, she disappeared from sight.

Hansrai blinked. "The illusion is going to become highly annoying."

"Should we follow her?" Jared questioned.

Hansrai started to answer, when he hesitated. "She'll be fine, won't she? Arella is your sister, you know her better than I do."

Jared grimaced. "Yeah, you are right. She probably already has the bags and is heading this way right now." He looked confused for a moment. "Remind me again why we left the packs back in the tunnel?"

Hansrai's face went blank. "I...don't remember." Then his eyes widened as he lifted his sword. "Hurry."

Jared nodded and they both ran into the tunnel. They didn't know exactly what was going on, but something told them that Seuderak was messing with them.

Chapter 24
Leaving Home

Xanthias didn't waist a moment more. He snatched Caspar's staff, rushed forward, and raised the thick rod, his eyes burning with determination. A glowing net started to appear beneath the boys, growing fast. It stretched out, floating in midair and appeared as if it wouldn't be able to keep the boys from falling.

As soon as Kiran hit the net, it started to sway, and then bounced, sending him flying upward and knocking into his older brother. The two boys hollered in alarm as they fell onto the net, bounced up into the air, and then tumbled back down onto the netting. They started to fly upward again, when the net closed around them, then slowly started to lower.

As soon as the net was safely on the ground, Xanthias dropped the staff and rushed forward. He peeled away the netting, the now-web-like substance tearing away at his touch. In moments he had Kirrat and Kiran out, both boys still looking as if they were in shock.

"Are you alright?" Xanthias asked, grabbing Kiran's shoulders.

"Y-yes father," the boy muttered, seeming to be in a daze. Then he smiled. "Can I do that again?"

His father stared back at him, before shaking his head. "No, you *cannot*."

"Aw," Kiran whimpered.

"Xanthias, monsters have been spotted near the border," Lilith warned as she appeared next to him. "We have to get everyone out of here."

The wizard nodded. "How long do we have?"

"Fifteen minutes," Lilith answered darkly. "Unless those monsters are following others."

Xanthias knew what she was getting at and nodded again. "How many villagers have gone through the portal?"

"About a third," Lilith answered. "I sent some of my guards with them."

"Good. Start moving everyone through, *now*," Xanthias ordered, searching the sky where the cloud that had morphed into Seuderak had been. "We don't have much time."

"Why do you say it like that?" Caspar asked as he walked up to them after Lilith had left, holding his staff tightly as if he were afraid that Xanthias would take it again. "You make it sound all dark and mysterious and as if we have run out of time. As if all hope is lost. As if-"

Xanthias looked at him as if to say, "We get the idea."

"Yes, well," Caspar puffed out his chest. "Xanthias, the chosen are in the labyrinth-" Xanthias grimaced slightly when he said this, remembering what had happened earlier when they had discussed it "-and will vanquish the enemy. The portal is prepared and we are evacuating the villagers. We are uniting the mighty and powerful wizards, huzzah! Well, more like re-uniting the mighty first chosen ones-which I and you are part of-is more like it!"

"Sorry, don't you mean *you and I*?" Kirrat corrected.

"Don't interrupt, boy," Caspar said, waving a hand distastefully in Kirrat's direction. "What could go wrong?! I mean-"

"You shouldn't say that," Kiran cut in.

Caspar glanced at him, slightly annoyed. After a moment, he took a deep breath and then grabbed Xanthias's shoulders, trying to shake him like a madman would. "Xanthias we are mighty warriors! POWERFUL WIZARDS!"

Xanthias stood as still as a rock as he stared at his friend. He scowled when Caspar said the last part.

"Caspar?"

"Yes?"

"Have you been drinking?"

Caspar stopped and thought for a moment. "No." Then he frowned, looking shocked that his friend had asked him that. "Xanthias, you fool, you know I don't drink! I've just had...too much bacon...and I've lost my marbles..."

Xanthias made a face as if he would be raising an eyebrow, though he didn't have any hair on his face.

"We have almost everyone through," Lilith announced as she ran up to them. "The last few villagers are going through the portal as we speak. The rest of my warriors are ready for departure, as well as Akira's Drago Warriors."

Xanthias nodded. "Thank you, Lilith. Please take my sons to the portal."

The fairy bowed her head, turned to Kirrat and Kiran, narrowed her eyes, and then started walking. Kirrat followed reluctantly, but Kiran hesitated. He turned to his father with pleading eyes.

"If you won't come, why can't we go with you?"

Xanthias sighed and knelt down. "It is too dangerous."

"Father-" Kiran was cut short as Kirrat grabbed him and dragged him away.

"You will be safe at the haven!" Xanthias called to his boys. "I *will* see you again!"

"Again, with the dramatic statements," Caspar said, shaking his head. "Goodbye, boys." He waved to them as he said to Xanthias, "Do you suppose any of the other wizards will come to aid us? Perhaps my twin brother, Drystan. Or Lillian...she is one of the best cooks around." He sighed and closed his eyes, imagining all the food she could make.

"Lillian would not come. It is not safe for her. She is not one of us," Xanthias said, watching Caspar carefully. "She is Santxo's child. Just because she is the daughter of a wizard does not mean that she has acquired his powers."

Caspar sighed. "And this is about the time when the monsters rush into the village, chasing down any villagers that have not made it to the portal. I and you will run up to the fairies, elves, and others in distress, heroically save them, and then leave to save other villagers from the nasty creatures."

As he finished saying this, a smaller of the monster lizards rushed around one of the huts and charged at them. Caspar sighed and raised his staff. A bolt of lightning struck down, frying the lizard and turning it to ashes. Caspar half coughed, half chuckled. He turned to Xanthias, his hair singed and standing on end. "Just like old times, eh?"

Xanthias shook his head as he drew his claymore. "*Just* like old times." He turned and watched as one of the bear-like creatures rushed him head on. He easily brought his sword up to strike the bear, killing it immediately.

"Do you still call your sword *Ayla, The Guiding Star*?" Caspar asked as he swung his staff around, sending random lightning bolts to fry monsters.

Xanthias gritted his teeth, feeling a sharp pain in his heart. "Perhaps, why?"

"I always found it an odd name," Caspar said, his eyes widening when one of the lizards hissed at him. "Ugly beast," he muttered, before scorching it. He then glanced at Xanthias. "Behind you."

His friend spun around and stabbed a giant wolf which had crept up behind him.

"It wasn't like she was a guardian or anything," Caspar said, blinking. "So why did you call your sword that?"

Xanthias sighed, cutting his way towards the part of the village where the portal was. "This isn't the time for this."

"Ah, but I'd like to know!" Caspar said, following as he twirled his staff. No beast seemed able to reach three yards near the half mad wizard, before being fried.

"Because Ayla was the star that guided me out of the darkness!" Xanthias hollered. Suddenly he seemed to have a burst of energy and he quickly attacked the monsters with more vigor.

"Ah, true love," Caspar said, shaking his head sadly. "I hope when I find my true love, she will be an expert on cooking bacon and ham." He licked his lips, trying to imagine the taste of bacon.

Xanthias looked at him strangely for a moment.

"Oh, we're almost to the portal, I can see it!" Caspar frowned slightly. "Oh bother, I do see that not all the villagers have gone through it yet…It appears the last few are struggling to get there…yes…Mm, this is not good…Oh look, Lilith's fairies are helping them. They're almost there."

Xanthias took out the last few monsters that were near him and rushed to his friend's side. "By the time they get through the portal, the doorway will take forever to close…unless the fairies that are keeping it open allow the portal to shut too quickly and die." He looked at his friend. "There are just a few monsters now, but there will be more. You must go find more help."

Caspar stroked his beard. "This is enough monsters for me for a whole month!" He scowled at a monster, pointed his staff at it, and then nodded after the creature turned to dust. "Should I fetch my brother?"

"No-"

"Conrad?"

"N-"

"Santxo?"

Xanthias glared at him.

"Dante?"

"No, Caspar."

"Illusion?"

"Caspar…" Xanthias growled.

"Onyx?"

"Yes, Caspar, I want you to go get Onyx!"

Caspar sighed. "What a wizard."

"CASPAR!"

"Ah?"

"Go find Onyx," Xanthias ordered. "Quickly!"

"What a *woman*, that Onyx is," Caspar said, raising his staff. There was a bright flash, and then he was gone.

Caspar appeared in a golden hall, his clothes charred. He coughed and dusted off his robes, scowling at the burning in his nose. He stuffed his free hand into his pocket and dug out a handkerchief, his nose twitching.

"Dirt and ashes on the floor," a female's

voice said from behind Caspar. "Tsk, tsk. You have entered the Golden Halls of SoundHarbor…I expect you to be dressed much more…well, properly than this. I will have to speak to Conrad about this situation. Tell me who you are, or I will have to attack."

"Onyx?" Caspar asked as he spun around, still rubbing his nose. "On-Onyx, it-it's m-me," he said, grinning wildly. Then his smile faded and his mouth dropped wide open when he saw the young woman standing before him. She wore a flowing emerald green dress that matched her eyes, a dark burgundy cape, and knee high black boots. Her raven black hair was tied in an ornate braid that rested over her right shoulder, decorated with beads and silk ribbons.

"*Me* is not the correct answer. Unless your parents had no sense of style when it came to names," the female wizard said, looking disdained. But even her scowl looked beautiful on that fair face of hers.

"Caspar." He raised his staff. "I can't believe you don't recognize me! How could we have called one another friends?"

Onyx stiffed and her right hand immediately went to her left hip, as if she was reaching for a sword, though it appeared that no weapon was there. "*We*, as in you and I, were *never* friends." She frowned as she looked him over, her contempt growing. "You look quite old."

"Yes…I have lost my marbles," Caspar answered, before dropping his handkerchief. He started searching his pockets.

"Marbles?" Onyx asked, placing her hands

on her hips.

"Where I keep my sanity," Caspar added, glancing up. "You know...the stuff that keeps us wizards young-"

Onyx rolled her eyes. "I know what it is, Caspar. Now, what do you want? Weren't you supposed to be with Xanthias and Akira?"

Caspar nodded as he pulled two pieces of bacon from his pocket. He started to munch on one and offered the other to Onyx, which she angrily denied. Caspar seemed lost in thought as he slowly chewed, trying to remember what it was that he was supposed to do. He seemed not to be able to remember anything right now...That was what happened when one was near Onyx. She was like an enchantress. Just the sight of her could capture the full attention of a man, even if he was the most cunning of men.

"Caspar, if I remember right," Onyx began, now crossing her arms as she circled around Caspar, "Lilith was to find us, but Conrad found her first. You were with him. He sent you with Lilith to be with Xanthias, am I right? With your help, along with Akira and Lilith's, Xanthias would most likely be fine, while Conrad and the rest of us united and came here to prepare for the others to come. So, please do tell, *why are you here?*"

Suddenly Caspar remembered. "Oh, Xanthias needs you. There are monsters attacking his home and almost everyone should have gone through the portal and should be here as we speak. But Xanthias fears that the portal will not close in time. If that happens, then the monsters will make it through."

Onyx's eyes widened in horror. "Caspar, you fool!" She quickly pushed past him and rushed down the hall, toward a door to the left. As she rested her hand on the doorknob, she said, "You should not have taken so long in telling me. For all I know Xanthias and Akira could be dead now."

Chapter 25
Cave Trolls

"Arella!" Jared and Hansrai called, rushing down the passageway.

A moment later Arella was standing in front of them, holding the packs and looking disappointed. "You have to be quiet!"

"We were worried about you," Hansrai said, sheathing his sword to help hold some of the bags. "Both of us couldn't remember why we had left the packs…My mind continues to draw a blank when I think back on it."

"And that surprises you," Arella said, raising an eyebrow.

"We think Seuderak is behind it," Jared added, ignoring what Arella had said and panting as he offered to take a pack.

Arella sighed. "That surprises you also?"

"Why don't you seem worried?" Hansrai asked.

"I do not see the point in worrying over it," Arella said, scowling. "We just have to be careful." She quickly placed the last pack on her back, making sure the straps were secure. "Ready to head out? We don't have time to be standing around."

Hansrai watched her in disbelief as he strapped his pack on and then slung a smaller one over his shoulder. "Yeah, I'm ready. Though, I think I should be the one who-"

"Who what, princey boy?" Arella said, batting her eyes. "Just because you are-or *once* was-a king of someplace, doesn't mean you can tell me what to do."

Hansrai stiffened. "I would at least like some respect."

Arella raised both eyebrows and turned to Jared. "He wants respect." She then looked back to Hansrai. "Oh, I'm giving you plenty of respect. I haven't killed you yet."

Hansrai clenched his jaw and glared at her.

"Did you hear that?" Jared asked, standing in a strange stance, looking both ways down the tunnel.

"Don't interrupt," Arella snapped.

"No, I'm serious," Jared told his sister, his voice thick with worry. "There is something else in here…I think we should leave."

There was a somewhat dull sound of something making a groaning noise, then the echo of something being scraped along the rock floor. The noises were coming from up ahead, where they were supposed to be going.

"What…" Hansrai's voice trailed off as he reached for his sword.

"Cave troll," Arella answered the unfinished question.

"Cave troll?!"

There was a moment of silence after Jared and Hansrai had said the words a little too loudly. Then an unintelligent half roar, half yawn. Heavy footfalls resounded down the tunnel, growing louder as the troll advanced.

"Great," Arella grumbled, drawing her sword. "Come on, let's face it head on-"

"Or hide quietly until it passes us," Hansrai said, quickly searching for a crack in the wall big enough for them to slide through.

"No time," Arella muttered, rushing forward. She swung her sword upward and sent a force field racing towards the cave troll, but instead of the troll flying back, it just started having trouble walking forward.

"Arrg?" the cave troll grunted, completely confused. Then it saw Arella and growled, struggling to move forward. It roared and tried to beat its club on the invisible force that was pushing it back.

Arella grimaced as her feet almost slipped

on the rock as she wrestled to keep the shield up.

"Hey, you big ugly beast!" Jared hollered as he chunked a rock at the troll, which bounced off of the inside of the shield, not able to go through. Arella ducked to dodge the rock that bounced back at her and then sent a hazardous look Jared's way.

"Sorry," he said, smiling nervously.

Arella shook her head, turned her attention back to the troll, and then gasped as he brought his club around again, smashing the force field. It shattered and sent a force knocking into Arella, which sent her flying back. She flew straight into Hansrai, who was standing not far behind her, and they both went sprawling out onto the floor.

"Look out!" Jared hollered, hoping to warn his sister in time as he watched the troll run forward, raising his club.

Arella's eyes widened and she quickly tried to stand, kicking Hansrai and then stepping on his arm.

"Ow!" Hansrai complained, rubbing his arm.

"Oh stop complaining and stand!" Arella shouted. The troll brought his club down, planning on smashing the two humans, but Arella leapt out of the way. Hansrai let out a startled yelp and rolled out of the way just in time as well.

"Arg!" the troll exclaimed, turning to Arella.

"Yeah, I'm sure you want to kill me," she said, backing away and keeping her sword at the ready. "But, hey, ugly dear, what's the point? Kill him instead!" She pointed at Hansrai. "He's the king! The *leader* of this expedition!!"

The troll seemed confused as it looked from

Arella to Hansrai. Then it rushed at Hansrai, swinging its club wildly. Hansrai's eyes popped wide open as he jumped back. He looked to Arella, stunned, and then started running.

"Why'd you do that?" Jared asked as he rushed to his sister's side. "We need him too."

"I know," Arella said. "I just wanted to see him scared." She grabbed Jared and moved him in front of her.

"H-hey…Arella, w-what are you d-doing?" Jared asked, trying to turn around to look at her. "I am not about to be your shield-"

"Hold still," Arella growled. "I just need to find something that's in your pack…"

"What are you getting?"

"Ah-ha!" Arella held up a glowing orb, like the ones that the Drago Warriors had had. "Akira gave me this."

"Aaah!" Hansrai hollered from down the tunnel. Arella sighed and rushed toward the sound, hoping her plan would work. Of course, when ever did a plan of hers go wrong? Just recently it had…

Arella shrugged it off. This time it would work, and if didn't, they'd find a way out. If Hansrai received some scars, or minor injuries, it wasn't her problem.

When Arella spotted the troll, she started yelling. The cave troll, which had been raising its club to clobber the young king, turned around and grunted. Arella smirked and waved the orb of light in the air. "Look at the pretty light!" she called.

"Arg?" The troll raised a large, burly hand to shield his eyes. "Arg!" He started running forward blindly, swinging his giant club around in a mad attempt to hit Arella.

"Hansrai!" Arella hollered, jumping back and then ducking to avoid the club. "*Get up!*"

The young king scrambled to get to his feet, desperately searching for his sword in the process. He remembered falling to the cave floor and dropping his weapon, but where it had gone, he didn't know. What he did know was that he needed to find it.

"Hansrai!"

He couldn't think clearly. Arella needed his help, but he had to find his weapon to be of any use. Of course, Arella had sent the troll on him in the first place. He knew that she wanted him dead. She could take care of herself, and if she got hurt, it technically would *not* be his fault. On the other hand, that wouldn't be very leader-like of him. How could he call himself a king? Yet…he didn't really *want* to be king.

Hansrai sighed when he found his sword and picked it up. He looked over the arming sword, feeling as if he did not deserve such a knightly sword as this. He wasn't even that good at wielding it…

Yet, he would never be ready to give away this weapon. It was beautiful…A golden cross-guard and pommel, a dark brown leather grip, and rare markings inscribed onto the sharp blade….Hansrai never seemed able to remember what the symbols meant. No one really knew. The sword had just been found in the chambers of King Hansrai the II. It had been a prized possession of his, one that rarely anyone would have had the pleasure of laying their eyes on.

After he had died, the secret hiding place of the cherished weapon found, and the sword retrieved, Hansrai had been given the sword. No one knew if the old king had wanted his son to have the weapon, but once Hansrai had discovered that the sword had been found, he had wanted it.

"*Hansrai*!!" Arella's voice echoed down the tunnel.

The young king looked up and searched for where Arella and the troll had gone, but they were no where in sight. Hansrai shook his head, berating himself. Arella, her brother, and the troll must have already left the channel while he had been lost in thought. Still silently scolding himself, Hansrai started running forward.

Arella and Jared stood side by side, facing the troll, back in the chamber with the many different tunnels branching off from it. Arella held the orb in one hand, with her sword in the other. Jared held his short sword in front of him, glaring at the beast, though he trembled slightly from being anxious. The troll continued to swing his large club, groaning and grunting the whole time.

"He really hates the light," Jared said, right as he and his sister ducked as the club came around again, "and really wants to destroy it."

His sister scowled as she jumped out of the way of another strike. "Yeah?"

"Well, is there some way you can move it away from us?" Jared asked. "If you could do that, it could distract the *ugly thing* so we can get out of here!"

Arella nodded. "I think I can do it." She tossed him the orb. "Distract him!"

"W-wait!" Jared's arms flailed as he struggled to catch the glowing sphere.

Arella knelt down and started to wave her hands in a circle, keeping her hands a few inches apart. "I'm going to create a force field that we can set the orb on, hold it for me for just a moment..."

Jared glanced at the troll, who was looking confused. When Arella had thrown the orb, he started looking back and forth, as if he couldn't tell where it had gone. Finally the troll found which human had the orb and grunted. Jared gulped and then started running down one of the tunnels, the troll right behind him.

Arella glanced up from her work and her eyes widened as she saw the troll disappear into one of the tunnels. She leapt to her feet and the force field that she had been creating vaporized. "Jared, no!" Without hesitating, she rushed after them, completely forgetting about Hansrai.

The chamber. Finally, he had made it. But where was Arella and Jared?

Hansrai groaned and leaned against the cave wall to catch his breath. If they had gone down one of the tunnels, he would never find them. There were too many to choose from, and if this really was a labyrinth, then it would continue to branch off. There would be a million different twists and turns. At one point he maybe would be on the right trail, but if he made one wrong turn, he might never find them. Ever.

Then…he had something to give him a clue as to which tunnel they had gone to.

A loud crashing sound echoed down one of the tunnels to his right, then a dumb sounding roar. A troll's roar. *The* troll's roar.

Hansrai sighed and started jogging down the tunnel where the noises had come from, hoping they wouldn't go into anymore tunnels before he reached them.

As Hansrai left the chamber, he didn't notice another troll coming out of one of the left tunnels. A much larger, much brighter troll, who somehow made his way into the chambers without hardly making a sound. The giant troll held his club with the end resting on his shoulder, inspecting the chamber silently, as if he did this all the time.

The troll noticed something moving out of the corner of its eye, and quietly grunting, turned to see what it was. The figure quickly disappeared as it ran off down the tunnel, something holding what looked like a sword. The troll narrowed its eyes and growled.

The large cave troll was like a giant guard dog, ready to take down any intruders. Now there were trespassers in the tunnels, after years of there just being the trolls and cave rats. Finally, something to hunt…something to chase besides the rats that would always slip away unharmed.

These pesky humans would *not* get away.

Jared cried for help as he looked over his shoulder and saw the troll advancing. "Arellaaa!!"

His sister shook her head and ran faster, until she was behind the troll. She dove to the floor and slid between the troll's feet, before skidding to a stop beside Jared. She quickly leapt to her feet and pointed behind the troll. "Look!"

The troll came to a quick stop and started looking left and right.

"He's still blinded," Arella said, snatching the orb from Jared and quickly hiding it in her cape. She looked around, before spotting a medium sized rock. She picked it up and tossed it over the shoulder of the troll, before moving closer to Jared and covering his mouth with her hand. "Be quiet," she whispered in his ear.

Jared gave a weak nod and watched as the rock hit the stone floor, the impact creating a dull echo. The troll froze in place, listening.

The rock rolled, before coming to a stop. Right at the feet of Hansrai. The young king frowned and picked up the rock, looking over it.

"Raarr!" the troll exclaimed, turning to face the direction where the rock had fallen. It rubbed its eyes, but when that didn't work, it growled. Gripping its giant club, the troll grinned slightly.

Hansrai's eyes widened, then he looked past the troll and glared at Arella. He mouthed something to her and she grimaced.

"Oops," she said.

Jared gave her a nervous side-glance. "Din't you saef non to saef ninythin?!"

Arella quickly removed her hand from covering his mouth. "Run!"

He didn't have to be told twice. Both siblings started running.

The troll looked back and forth, before going after Hansrai. The young king groaned and started to run, when he came to a quick stop. He was going the wrong way to get away from the troll. He needed to be following Arella and Jared. They had to stick together and find their way through the labyrinth. They were wasting their time with this troll and needed to get a move on.

"Rrr."

Hansrai looked up to see the ugly face of a much *larger* troll. For a moment both stood still, staring at the other. Then Hansrai jumped back, swinging his sword wildly at the troll and then quickly spinning around to run off. The other troll was in front of him, rushing at him and swinging his club.

Not knowing what else to do, Hansrai continued to rush at the smaller troll, before diving to the ground and sliding between the troll's feet, barely avoiding the troll's massive club. The two trolls collided, while Hansrai rolled over to his hands and knees and thrust himself up onto his feet.

As the trolls were distracted with untangling themselves, Hansrai ran down the tunnel, hoping he would find Arella and Jared soon, and that they hadn't gone too far.

After heading down the tunnel, he came to a fork in the path, the tunnel leading left and right. He glanced down the left tunnel first. It went on a ways, before turning right. At least, it appeared to go that way from where Hansrai stood. It was either go down that passage way, or go to the right tunnel-

The trolls were up and angry, searching for Hansrai, by the sounds of it. Hansrai didn't dare look over his shoulder to see and started running down the left tunnel. Not the right the right tunnel, where Arella and Jared had gone. No, he went down the *left* tunnel, the *wrong* tunnel.

Arella bit her lip, losing track of all the left turns, right turns, spiraling stairs-yes, there were stairs in the labyrinth, spiral staircases like no other stairs Arella had ever seen (they actually spiraled upward! Without ever leaving the ground) that lead to another level of the labyrinth-trap doors, the invisible walls, the walls that appeared to be there but weren't there, the overlapping roads (so that you had to climb to get over it and to be able to continue on your way). There were so many different tricks to the labyrinth that you couldn't keep your mind thinking straight. Sometimes you had to travel in complete darkness, forcing you to have to slowly feel your way along. Other times the passage would be lit up so brightly, you would be blinded. But what the siblings found to be worse were the times when they traveled down a passage way that seemed to circle around and around, until coming to a dead end in the center. Though, you would never be able to notice that the passage way was slowly circling around, because of the shadows. These passages were dark, with shadows continually moving around you, giving you the sensation that you were being followed. There were even low, hissing whispers floating around them. Whispers that seemed to belong to their past, of things that had left scars in their memories forever. More than a few times Arella or Jared would become lost in this nightmare and stumble, before falling to the cold, rough, stone floor and the shadows would seem to morph into hands, reaching out as frightening cries would echo down the hall.

Once when Arella had been the victim of this, the voice that had called to her was the voice of someone she had loved. A voice that she dearly hoped to never forget, though she hardly ever spoke of the person of whom the voice belonged to. From the better memories, the voice had been rich and joyful, but the voice that whispered to her in that dark, depressing tunnel was far from that. It was raspy and hardly audible-yet Arella knew it belonged to him…

Her father.

"Arella," grated the sickly sounding voice. "You should not have run…You should have stayed. You should have protected us. You *know* you could have, but you didn't."

"No!" Arella shook her head and tried to get to her hands and knees, so at least she could crawl forward, but the whispers seemed to not just have mental power over her, but physical. They seemed to push her down, pinning her to the ground as they murmured harsh or pleading remarks to her.

She heard her father's, her mother's, her brother's, and even Hansrai's voices. Some sounded disappointed, others sounded desperate, and a few sounded enraged. She would hear her mother pleading for help, while Hansrai would be shouting at her. He spoke harshly, nagging at her continually. Her brother would be asking her questions; one after the other. Her father was relentless on scorning her for running away with her brother, instead of staying and fighting. As the whispers continued to crash into her, she was knocked lower to the ground, until she felt as if she were being pressed into the solid surface. Her heart ached and her head seemed to spin.

More voices joined, until she could not understand any of them. The voices became muddled, until they seemed distant and unclear, as if she was hearing them from underwater. It even got to the point of her not being able to breath. Her lungs burning, Arella slowly closed her eyes as she drifted into unconsciousness...

The ground was warm, unlike the cold stone floor she had been trapped against, plus, it didn't feel like stone. No, she was somewhere completely different. There was sun shining down on her. Warm, pleasant sunlight that streamed down and gently touched her face.

Arella didn't open her eyes or move yet, but softly ran her hand over the warm surface she was lying upon. She then closed her hand around some of the small granules of sand. That's when she heard the gentle lapping of water and smelt the ocean breeze, as her senses started to come back. She was on a beach, she was sure of it.

Quickly sitting up, Arella opened her eyes and grimaced. After being back in that dark, terrifying tunnel, her eyes had to get adjusted to the bright light. She blinked and then rubbed her eyes.

She muttered something to herself as she leaned forward and bowed her head, rubbing ferociously at her face. When she felt as if she might actually be able to see something, she slowly lifted her head. Still having to squint to see something, Arella saw a beautiful stretch of blue green ocean, just inviting her to come and cool off in its refreshing waters.

Arella carefully stood, staring out over the ocean, before looking at the white sandy beach that she stood on, grimacing as the sunlight shone brightly upon the sand. She quickly glanced up at the sky and frowned.

The sky was very odd, for it was the exact same color as the ocean, and appeared to be moving, with waves crashing down in the distance, if Arella saw right. It was as if there was a giant mirror stretching out over the ocean…

Arella looked directly above her and her eyes widened. She saw herself-upside down-looking back down at her. She could see the white beach, then the reflection of palm trees behind her, and a great big ball of floating light…that was *not* a reflection. It was just a big ball of pure white light, floating near the mirror sky.

"Where am I?" Arella muttered. This was a very strange place and the first thought that came to Arella was: *Am I dead?*

"Arella."

Swiftly turning around, Arella reached for her sword. "Who's there?"

Eight figures stood near a clump of palm trees, silently watching her, their features obscured by black cloaks. Each one had their own unique weapon, that none of the others had. Two stood before the other six. The one to Arella's left held a claymore sword, while the one to the right had a sword like no other Arella had seen. It was longer than the claymore, and at least three times as wide. The hilt was a navy blue, with a single crystal embedded on the silver cross guard.

Out of the other six figures, the one to the far left wielded a giant war hammer, with a battle axe strapped to his back. The one to his left held a crossbow, the one after him had a grasp on the snath and a grip on his scythe, the next had mace, then next stood a woman with a silver spear, and then the one to Arella's right, the last cloaked figure, stood proudly, holding a morning star in each hand.

Arella puckered her brow as she looked them over suspiciously. "Who are you and where am I?" she asked, threateningly drawing her sword.

"Silence, chosen one," the female warrior of the odd group said, still motionless. "We have come to help you through the labyrinth."

Arella narrowed her eyes. "I highly doubt you know your way through the enigma maze."

"No," the warrior with the scythe answered for her.

"Though we do have important information that will help you through the part of which you find yourself trapped," explained one of the men that stood in the front; the one with the large sword.

"This is a joke," Arella said, scowling. "I am no longer in the labyrinth, but in some strange...*place*. How about you stop fooling around and tell me how to get out of here, before I decide to slit your throat."

The warrior with the claymore sword stepped forward. Or, at least, he moved forward, yet he didn't move a muscle. It was as if he was floating forward. "This, young one, will guide you through the *web of remorse*: Success is not what has made me, but my failures; do not dwell on your mistakes but learn from them. What has happened has happened, and no matter how hard we regret our past choices, we cannot undo what has been done.

"Each part of the labyrinth will test you. This is the only time of which I can help you, though. You must learn how to overcome each obstacle. Do not bicker with your companions, for the enemy will use that against you...."

Arella slowly lowered her sword as she glared at the warrior who had just spoke. "I recognize your voice. You...you're that chief, or whatever, from the village in the West. What game are you playing-"

"Go, now, child." The warrior raised his claymore and bowed his head-his first movements since they had appeared.

"Wait-" Before Arella could finish her question, she felt a force pulling her back, towards the water. Arella struggled against it, slashing her sword around, violently fighting to get back to where the mysterious warriors were. It was to no avail. In moments she was being dragged through the water, until it was up to her waist.

"XANTHIAS!" Arella screamed furiously, before the warrior with the massive sword raised his hand and another force knocked into Arella, sending her soaring out over the water and then crashing into the depths of the ocean of the mirror beach.

Suddenly the water seemed to evaporate around her, and the next thing she knew, she was back on the cold stone floor in the tunnels of the *web of remorse*. Her eyes shut tight, she could hear the haunting whispers still moaning and taunting her. She sensed her brother not far away, crying for help as he fell to his knees.

When it seemed as if the shadows would prevail, Arella's eyelids fluttered open, her eyes glowing with an angry and determined gleam.

Chapter 26
Track of Thorns

Smoke and ashes blew through the ruins of the village, small fires still burning throughout the wreckage. Bodies of monsters, fairies, and Drago Warriors alike scattered the ground, some so badly burnt, no one could distinguish what exactly it was...or once was.

A half dead monster growled as it clawed its way forward, its hind legs completely useless. It had its eerie green eyes set on a young Nyx fairy who lay on the ground, breathing, but unconscious. Baring its fangs, the evil creature reached out, dug its sharps claws into the ground, and pulled itself forward, only a few feet away from the fairy now...

Something from its right caught the monster's attention and it quickly looked to where the movement had come from. A long, silver spear sliced through the air, then coming downward, turning at such a sharp angle, it seemed impossible. Before the monster could react, the spear struck it, being embedded deeply in the monster's neck, the end going through and sticking out of its right shoulder.

Instantly on impact the monster died.

"Good aim," Xanthias's voice said, moments before the wizard stepped through a drifting pillar of smoke and walking towards the dead monster.

Onyx came into sight, scowling at the ugly beast. "It takes concentration, of which I have."

"Is that the last of them?" Caspar asked as he stumbled forward, coughing and waving his hand wildly through the smoke. Then he stopped and sniffed the air. "I smell bacon."

Onyx turned towards him and glared. "You always smell bacon and that is becoming highly exasperating. For once in your miserable life, do something useful."

"Like not being late to find help," Xanthias growled. He then looked away from his friend and called for Lilith. A few moments later the fairy landed a few feet away from him. Xanthias didn't have to tell her what she was called for. As soon as she saw the unconscious fairy, she gently picked up the young girl and shook her head.

"I thought we had everyone through."

Xanthias bowed his head. "Take her to the haven, Lilith."

Lilith nodded and started to walk away, when Onyx stopped her by laying her hand on the fairy's shoulder.

"Your warriors are valiant," the wizard said, looking the fairy in the eyes. "I am honored to have your kind fighting beside us."

Lilith bowed her head in respect. "Thank you, Lady Onyx."

The wizard gave a slight nod and the fairy walked away, quickly disappearing from sight, leaving the wizards alone in the ruins.

Akira stood outside of the destroyed village, along with the rest of her warriors that had survived the attack. The fairies that had created the portal looked exhausted, as if creating the gateway had drained all their energy.

"We must head out," Xanthias said as he walked up to stand beside Akira.

She nodded, though she seemed to be hesitating to ask a question. When Xanthias looked at her questioningly, she decided to ask. "What about the fairies?"

The wizard looked to the weary fairies, his face void of any emotions. "They can go to the haven if they wish."

Akira turned to her warriors and raised her sword. "Drago Warriors out! Start heading towards Aselda."

As Akira and her warriors left, some of the fairies followed, while some created small portals and transported themselves to the haven, hardly even having the energy to make a portal. Xanthias watched silently, before noticing Caspar standing far off from everyone else, sadly munching on his favorite snack.

"He has not changed," Onyx said as she brushed past Xanthias. She scowled. "Except for the fact that he has lost his *Sanity* and has grown old."

"You are right, but he is still my friend," Xanthias said, crossing his arms over his muscular chest. "Even though he is foolish and often times forgets to do his job."

Onyx's scowl deepened. "I do not see how one like you could stay a faithful friend to one like *him*."

Xanthias grinned slightly, but didn't say anything.

Onyx sighed. "Well, I suppose I should be getting back to the haven. Conrad will want to know where you are at and that the chosen are in the labyrinth. If you need me again, just send me a message and I will come. Do not *ever* send Caspar for something so important." She handed him a small bundle and then straightened her cloak. "Farwell, Xanthias."

The wizard smiled at her as her skin started glowing. She caught sight of his smile and frowned, before vanishing.

"Why can't she stay with us?" Caspar asked, suddenly standing next to Xanthias. "We could use someone like that woman."

Xanthias grunted. "I would rather not have her around."

Caspar sighed, not hearing Xanthias. "Beautiful. Absolutely beautiful..."

Xanthias cast a disgusted side-glance in Caspar's direction. "Come on, we have a lot to do."

"Does it involve bacon?"

"No."

"I suppose I could go..."

"*Caspar.*"

The crazy wizard nodded. "Yes, I'm coming. Do you suppose I could have bacon once we reach the haven...?" Their voices drifted off on the gentle breeze as they started heading east. The last few stragglers followed, none of them noticing a cloaked figure standing in the shadows, silently watching.

The mysterious figure glared as dawn approached, before quickly turning and walking towards the ruins of the village.

"Brother, I cannot enter the labyrinth," Zara Cyan hissed angrily as she walked through the village. "The entrance can only open when it is midnight."

I can get you through.

Zara came to a halt in the middle of the village, staring with delight as the houses burned. A loud crackling sound came from one of the huts, before it exploded, fire enveloping Zara as she smiled coldly.

Akira landed next to Caspar and Xanthias after an hour of traveling, still in her dragon form. "Some of my warriors say that this will take too long, that the warriors we wish to free will be dead by the time we make it to Aselda."

Xanthias didn't say anything, but watched her carefully, waiting for her to finish.

"I think…" Akira looked towards the mass of dragons that were still flying. "I think that they have enough energy."

"To do what?" Xanthias asked, bowing his head. "That is dangerous."

"What is?" Caspar asked, feeling puzzled.

Akira sent him a dangerous look. As a

dragon, she could swallow him whole, though she wouldn't want to actually *eat* someone. She could threaten someone with that though.

"It is basically when the Drago Warriors can zip through the air, combining their powers to create a massive push that catapults them forward at the speed that could instantly kill you, unless you are in the shield which they enclose you with," Xanthias explained.

"Ah," Caspar said, nodding, though he didn't seem to really understand what was going on still.

"If we do that, we could be in Aselda within less than an hour," Akira said.

Xanthias thought about it, silent for a long moment. When he finally spoke, he looked somewhat hesitant. "Where is the Baldhart bat?" he asked.

"Following us, but at a slow pace," Akira answered, before her expression softened. "He misses his son."

Xanthias nodded. "We will wait for him and then...we will do it."

Chapter 27
Left Turn at Destruction, Right turn at Delusion

He was growing tired. Everything was so confusing about this maze. He had made countless turns and now the labyrinth was becoming even more baffling.

This *Midnight Labyrinth* was definitely not like anything Hansrai had imaged it would be. Strange stairs, invisible walls, or walls that weren't even there, though his eyes made it appear that they were...Trick after trick threw Hansrai for a loop. No matter how hard he tried, he just couldn't figure out anything. Every time he went down a new tunnel, something was telling him that he was going the *wrong* way. It had been hours since Arella and Jared had disappeared and he still hadn't found them. He was beginning to feel like giving up.

"What was the point of chosen ones if they just get lost in this stupid labyrinth?" Hansrai thought aloud as he collapsed onto a large rock, not caring if it was comfortable or not. It was covered in lichen, though Hansrai didn't pay attention to it. All he was thinking about was having a quick rest.

As he sat in the dim lit tunnel, he thought about his home. Sure he didn't like being a king, but it was better than *this*. He hadn't even traveled in the labyrinth for a whole day and he was sick of it. He wanted to go home and forget that any of this had ever happened.

But of course he would never find his way out and even if he could, Abraxas would kill him as soon as he entered back into his homeland. Though, the more Hansrai thought about it, the more he doubted that being killed by his royal advisor sounded so bad. It was either him being murdered by Abraxas or being killed in this forsaken labyrinth.

Closing his eyes, he rested his head against the tunnel wall. He didn't know what to do, so he was just going to sit here and rest…Maybe if he was able to relax a little, he could think more clearly.

As he rested, he suddenly noticed how silent the tunnel was, aside from the quiet echo of dripping water from up ahead. Hansrai went completely still, listening hard for the sound. Sure enough, moments later, he heard the sound again.

Sitting up, Hansrai rubbed his soar throat. *Water…*

Arella and Jared had the canteens and since they had been separated, Hansrai had had nothing to drink. He frowned, terrible thoughts swirling around in his confused mind. After slowly standing, Hansrai started to stumble forward.

"That thief and good for nothing brother of hers left me on purpose…" Hansrai thought aloud, his voice hoarse. "Of course she would take the water and then they would disappear…they knew that I wouldn't be able to find them…"

His eyes were bloodshot and he had a wild expression, as if he wanted to kill Arella and Jared himself.

He quickly rushed forward as he started to see green and plants among the grey, dull tunnels. Soon he noticed more plants growing and instead of the stone flooring, he was walking on solid ground. Hansrai took in a deep breath, enjoying the smell of the dirt and plants. As he walked down the beautiful passageway, he came upon large chunks of stone, covered in moss. When he saw this, he glanced up to see the night atmosphere stretching out above him. Part of the ceiling had collapsed, revealing the tranquil sky. For some reason, the stars seemed closer than they ever had before.

I must be getting closer to leaving this bizarre maze, Hansrai thought, taking another deep breath.

Then he saw the water…and the greed came back to him.

He saw a lake, but what was strange was that in the crystal blue lake were many walls, creating a maze that went through the water. Hansrai scowled and looked to his right, where a small waterfall was. The cool water gushed out of a rock and spilled down into a large silver bowl that rested on a bronze pedestal. Hansrai ran to the basin and dipped his hands into the water-

He frowned when he didn't feel any water touch his fingers, though it appeared that his hand was resting in the water.

"Ask and it will be given to you," said a quiet voice.

Hansrai spun around to see a young woman with golden blond hair standing in the lake, the water just above her waist. She wore a pale blue sleeveless dress and had fair skin, with light pink lips and rosy cheeks. The woman cast a glance in his direction, her silver eyes seeming to see right through him. She held up a silver pitcher and cocked her head to the side, waiting to see what he would do.

For a minute Hansrai didn't know what to say. He just stood and stared at her, before clenching his fists. "Give me some water!"

The woman pursed her lips. "Say it nicer."

Hansrai glared at her. "I want some water. My traveling companions took the water and ran off."

"Are you sure about that?" the woman asked, slowly tipping the pitcher, until a stream of water flowed off of the lip of the jug.

"Yes, I am sure about it!" Hansrai hollered, his face turning red. "She has been trying to kill me since we met!"

The woman sighed, before dipping the pitcher into the water. "Anger solves nothing."

Hansrai growled. "Can I have the water or not?!"

With another sigh, the woman nodded. "The sweetener might taste sweet, but goes down the throat like thorns."

Hansrai ignored her and dipped his hands into the water. He sighed as he felt the cool touch. He quickly took several drinks, savoring the sweetness of the water. After he had his fill, he turned to the woman in the water, who hadn't moved from her spot and was continuing to fill and then dump water from her pitcher.

"Which way leads out of here?" Hansrai demanded, pointing to the maze that stretched through the water.

The woman ignored him and continued on with what she was doing.

"I said, *WHICH WAY LEADS OUT OF HERE*?!" Hansrai hollered at the woman, who flinched.

She glanced up and then nodded towards the left passage.

Hansrai wiped his mouth with the sleeve of his shirt and then ventured out into the water, wading past the woman and into the left passage. The woman acted as if he wasn't there, dipping her pitcher back into the water. When Hansrai was gone, she dropped her pitcher and looked up, her eyes gleaming with malice.

Arella kept her arm around Jared, helping him along down the passage. The *web of remorse* had taken its toll on him and now he looked dangerously weak. Arella feared that if he wouldn't regain his strength, he wouldn't make it through the labyrinth.

"Arella," Jared groaned.

"Shh, Jared," Arella said sharply, only to keep him from talking.

"Plant," he muttered, pointing ahead.

Arella frowned and looked to where he was pointing. At first she didn't see it, because it was so small, but then she spotted it. A small sprout growing from a pile of dirt. That's when she also noticed a small stream of water gushing out of the wall and running down a crack in the cave floor. She quickly started following it, not even thinking about going down any of the other tunnels. She just followed the small stream and growing vegetation.

After a while Arella noticed parts of the ceiling that had collapsed and was able to see parts of the night sky.

"Jared, I think we are almost through!" Arella said, smiling at her brother. She hadn't smiled like that in a long time. "Then I'll be able to help you."

Jared frowned. "What about Hansrai?"

Arella hesitated. "I don't know, Jared. My main concern right now is to get you to safety…then I will try to find Hansrai."

Jared nodded weakly. His face was so pale, he almost looked like a ghost, which worried Arella. She tried to pull him along, but with his weight and the extra weight of the packs, it was becoming extremely hard.

As she struggled onward, she heard soft humming coming from up ahead. Frowning, Arella wondered if the person would be friendly, or would she have to fight?

Moments later they were in the lush cavern, with the lake, maze, small waterfall, silver bowl, and bronze pedestal. The woman that Hansrai had spoke to was still in the place where she had been when the young king had passed through, except for her hair was now in braids, she looked kinder, and her eyes were harvest gold.

When the woman didn't look up, Arella started to move towards the waterfall, keeping a careful eye on the woman, just in case she suddenly decided to attack.

After gently propping Jared against a large rock covered in moss, along with the packs, Arella dipped her hands into the silver bowl. Her brow furrowed when her hand seemed to go straight through the water, as if it wasn't there at all.

"Ask and it will be given to you," the woman said softly.

"Look, I need the water for my brother-"

"Ask and it will be given to you," the woman repeated, seeming annoyed. She turned to look at Arella for just a moment, before looking back down at the water. "Is it that hard of a task for me to request?"

Arella rolled her eyes. "Can I *please* have some of the water for my brother?"

"Ask nicely," the woman muttered, before bringing her cupped hands to her head and letting the cool water run over her face.

Arella bit her tongue to keep from saying something unpleasant. After trying to calm herself, she nodded grimly. "Forgive me, may I have some of your water?"

The woman looked back up and smiled. "Yes, you may."

Arella stood still for a moment, glaring at

the woman, before turning back to the basin. She stuck a finger in, cautious at first.

The woman chuckled. "Do you think that I poisoned it?"

"You can never be too careful," Arella replied coldly, before placing both hands in the water, cupping her hands, and then bringing them up to take a sip. Arella scowled as the sour taste invaded her mouth. She coughed and then spat it out.

"It does not have a pleasant taste," the woman said, running her hand through the water, "but has healing properties."

Arella rested her hands on the edge of the large bowl and doubled over, trying to spit out any of the other water that was still in her mouth. "Why does it taste so bad?"

The woman sighed. "Why does life have to be so hard on us?"

Arella glanced in the woman's direction, though she said nothing.

"It will help your brother," the woman said, staring at her reflection in the water.

Arella narrowed her eyes. "Why are you in the labyrinth?" she asked. "Are you some spy of Seuderak?"

The woman grimaced. "It is true that, because of Seuderak I am here, but I am no spy…he dragged me down here when he was banished. While he cannot leave, I too, am doomed to be trapped here."

"Who are you?" Arella questioned, standing up straighter and walking towards the lake.

"That does not matter," the woman

answered slowly. "Give your brother the water, it will heal him. Then, you must be on your way. The right tunnel leads out of here, if you follow it correctly. Listen to your heart, not your mind, and you will be able to make it out."

Arella nodded and started to go back to her brother, when she hesitated. "Have you seen our companion? We were separated…"

The woman raised an eyebrow. "A hotheaded young man?"

Arella thought for a moment. "He is King Hansrai the III…Tall, brown hair, brown eyes, stubby beard, I think…I haven't paid much attention to his face. The only time I really look at it is when I'm glaring at him…"

"He went down the left tunnel," the woman said, giving a slight nod in the direction of the passage of which she spoke of.

"But you said to go down the right tunnel if we wanted to make it out of here," Arella said, her hand instinctively resting on the hilt of her sword.

"Yes, yes I did." The woman looked back to Arella. "He was harsh and hotheaded, like I mentioned before. *Ask and it will be given to you.* He asked for something in a very angry way and received what he deserved."

"But we *need* him," Arella said, grimacing as the words left her mouth. She really didn't want him around, but if they really were the chosen, then they had to stick together.

The woman frowned. "Wait…you must be the chosen ones."

Arella nodded. "And you sent one of us down that tunnel." She rushed back to the basin, fetched some of the water, and then forced the drink into Jared's mouth. "Come on, Jared, we have to go find princey boy," she muttered, shaking his shoulders. "Swallow it."

Jared tried to spit it out, but started to swallow. He coughed and his eyes started watering. "I swall-" He coughed, trembling. "I swallowed wrong!"

"You'll get over it," Arella said as she started picking up the packs. "We have to hurry so get to your feet."

The woman had silently been watching them. "I am so sorry," she whispered, shaking her head. "I did not that he was a chosen one…and that you cared for him."

Arella stiffened. "I don't care for him. Actually, when we're done killing Seuderak and saving Ardara, I wouldn't mind dumping him back in this forsaken labyrinth."

"You quarrel a great deal?" the woman asked.

Arella nodded. "Yeah, I guess you could say that. I've tried to kill him, so…yeah." When she had Jared to his feet, they started making their way towards the lake.

The woman raised an eyebrow. "So you would not be greatly upset if you knew that Maglorix's sister is after him?"

"Who?" Arella snapped as they started wading in the water. At first Jared was slow, but he seemed to be regaining his energy.

"Zara Cyan. Maglorix Cyan is her brother…Maglorix was his name, before he turned on *them*," the woman answered.

Arella froze, a shiver slithering up her spine. "Seuderak."

Hansrai gave another stroke of his arm, before rolling over onto his back and allowing himself to float along with the current. After drinking that water from the silver basin, he was beginning to feel awfully drained. His throat felt even more dry than it had before he had drank anything. He tried to drink of the water of which he swam in, but it only caused the pain and dryness to increase.

His thoughts became disorientated and the only clear thought that he could think of gave him a headache. Why had he done that? Why had he spoken so harshly?

He started to slip under the water and quickly rolled over again, struggling to swim forward. After what seemed like an eternity, he saw an almost flat rock surface that was just a few inches away up from the water. He quickly swam towards it, before pulling himself up onto the rock surface.

Grimacing, he set his pack down, unbuckled his belt, laid it next to the pack, unbuttoned his shirt, and carefully pulled it off, cringing at the pain that shot up his spine. After wringing out his shirt, he stretched it out over the face of the rock surface to the right and then propped himself up against the pack, his eyes slowly closing.

He soon fell into a troubled sleep, his pain increasing. He stirred restlessly, never finding a spot where he felt comfortable. For almost an hour he lay there, lost in his nightmares.

A cloaked figure swam silently through the water, before stopping ten feet away from where Hansrai was resting. Zara smiled coldly and then slipped back under the water. Moments later she was softly climbing up on the rock surface, keeping her golden eyes on Hansrai. When she was up on the rock, she slipped her hand in her cloak and then withdrew it, holding a dagger.

Stealthily creeping towards Hansrai, Zara twirled her knife, before she was right next to Hansrai. She hovered her face over his, smirking at his troubled countenance as she lifted her dagger to kill him.

Chapter 28
Clash of the Thief and Assassin

Arella acted quickly when she saw the dagger. She had to. It was that, or let Hansrai die.

She created a small circling force and threw it at the weapon, hoping she wasn't too late.

Time seemed to slow as the circling force

spun through the air, heading straight towards the lowering blade. Zara's eyes closed and then opened, right as the force hit the dagger and knocked it out of her hand.

There was a moment of silence, before Zara suddenly looked towards Arella, a smug grin on her pale face. She rushed to the edge of the rock surface and then plunged into the dark water, quickly disappearing from sight. Arella blinked, unsure if she had seen it all clearly. She thought she had seen two sharp teeth that were longer than the others in Zara's mouth. And how Zara had moved…it was like she was an animal.

Arella narrowed her eyes and looked at the water, though it was impossible to see anything now. She started kicking and swinging her arms wildly, while still trying to keep an eye on Hansrai, but no matter what she did, she couldn't find Zara. She had just vanished.

Then suddenly something gripped her leg and pulled her under-so quickly that she didn't have time to hold her breath. Water quickly filled her mouth and lungs. She couldn't see anything, but she still fought against Zara, somehow managing to kick her in the stomach so that Zara released her. But then she couldn't tell which way was up or down.

Suddenly a powerful force hit her, pushing her up out of the water and crashing into the cave ceiling. She screamed as she was pressed against the hard surface, water spraying so hard it felt as if it was cutting into her skin.

Then, without warning, it all stopped and Arella started to fall back towards the water.

Seconds before impact, another force hit her from her right and tossed her through the air, before she sprawled out onto the rock island Hansrai was laying upon. Arella groaned as she writhed, feeling only pain.

There was a loud whoosh and Arella saw a torrent of spiraling water reach upward. As soon as the tip touched the ceiling, it split down the middle, revealing Zara who seemed to just be floating in the midst of the swirling water. Her hood was still up, covering her face almost completely. She had her arms stretched out, holding an end of her cape in each hand. How the cape was extended, it almost appeared that she had bat wings.

"My powers are limitless here," Zara hissed. The water surged forward until Zara was only a few feet away from Arella. Arella's body was lifted suddenly off of the ground and then thrown to the water. As she hit the surface, Zara leapt out of the spiraling water and landed on top of Arella, gripping Arella's throat and squeezing as they both plunged into the water.

Arella was quickly losing consciousness, but she knew that she had to do something. She moved her hand towards Zara and knocked a weak force into the assassin. It wasn't incredibly strong, but had just enough power to force the assassin to release her grip and be shot out of the water.

Arella quickly swam upward, gasping for air as her head broke through the surface of the water. It was becoming hard to breath and concentrate, the world seeming unclear. She started swimming, not knowing exactly which direction she was heading, until she reached a rock island that was in the middle of the passageway. She quickly heaved herself up onto the little island and rolled over onto her back.

She's too powerful...I can't fight her by myself, Arella thought as she tried to inhale, but started coughing.

"Weak," came the quiet, hissing sound of Zara's voice as she stepped onto the island. She reached into her cape, retrieving three sharp objects which she could hold between her fingers. As she started to extend her hand and release her weapons, Arella quickly rolled to her right, before using her arms to thrust herself up to her feet, barely avoiding the sharp objects that flew her way.

She stumbled when she got to her feet, almost falling into the water that surrounded the small island that she stood on. Arella quickly moved to her right, further away from the edge, and steadied herself as she drew her sword.

The assassin swiftly spun around to face Arella, again sending darts hurtling her way. Arella blocked most of them, dodging the small, sharp objects, and then gritting her teeth when one punctured her left arm. Ignoring the pain, she brought her sword around and stopped the blade once it was inches away from the assassin's face.

Zara smiled slightly and Arella glanced down. The tip of the assassin's blade was within inches of piercing Arella's stomach. Arella quickly looked back at the assassin's face, to see the assassin shaking her head just slightly.

"Never has my brother sent me to kill someone that could put up a fight," she said, her voice as cold as ever.

The assassin withdrew, before twirling around to face the direction which Arella had come, throwing three more of her weapons. As the assassin's cape waved in front of her and then slowly came to gently touch the rock surface, Arella spotted the assassin's target.

Her brother.

He clung to the cave walls, slowly moving forward on a small rock ledge that was a few feet above the water. She had told him to stay put, but of course, he hadn't listened. And now he seemed completely oblivious to the dangerously sharp projectiles flying towards him.

"*Jared*! No!!" Arella screamed, lunging forward and reaching out, she concentrated hard on the three sharp objects. She had never tried to focus on something so hard in her life, but she wasn't willing to let those darts hit her brother, even if it wouldn't kill him. As she stared at the darts, her hands started glowing and then, suddenly, the small weapons turned to dust.

In the next few moments, two things happened:

Jared, startled by his sister's cry, lost his footing and fell to the cold water. Before Arella hit the rock surface of the island she had been standing on, the assassin brought her hand around and a strong force knocked into her. She was flung onto the rock island of which Hansrai lay on, still unconscious and deathly pale.

Zara leapt off of her rock island and skidded over the water, seeming to ride upon an invisible force that tore through the water. Once she was within six feet of the first rock island, she jumped into the air and then landed three feet away from Arella.

The young thief watched as Zara pulled a sword from her cloak, where it seemed like a weapon should not be able to be concealed. She tried to get up, but she felt too weak. After being thrown around like that, her body just wouldn't move.

The assassin twirled her sword and lifted it for her final strike…and then Arella knew it was her end.

That's when she heard something that she was not expecting: Hansrai's cry and then the sound of a sword piercing *someone*. Zara's own blade stopped within inches of stabbing Arella's throat. The assassin stood motionless, a wicked grin spreading across her face as she noticed the sword that had stabbed her back and the point that had gone completely through.

After that, she exploded. As in, her body turned to millions of ashes and quickly scattered.

Now Hansrai stood over her. When he saw that the assassin was gone, he quickly tossed his sword to the side and knelt down beside Arella. "Are you all right?"

She gave a slight nod, though just that movement sent pain through her whole entire body. "Jared," she whispered, looking back to the way they had come through.

Hansrai nodded and quickly dove into the water.

Arella lay on the wet rock, lost between losing consciousness and staying awake. She didn't know how long she was there before Hansrai and her brother returned to find her, but she found herself startled when they woke her.

"We're going to set you on the raft," Hansrai explained as he and Jared knelt down at both sides of Arella.

Boat. What boat? Arella grimaced as Hansrai and her brother started to lift her.

"You know…that the woman lent to us…said it would help us through this part of the maze…gave us some of the healing water…you'll be fine." Jared's voice drifted in and out of Arella's thoughts as she was gently placed upon a cushioned part on the raft. Though she was losing consciousness again, one thought continued to plaque her.

How had Hansrai suddenly been able to save her, when he had looked practically dead moments before that?

As they drifted down the current, Arella thought she spotted the woman from the lush cave standing in the water. Though, that would have been impossible since that part of the underground river was too deep for someone to stand in. Yet, it appeared to be her, the water just above her waist, just like how she had seen her earlier…

Chapter 29
The End of the Splendor

Xanthias rode on the Baldhart bat's left shoulder, silently watching the young Drago Warriors around him. Akira was in the lead, helping some of the stronger of her warriors with keeping the safeguard bubble around them. Caspar rode upon one of the shape shifters in the back, seemingly content as he munched on his bacon.

No one could see what was going on in the world that they were soaring over, except for Akira and Xanthias. Akira, because she was controlling the bubble. Xanthias's eyesight aided him in seeing his surroundings outside of the protective bubble. Everything was going by too quickly for even Akira to fully understand, but Xanthias's mind swiftly sorted through the blurred images and set them in the right order to create images of the landscapes below.

Not long afterwards he noticed that they were out of the West heading straight for Aselda. As they moved quickly along, Xanthias looked ahead, until he could spot the edge of the woods of the Elganté forest.

Suddenly Xanthias stiffened. It was hard to tell exactly, but he thought he saw smoke in the distance, where the forest was. Leaning forward, he squinted his eyes.

"What is it?" the giant humanoid bat asked.

"Nothing good," Xanthias said, before standing, somehow managing to keep his balance. There was a moment of silence between the two, before Xanthias leapt off of the bat's shoulder and landed on the back of one of the dragons. The medium sized dragon did not seem to notice, for as soon as Xanthias touched down, he leapt again. He continued to do this, until he was standing on a dragon that flew near where Akira was.

"Akira!" Xanthias hollered to her.

The red dragon growled. "What is it?"

"Land *now*!"

Akira didn't seem pleased with this, but obeyed, careful not to land too quickly and crash. Instead of the bubble reaching down to the earth though, one by one the dragons disappeared, evaporating into thin air. This happened to Xanthias soon afterward. He couldn't see anything but darkness, which seemed to disagree with his eyesight. There was *nothing* else there but air as he was transported to the ground with the rest of the warriors.

When he finally felt his feet touch the ground and could see, he found himself in what appeared to have been a battle field. Twisted and deformed bodies of the Royal Guard and monsters scattered the forest floor, some even up in the limbs of the trees. But what Xanthias found most disturbing was a different kind of creature that was mixed with the others. A large, white beast…

"Saber Killers," Akira said. Her form was still appearing, parts of her leg seeming almost transparent as the rest of her came into view.

"The village!" came the gruff call of one of the older Drago Warriors, who pointed to a pillar of smoke.

An arachnid leisurely made its way across its web,

carefully going through the complex network of lattice. A group of the Royal guard marched down the long, dark underground passageway to the dungeons that lay beneath Mt. Edavni. They were the last few stragglers that were trying to escape before the Saber Killers found the dungeons.

"What about the prisoners," one said as they past the cells.

"We want them dead," another of the guards answered. "Leave them here for the Saber Killers to find."

A girl of about fifteen leaned forward, watching as the guards disappeared down a tunnel, her orange eyes glinting with rage. She had flaming red hair, a dark beautiful tan, a short red sleeveless dress, dark yellow leggings, and brown boots. Though she looked gorgeous and delicate, she was a fighter. A fighter who desperately wanted to follow the guards and teach them a lesson, but the bars were standing between her and her enemies.

Another girl that was in the dungeons coughed. She had short light blue hair, the ends just barely reaching her chin, dark blue eyes, and skin like the first girl's. She wore a long dark blue shirt, grey pants, and blue boots, with peal earrings. "W-why are they leaving us here?"

"Ocean, it's 'cause we're Drago Warriors," said one of the boys of about sixteen. He ran a hand through his jet black and slightly curly hair. He studied her with his dark eyes, before sighing. "Are you really surprised?" Even in the dark one could tell that he had pale skin, as if he never spent anytime outside. The boy absent mindedly pulled at his black shirt, feeling as if all hope was lost.

Once they were sure that the guards were gone, the girl with the blue hair perked up. "Cole, what's the escape plan?"

The pale skinned boy glanced up, before shaking his head. "You think I have an idea? If Adrian was here, I might, but he's not. Blaze? Violet?"

The red head sprawled out on the cell floor on the other side of the tunnel. "Nope." She glanced at a girl who sat in the corner. The girl wore a dark purple cape that obscured her identity. Violet slowly shook her head, not muttering a single word.

"If Wolf was here he'd know what to do," Ocean muttered to herself, playing with the rim of her shirt. When everyone was staring at her, she glanced up and blushed. "What? He and Adrian are very smart. So is Jack though…"

"My brother is," a girl whispered. She lay against one of the walls, her dark curly brown hair covering her face.

"Dakota, I'm sure he's fine," Blaze said, sitting up. "I think he escaped. Which…is good. He'll go find Akira, then we'll all be saved."

"Unless we're dead before they make it," said a deep voice from the shadows. A boy of about nineteen stepped out of the gloom, his dark skin seeming to melt into the shadows. He was a massive warrior with barrel like arms and chest. "We have to find a way out ourselves."

Cole sighed as he rubbed his forehead. "Calder, unless you can think of something, we are stuck here until we die. None of us can break out of here…"

"Wolf could," Ocean said, smiling slightly. "He will come and save us."

Calder growled and started to lunge at Ocean, but Cole leapt in his way, raising his fists. Immediately the stone floor cracked and the big guy tripped. "Leave her out of this, Calder," Cole said, keeping his fists raised.

"You know...That is why we are here. Because we were on a mission with girls," Calder spat, gradually standing. He glared at everyone. "Blaze, Ocean, and Dakota. It is because of them!"

"No! It is because you wouldn't follow the orders that Adrian gave us!" Cole shouted, the ground beneath him trembling. He jabbed a finger in Calder's direction. "You are stubborn, arrogant, and hotheaded."

Calder growled and cracked his knuckles, before charging at Cole. The younger teenager leapt backward, swiping his hand at the larger warrior. A stone wall shot upward, smacking Calder in the jaw. The large warrior stumbled back grabbing at his face. When he was able to steady himself, he glowered at Cole, staring death at him. "How about you save us then? Use your power over the rocks to get us out of here. Then you'd be a hero. Isn't that what you've always wanted?"

Cole shook with rage. "I can't...the prison is spellbound. I can hardly lift a few stones up-"

"Coward," Calder coughed. "That's what you are. A wimpy little Drago Warrior who is trying to prove himself worthy of the Royal court. Akira will never take you-"

"Shut up!" Cole yelled, picking up a rock that lay on the floor and throwing it at Calder. The warrior easily dodged, snorting as he shook his head. Next he grabbed a rock and hurled it towards the weaker opponent.

Cole lifted his hand and stopped it. He glared at Calder, thinking about either putting the rock down or sending it back at Calder.

"Stop this!" Dakota screamed as she jumped between the two. "This is *not* going to help us to get out of here."

Cole and Calder glared at each other, before Cole nodded and walked over to a corner to sit down. Calder didn't move, his eyes following Cole. Part of him wanted to rush forward, but with Dakota standing in the way, he knew he shouldn't.

CLANK!

Blaze sat up suddenly. "Guys...did you hear that?"

They all went completely silent, afraid to even breathe. The sound of heavy breathing and claws scraping against the rock floors echoed down the tunnel, sending chills up their spines. Blaze bit her lip and reached for where she kept her knife, when she remembered that the guards had taken all their weapons.

"Saber Killers," Violet said quietly, not moving from her spot. "Don't move."

Akira stared in horror at the burning village, grimacing at the screams that echoed down the street. "Xanthias..."

The wizard nodded. "Find your warriors, the rest of us will find any survivors."

The Drago warrioress nodded and started running towards the castle. She hadn't gone far when one of the Saber Killers pounced her. As it lunged at her, she swiftly spun around, drawing her sword and bringing it up to slice its throat. The Saber Killer crashed into her and skidded across the ground. When it finally came to a stop, Akira found herself beneath the heavy creature trapped.

Gritting her teeth, she tried to push the carcass off, but it was to no avail.

"Need some help?"

Akira froze, recognizing the voice immediately. She started to answer, when the body of the Saber Killer was suddenly lifted and tossed to the side. Standing beside her was a tall and brawny teenager. He had black spiky hair with sideburns, metallic grey eyes, and dark tan skin, with a scar on the right side of his face running down from his forehead to his chin. He wore a shirt with the sleeves cut off, black pants, a belt, and boots. He grinned slightly as he offered her a hand. "About time you showed up."

Akira slapped his hand away and slowly stood. She looked hopeful for a minute. "Did the rest escape?" she asked.

"No," the warrior said, crossing his arms. "Adrian, Dawn, and I have been handling the Saber Killers."

"And doing a terrible job," Akira said. "Xanthias and Caspar are here. They'll deal with the monsters. You need to help me find a way to the dungeons."

"Caspar?" He spat at the ground. "Fool."

Akira nodded. "Yes, he is, but he can do it.

Now follow me."

The warrior nodded and quickly followed Akira, knocking any Saber Killers aside that tried to attack them.

The Saber Killers entered the dungeons, sniffing for their prey. They were following the trail of blood that the guards had drenched on the walls and flooring. A few of the last Saber Killers that entered into the underground tunnels licked at the blood, slowly following the others that were running down the passageways.

As another scent mixed with the smell of the blood, the Saber Killers began to become frantic. The ones in the lead rushed forward, but came to a quick halt when they entered the dungeons. They could smell that something else was there, but the cells were empty.

Ocean held her breath as she watched the Saber Killers prowl around. They looked like a strange mix of a white wolf and some other creature…The bizarre canines' eyes were a sickly red, with black slits in the middle, almost like a cat's eyes.

The Saber Killer nearest to her cell growled, baring its sharp fangs. Ocean started to gasp, when she stopped herself. As long as she stayed in the shadows and didn't move, Violet would be able to keep her unseen by the Saber Killers.

Without warning the Saber Killer started attacking the bars to her cell, somehow biting through the metal. Ocean screamed and fell back, suddenly becoming visible. Cole hollered something and ran forward, also becoming visible.

The Saber Killers looked from Cole, to Ocean, before attacking both. Ocean screamed and ducked as one leapt at her. The others started fighting. All but Violet. She was no where to be seen, but the young warriors could tell that she was there. Whenever a Saber Killer stepped too close to the shadows, the shadows morphed into the shape of a sword, and then, suddenly, the beast would be dead.

"Take this and this and this!" Blaze shouted, her hands catching on fire as she punched at the face of a Saber Killer. It growled, glaring at her with its menacing eyes, and then bit her arm, paying no attention to the burning in its mouth. Blaze screamed as the Saber Killer's sharp fangs tore into her skin, trying to keep the fire burning. She gritted her teeth, closed her eyes, and let the fire burn hotter. The Saber Killer immediately released its jaws and started running, whimpering, before falling over dead.

Blaze grimaced and held her wounded arm, before turning around to see another Saber Killer running at her. Blaze's eyes went wide as she started to step back. The Saber Killer had its eyes set on Blaze as it leapt into the air, ready to pounce on her-

Suddenly the wall exploded, the majority of it knocking into the Saber Killer and tossing it to the side. Blaze blinked and then slowly looked to the hole in the wall, where a massive warrior and a cloaked figure stood. A smile crept across her face. "Wolf!"

Ocean looked up from battling. "Wolf?" When she saw him, she blushed. "Wolf, you are alive-"

A Saber Killer leapt at her, knocking her to the floor and opening its mouth wide to bite her throat. Wolf narrowed his eyes, cracked his knuckles, and ran forward punching the Saber Killer full force in the jaw. The canine beast growled as it stumbled off, its jaw slack.

"Get up," Wolf said, moving in front of Ocean. "I'll take care of this."

As the Saber Killer regained its balance, it turned to Wolf. The young Drago Warrior waited, staring the Saber Killer in the eyes, not cowering away. Without warning three more Saber Killers attacked him from his left and right. Wolf growled as he fell to his knees. He reached out and grabbed one of the beast's by its neck and threw it to the side.

Akira rushed to his side, stabbing the Saber Killers and then kicking their dead carcass's away. "Be thankful that there weren't more here and that I was here to help you," she said as she withdrew her swords from the last Saber Killer.

She turned to the others. "If you have the energy, we need your help to defend the villagers."

Blaze bowed her head. "I will help as well as I can," she said, still holding her bleeding arm.

Akira's expression softened. "Be careful." She turned to walk down the tunnel. "Wolf, take the lead. Something tells me more of the Saber Killers will be coming down this way."

Wolf nodded and took the lead, cracking his knuckles and ready for another fight.

The village was a depressing sight, to say in the least. Homes were burning, carcasses littered the streets, and panicking villagers were either trapped, or trying to flee. Smoke billowed out of the buildings, cries for help coming from inside.

A black dragon swooped down low, searching for Saber Killers to fight. The dragon was large, with dark red wings that caught fire one moment, before turning shadow the next. He had two long black horns on his head that curved backward, black spikes that ran across the back of his neck, yellow eyes with red slits, and streaks of red scales through the black ones. He looked strong and mighty, a young and feisty Drago Warrior.

He was Adrian Raven Shadow.

From his point of view, Adrian could see almost everything that was going on below. The Drago Warriors and two wizards fighting, the villagers trying to flee from the attacking monsters, and the Saber Killers. As he watched, he noticed the Saber Killers beginning to retreat. Narrowing his eyes, Adrian watched the Saber Killers starting to flee, then looked to his right, where the castle was. A group of Drago Warriors were flying towards the village…

The dragon's lips curled slightly as if he were trying to smile. Figuring that he was no longer needed there, Adrian turned to the east and started flying towards the havens, before he slowly faded and then completely disappeared.

Akira flew into the middle of the village,

taking her human form as soon as she landed. Her eyes widening in horror, she looked around the burning village. Two girls were running by a watch tower, when the bell tower started to collapse. The girls screamed and started to run, but one of the girls tripped. The other tried to help her up, but Akira knew they wouldn't make it. Before she could help them, Wolf soared over, flying beneath the toppling tower. He used his front feet and claws to keep it from falling all the way, giving the girls enough time to escape. As soon as the girls were safe, Wolf let the tower finish falling. He flew off quickly in search of others he could help.

The two girls ran up to Akira, sobbing as they reached her. "Our mum is dead!" one wailed.

"Please help us, ma'am!" the other pleaded.

Akira choked on her tears as she looked down in pity at the girls. "It is all right, I will take care of you...Help me find any other survivors, so we can get out of here."

The two girls nodded, sniffling as they wiped their tears away. Akira lead them through the village, giving aid to anyone that was alive.

After turning to her human form, Ocean ran down a street, before stopping to look around. So far she hadn't found anyone who needed help, or they were dead. Then she saw a little blond head bobbing around as a little boy screamed, sitting down beside one of the buildings, calling for his parents.

Her heart feeling like it was about to shatter, Ocean rushed over, kneeling down in front of the little one. "Shh, shh," Ocean whispered, gently picking the baby up into her arms. "It is ok, I got you..."

"Momma," the little boy sniffled, rubbing his left eye, which looked bloodshot.

"Where is your mommy?" Ocean asked, holding the baby close to her.

"Momma," was all he said.

Ocean closed her eyes, a tear slipping down her cheek. She stood and started to walk away, when she sensed someone standing behind her. Slowly turning around, Ocean saw a boy of about twelve standing there, his face pale. "Help me, please?" the boy muttered.

"Yes, of course, come along," Ocean beckoned.

"My sister is stuck," the boy murmured, as if in a daze. "My sister...she might die."

"Wh-what...where is she?" Ocean stammered, her eyes burning from her tears and the smoke.

"Under a wagon," the boy answered, his shoulders slumped. He lowered his head, staring at his scrawny body. "I am not strong enough to lift it."

Ocean nodded. "I know someone who is. Show me where she is at."

The boy shook his head yes, before turning to leave. Ocean quickly followed, praying that the boy's sister would be all right. Once they reached the upturned wagon, she saw a small girl pinned under it, screaming for help.

Running over to the cart, Ocean and the boy knelt down beside it.

"It's ok, we're going to help you," Ocean told the girl.

"Hurry," the girl whimpered.

Ocean blinked back the tears that were threatening to blur her eye sight. She took a deep breath, before screaming, "Wolf!"

The baby started crying again. Ocean gasped, hugging the little boy. "Shh, it's ok," she whispered, before looking to the twelve year old. "I have a friend, he can save your sister."

"Please," the boy whispered, before his eyes drifted to see his sister. "My mum and dad are dead...she is the only family I have left."

Ocean sighed, muttering to herself, "Wolf, where are you?" She searched the sky, hoping to see Wolf coming. A moment later, she saw his large dragon form soaring towards her. He landed next to them, quickly taking his human form. Ocean didn't even have to say anything, Wolf knew what he had to do. He cracked his knuckles, before glancing at Ocean and the boy. "Back up," he said in his deep voice.

Nodding, Ocean and the boy quickly stood, backing away. Wolf lifted the wagon off the ground, then threw it away from them. He smiled kindly at the wee little girl as he gently lifted her up off the ground. "Are you all right?" he asked.

The little girl's eyes widened as she hugged him around the neck. "Thank you," she whispered. Wolf stood there, a little stunned. "Uh...you're welcome..." he finally said.

A chunk of burning wood fell at her feet, smoke rising up into her face.

Dakota stumbled back, coughing as she leaned against one of the wooden support beams of the porch.

"Cole!" she screamed, turning her head as another cloud of smoke came out from the front door of the home. "Cole, where are you?!"

The house groaned, threatening to collapse. "Cole, c'mon!" Dakota shouted again.

No answer.

"Cole!"

The roof let out a loud moan, before starting to cave in. Dakota held onto the support beam, closing her eyes. *Come on Cole, where are you?* She opened her eyes for just a moment. She saw a dark shadow moving through the fire, before a black dragon shot forth from the fire, snatching Dakota up as he flew into the sky; behind them the house caved in.

Dakota let out a terrified yelp, gripping one of Cole's claws, though she knew he wouldn't let her fall. Cole swiftly made his way to where Caspar and Xanthias were. The two wizards stood near a group of the survivors that had gathered in the town square.

"...the Saber Killers have retreated, sir," Cole heard one of his fellow Drago Warriors say to Xanthias.

The wizard nodded. "We must hurry to get everyone out of here. The Saber Killers will be back."

Caspar gently patted a small boy on the head and then walked over to his friend. "I will fetch Lilith and one of her friends. They can help create a portal-"

"That is not necessary," came the Nyx fairy's soft voice. The two wizards turned to see her walking out of the shadows of the ruins of a building. There was a loud crackling sound, before a Siria fairy appeared in the flames of one of the many raging fires. She stepped out of the inferno, unharmed.

Xanthias sighed in relief. "Thank goodness."

Lilith smiled slightly and then turned to the Siria fairy, who nodded. Without wasting a moment more, they began working on the portal as the others joined them in the town square. Ocean and Wolf walked up, helping the children along that they had rescued. Akira showed up not long after, followed by a small group of people that she had saved.

Xanthias looked around at the sad faces of the survivors of Aselda, his heart feeling heavy. He started to walk away, when an old woman stopped him. After comforting her, Xanthias continued to move away from the others, walking towards one part of the village. He didn't know why exactly, but something told him that he needed to.

Then he saw her.

Harmony sat on a crate, hugging one knee, while her other leg dangled off the edge. She rubbed her face on the rim of her dress and wept, at first not noticing Xanthias. When she did notice him, she slowly looked up, her face grim, as if she was about to deliver horrible news to him.

Chapter 30
The Cave Trolls' Return

Arella didn't know how long she had slept for, but when she finally woke, she saw stars…

Frowning, Arella slowly sat up and stared at the night sky, the stars seeming so close…It even looked as if she could just reach up and grab one. She shook her head, and when she looked back up, the starry sky had disappeared. Now she only saw the cave ceiling.

Quickly crawling to the edge of the raft, Arella looked to the large hole in the ceiling, wanting to gaze upon the night sky just one more time.

"You're finally awake," came her brother's voice from behind her, at the front of the raft. "Are you feeling any better?"

Arella sat down and let her legs dip into the water, before she slowly looked over her shoulder. "Yes…yes, I do."

Jared grinned. "That's good. You had us worried. That healing water really does work."

Arella wrapped a blanket around her shoulders and twisted slightly so that she could see both her brother and Hansrai. The young king knelt on the right side of the raft, holding a long pole to guide the boat along. Jared sat on the left, also holding a pole, though at the moment he was looking at his sister.

"You and Hansrai defeated the assassin," Jared said, smiling.

Arella hesitated, before shaking her head and looking the way they had come. "I don't think she's gone yet."

Jared watched her quietly for a long time and then sighed. He went back to steering the raft, feeling nervous as he continually cast anxious glances towards the shadows. How could the assassin still be out there? He had seen Hansrai stab her...

Jared opened his mouth to say something else, when he heard something. "Oh no," he groaned. "Not again."

Hansrai turned around and looked back the way they had come. "Cave trolls."

"*Trolls*?" Jared asked, setting his pole down and standing up. "Do you mean to tell me that there are more this time?"

"Yeah," Hansrai muttered, before he quickly went back to his kneeling position and stuck his pole back in the water. "Hurry up, it sounds like they're not that far behind us."

Jared nodded and sat back down, reaching for his pole. "Can cave trolls even swim?"

Arella slowly stood, the blanket falling from her shoulders. She watched in shock as a large raft turned and started floating down the passage they were in. A bulky green figure stood on the raft, using a giant bone to steer its raft. When the troll saw the smaller raft that the chosen were riding on, it narrowed its eyes and growled.

"Um, Jared, there's your answer," Arella stammered.

Jared looked over his shoulder and let out a startled yelp as more large rafts joined the first; about a dozen trolls were following them. "What are we going to do?!" Jared cried, desperately swinging his pole through the water, as if he thought it would move them along quicker. "We can't outrun them!"

Arella's eyes narrowed. "Just get down and hold on tight."

Hansrai looked at Jared questioningly, but the young bandit just stared back. Both boys threw down their poles and clung to the raft, unsure of what Arella was about to do. Whatever it was, it was best to hold on tight.

Arella smirked at the trolls as she raised both her hands. A powerful force blew them forward, while knocking into the other rafts and sending the cave trolls flying. Arella kept her hands up, somehow able to balance herself in the process.

"That should take care of them for a while," Arella muttered.

They raced forward, gaining speed. At one point she heard Hansrai and her brother holler, "Fork in the path!" A grin tugging at the corners of her lips, Arella moved her hands to the right just slightly. The raft shuddered, before quickly moving to her left and up onto the wall. Her brother started yelling, telling her to stop, but it was too late. The raft continued to climb up the wall, before skidding across the ceiling. The boys cried out and gripped the raft as they felt themselves start to fall. Before anything could happen to them, the boat was back on the water, only to go in a full loop again.

This happened a few more times, before they found themselves in the left tunnel. Jared groaned, feeling queasy.

"A-Arella," he moaned. "How much f-farther...*waterfall*!"

He looked over his shoulder, to see his sister looking back at him. Her lips were moving like she was trying to say something, but he couldn't hear her. "What?!" he yelled.

"Just *hold on*!" she shrieked.

Jared's face went pale as he clung to the raft as tightly as possible.

"She's crazy," Jared heard Hansrai shout over the sound of the upcoming waterfall. "She's not serious...is she?"

Jared glanced at him and nodded, not even worrying about trying to say anything.

The next thing they knew they were tumbling off the edge, along with the cascading water. Hansrai and Jared shouted at Arella to save them. As they reached the bottom, the young king and thief shut their eyes ready for the impact...that never came.

When they opened their eyes, they noticed the raft floating just a few feet over the water, before roughly touching down. The raft bounced, came back down, and then skipped over the water like a flat stone.

The raft groaned, threatening to break. Hansrai gritted his teeth and closed his eyes as a splash of water washed over the raft. "Arella, it can't hold up much longer!"

"Well it's going to have to!" Arella snapped back. "Er...don't look ahead of you."

He had heard the term, *don't look down*, but never before had he been told not to look ahead after almost falling to his death. Instead of listening to her, he looked ahead and his eyes widened. There was another drop...

As they approached it, he saw down into a large cavern, full of the water filled passages crisscrossing and swirling around.

It was a massive water ride...and their raft was *not* going to hold up through *that*.

"Arella-"

"I thought I told you not to look!"

This time all three of them screamed as they soared down the slope, the raft cracking and groaning more than ever. The channel took a sudden turn and Arella was almost thrown from the raft. "Hold on tight, this is going to be a real bumpy ride!"

Jared gritted his teeth, praying that it wouldn't last too long...

Arella stumbled to the left and right continually, her arms moving in every direction, causing the ride to be even worse as the force flung them around. More than once they almost crashed when they came to a turning point. They skipped over the water several times, the raft starting to splinter.

"Arella the raft doesn't need the boost anymore!" Hansrai called over his shoulder. "You're only making it worse!!"

On the next bump, Arella broke the force and fell back onto the raft, almost rolling off of it at the next turn. Her legs were dangling off the edge as they started to climb up the wall at the sharp turn, but she quickly gripped the raft to keep herself from flying off.

Once they had straightened again, she hurriedly pulled herself onto the raft and held on for dear life. She closed her eyes and waited, gritting her teeth as she was bumped around and almost thrown from the raft again.

"Oh no!" Jared yelled from the front of the raft. "Not that…not that…."

Arella lifted her head and her eyes widened when she saw another drop. The water gushed downward, before being shot up, following the riverbed to create a U.

"Everyone hold on tight! This time for sure!!" Arella screamed, before they plunged down. Her hands starting to slip, Arella gritted her teeth and concentrated on keeping a hold on the raft. If she slipped…

"Whoa-oh!" Jared hollered as they suddenly shot upward with the water. As they reached the top, the raft struck a rock and shattered, sending splinters, Jared, Hansrai, Arella, and their packs flying in different directions.

Chapter 31
SoundHarbor

Akira watched silently as the villagers were lead through the portal. She knew that there were many other villages to save, but they wouldn't be able to save all of them on their own. Her warriors were growing exhausted, even Xanthias seemed to be growing weary. They needed help…

"Do we stay here, Akira?" one of the Drago Warriors asked.

Akira hesitated to answer. If the Guardians would come to aid them in saving the villages, then they would, but if they wouldn't…

"Stay here for now, until Xanthias comes

back," she answered.

The young warrior watched her carefully, but when she cast an irritated look in his direction, he quickly left.

Sighing, Akira turned her full attention back to the fleeing villagers. Wolf and Ocean were helping a group of orphaned children along, talking gently to them. A young girl clung to Wolf, just like she had been when Akira had spotted them joining the rest. Wolf looked slightly uncomfortable, but he didn't try to put the little girl down.

A smile crept across Akira's face-something that rarely happened. But when she saw Xanthias walking up to her, looking grim, the smile was suddenly washed away. She stood still, preparing herself for what Xanthias was about to tell her.

As the wizard walked up to her, he looked shaken. He stopped next to her and said, "Take your warriors…go through the portal. Tell everyone to go through." Without waiting for her to answer, he walked away to find Caspar.

Akira turned and watched as he left, wanting to ask what had happened, but knew better. Sighing, she started to look for her warriors to deliver the news, when she saw Harmony standing near one of the destroyed buildings. The young guardian stared at Akira, as if she had been watching the whole time. Only…something was strangely different about Harmony.

Her form wasn't glowing. In fact, she looked completely human.

Onyx stood on the bridge, a hand resting on the white brick wall. Her eyes flickered when she saw the refugees filling the large courtyard below. Elves were helping to guide them to the infirmaries, or just to rooms where they could rest. All those grim faces…

"There should be more," she whispered.

"Why do you say that?" came a deep voice of a warrior as he walked out onto the bridge of the archway.

"If these people are from Aselda, there should be more of them," Onyx answered.

The warrior stood next to Onyx and rested his hands on the wall. "Aselda fell long ago," he answered. "Though they still think of Aselda as the capitol, Aselda has become one of the smaller cities in Ardara."

Onyx watched as Wolf and Ocean walked through the portal, followed by a group of children. She shook her head slightly and then looked to the warrior. "Even if that is so, I fear that Xanthias and Akira were delayed…"

The warrior nodded. When he saw Wolf and Ocean, along with other Drago Warriors, he frowned and stood straighter. "Something's not right."

Onyx turned back to him as he quickly walked away. "Nothing is right at the present time, Dante."

Dante slid the hood of his cape over his head,

before pushing on the large oak doors that stood in front of him. As he entered the long chamber, he looked straight forward, to where a large golden seat stood.

Though he saw no one there, he began walking towards the throne, his cape flowing behind him. This long chamber had no walls, but only silver and bronze pillars that held the golden and royal blue ceiling aloft, allowing anyone who entered the open chamber to look down upon the magnificent citadel below. If one studied the navy blue and jade flooring, they could see that it created a large map of not just Ardara, but the entire world of *Athlone*.

The wizard did not have time to study maps though, he had a much more important task. Once he reached the golden throne, he sat down upon it and closed his eyes. As he concentrated, his hands began glowing. He quickly slid his hands over a seal that was carved into both armrests of the throne. There was a moment of silence, followed by a quiet grating sound that came from under the floor. As the grinding noise continued, the chair began sinking into the ground, before it completely vanished from the open chamber.

Dante opened his eyes when the throne came to rest on a cold, stone surface. He stood and searched the dark cavity he was in, before he started moving forward confidently. He didn't need to see to know where he was going; he had trodden this path many times.

He soon found himself carefully descending a spiraling staircase, running his hand across the curving stone wall. He traveled down the long staircase, quickening his pace when he saw a flicker of light up ahead. Stepping from the last stair, he found himself in an underground cavern. Torches lined the walls, casting their light upon a large, round table that stood in the middle of the cavern. Surrounding the table were eight chairs with tall backs, red velvet cushions, and clawed legs.

Four cloaked figures were already there, waiting. When Dante entered the cavern, they all looked up from their hushed conversations.

After a moment of silence, one of the warriors spoke up. "Is it true? Have the villagers of Aselda come?"

Dante gave a slight nod as he took his seat. "Yes," he said gravely.

"Why do you sound so grim, Dante?" asked the tallest of the warriors, who sat in the most elaborate chair.

The wizard hesitated, before placing his arm on the table and leaning forward. "Something is not right."

One of the other warriors coughed, as if covering a laugh. "Speaking the obvious."

"Drystan," said the leader roughly, and the younger wizard immediately sobered. Turning back to Dante, he said, "Continue."

Dante drummed his fingers on the table, lost in thought for a long moment, before he finally answered. "I saw Drago Warriors come through the portal with the villagers…not like before, where a few followed to make sure that the villagers got to safety. Nay, I would swear that I saw many more than what we have seen before. Then, before I left, I noticed a girl that looked much like Harmony."

"What of it?" asked a dark, mysterious voice of the fourth figure.

Dante turned to him. "I believe it *was* Harmony."

The wizard stiffened, but said nothing more.

"I fear that I know where you are going, but I will ask, what are you getting at, Dante?" questioned the leader, sitting stiffly in his chair.

Dante sighed, before casting a glance in his leader's direction. "Master Conrad, she was not Guardian. She was human."

Conrad slowly bowed his head and leaned back in his chair.

"Uhh…what exactly does that mean?" Drystan asked, looking around at the others.

"It means that something is wrong with the guardians," Xanthias's voice said grimly as he entered the cavern. "Let us pray that the chosen can accomplish their mission, or else, all hope is lost."

The rest of the wizards in the chamber went silent, staring at Xanthias as he came closer to the large table.

Xanthias slowly looked up as he muttered one last, haunting sentence, "I created an even worse crisis; one that could be the end of Ardara."

Chapter 32
Heart of the Labyrinth in Sight

Arella groaned as she ran her hand over the wet surface that she lay on, struggling not to fall unconscious. Everything around her was just a blur of dark shades that seemed to be constantly moving. Groaning, Arella rolled over onto her back and stared up at the cave ceiling.

You have to get up, she told herself. *We must...destroy Seuderak...*

She tried to lift herself up to a sitting position, but she was too tired and her body was aching. Not just from the raft wreck, but from using her powers to propel the raft forward. All of it combined had taken its toll on her. She would be too weak to face the most evil sorcerer in all of Ardara. What would it hurt to just give up now?

Never give up.

Suddenly she saw a brilliant white light coming from out of no where. Grimacing, she turned to where the light was coming from and blinked. The light looked as if it were trying to show, but was covered by...

Arella furrowed her brow as she stared at the struggling light. It was coming from her right hand, which was still bandaged. Frowning, she slowly sat up, ignoring the pain, and then carefully unwrapped the bandaging.

As the binding slipped off of her hand and fell to the ground, the glowing light became brighter and brighter, until it blinded Arella. Scowling, Arella lifted her left hand to shield her eyes, wondering why her hand would be glowing...

That's when she felt the cool breeze as it swept through the cave. Sitting up straighter, Arella turned to where she sensed the fresh air coming from. After a long moment of hesitating, she quickly leapt to her feet and started limping forward. Behind her she could hear the rushing waters, where they had crashed. If she could find a way out, she would come back to look for her brother and Hansrai.

Arella stumbled along, holding her hand out in front of her, letting the vivid light aid her in traveling down the dark passageway. One thing she noticed was that the tunnel didn't ever branch off, or have many twists and turns to it. It was *not* a lengthy tunnel. Soon after she started to follow the passageway, she could see light up ahead and let her hands fall gently to her sides, no longer needing their light.

When she came to the end of the tunnel, her eyes widened. What she saw before her took her breath away. It was absolutely beautiful and…extremely enthralling.

She stood on a shelf rock surface, looking down upon the next part of the labyrinth. This part was built upon an extremely large slope, formed out of the orange rock that the small mountain was made out of. From her vantage point, it appeared that thick, dark vines covered the walls of the labyrinth, also growing in clumps in the middle of the paths, to create a blockage.

But what Arella found most interesting was not the labyrinth, but what the labyrinth was *in*.

It appeared to be floating in the dark sky, among thousands of stars. As she watched the stars drift slowly around the labyrinth, she figured that was why the stars had appeared so close. Yet…something didn't feel real about this place. The stars almost seemed fake, very unlike the stars in the night skies that stretched out over Ardara.

No, these stars seemed to have a mind of their own...

One of the stars trembled, before hovering towards Arella. As it approached, Arella noticed that it was *not* a star, but a small glowing figure with light blue skin and wings.

"Pixies," Arella muttered, staring at the little being as it smiled mischievously at her.

"Hansrai..."

The voice seemed far away and very unclear to the half unconscious king. He groaned and rolled over on the somewhat soft surface, not quite sure where he was. His memory was fuzzy and he was struggling to remember what had happened.

"Hansrai!"

Suddenly freezing cold water washed over his face and everything came back, hitting him so hard he felt as if he had just been struck with a giant war hammer. The images rushed through his mind, placing the pieces back together where they belonged.

He remembered the insane ride on the rapids, recalled when the raft had struck the rock, and recollected the memory of being tossed into the air.

Feeling his strength coming back to him, Hansrai shot up into a sitting position. Standing beside him was a very soggy and dripping Jared. The young bandit made a face as he stuck the opening of the canteen near one eye.

"Empty," he stated. Tossing it to the side,

he glanced back at Hansrai. "All the magical water is gone."

Hansrai frowned as he rubbed his head. "That could have come in handy while fighting Seuderak."

Jared shrugged. "I had to get you up."

The young king groaned as he stood. "Where's Arella?"

"I don't know," Jared answered, looking worried. "When I woke up, I saw a bright light coming from the other side of the rapids." He pointed to the rocky grounds on the other side of the fast-moving waters. "When I tried to look closer, the light had already gone down a tunnel. I think it has something to do with Arella."

"On the other side…" Hansrai sighed. How were they supposed to make it to the other side?

Can't quit now.

Giving a nod of determination, Hansrai started searching for a way to cross the torrents without being swept away. As his eyes followed the rushing water, he saw that up ahead the water shot into a large whole in the rock wall and smiled slightly.

"We'll scale the rock wall," Hansrai said, pointing towards it.

Jared's eyes widened. "Are you serious?"

Hansrai frowned. "Aren't you used to doing dangerous stuff with your sister?"

"Yeah," Jared answered, laughing nervously. "But she doesn't do stupid stuff and she has magical powers. You…you're just a king."

Just a king. Hansrai shook his head. "Well, we have to try something."

Jared sighed. "All right, let's try it."

Hansrai nodded and started walking towards the wall, unsure if his plan would really work. He had never really climbed any steep surfaces and didn't know if he would be able to, but he had to at least try. Anyhow, if he did fall into the water, get tossed around relentlessly and then die, he wouldn't have to fight the most evil wizard in all the land, right?

Hansrai shuddered. He would rather live to fight the sorcerer. He was one of the chosen after all. Unless…they had made a mistake. Or this all was just a trap to kill him because he was king. Maybe Arella had even been part of it. He knew how badly she wanted him dead.

Hansrai grimaced as a shiver ran up his spine. No. If Arella had wanted him dead, she would have killed him already. She had had plenty of chances to do so.

"You first."

Jared's statement brought Hansrai out of his thoughts as they arrived at the rock wall. Hansrai looked somewhat nervous as he stared up at the rough surface. "But you are the one who is used to doing this kind of stuff."

"You're a king," Jared said, crossing his arms defiantly.

"A king has someone to taste his food to make sure it has not been poisoned," Hansrai shot back.

Jared scowled. Then they both stood in awkward silence, as if waiting for Arella to barge in, yell something while starting to climb the wall herself, proving that it was all too easy. But of course Arella wasn't there with them. She didn't threaten them, or look at them as if they were wimpy. No, there was just the uncomfortable silence and the glares exchanged by the king and bandit.

After the long silence, Jared and Hansrai both nodded. "I'll go first," they said in unison.

There was another moment of hesitation, before Jared shrugged. "I am the youngest, so…"

Hansrai sighed. "All right, all right. I'll go first."

Jared smirked triumphantly as Hansrai began climbing the rock surface, grimacing as some of the sharper rock cut into his skin.

"It really runs in the family," Hansrai grumbled through gritted teeth.

"What does?" Jared questioned.

"You know what-" His sentence was cut short when his foot slipped and he fell back to the ground. As he groaned, Jared made a face, before attempting to climb the wall himself.

When Hansrai finally sat up, he watched with an annoyed countenance as Jared was almost to the other side.

"You're turn!" Jared called as he leapt to the ground.

"How…" Hansrai shook his head and went back to trying to scale the rock wall, grumbling to himself as he did so. It was hard for him to climb, with blood smeared all over his hands making the rock surface slick.

Once he was right over the torrents, his hands slipped. With a cry of alarm, Hansrai started to fall towards the rapids.

"Hansrai!" Jared called as he started to rush forward, though he wouldn't be able to do anything.

Coming within inches away of hitting the water, Hansrai suddenly came to a stop, floating just above the water. Hansrai slowly floated towards Jared and then was dropped roughly to the ground.

"You two wouldn't be able to survive without me."

Jared and Hansrai quickly turned to where Arella was standing behind them. She had her arms crossed and was glaring at them.

"I should have just started traveling through the last part of the labyrinth and left you to fall."

Hansrai started to thank her, ignoring what she had said, when he stopped. "Last part of the labyrinth?" he questioned, slowly getting back up to his feet.

Arella nodded. "Yes."

"How do you know if it's the last part?" Jared questioned, thinking that news was all too good to be true.

Arella gave another nod and turned to the tunnel she had come through. "Follow me."

"See just down the slope? Near the base is the edge, but it appears that there are small, floating islands right out from it. These islands stretch out to the next large piece of land, which is the next part of the labyrinth. Also, watch the stars. Some of these stars are creating a line that follows part of the labyrinth, before leading to a giant clump of stars," Arella explained, pointing towards the circling formation of stars.

"These stars..." Jared began, scowling at a giggling one that was swirling around his head. "They are very annoying."

"That is because they are pixies," Arella clarified. "And these pixies are attracted to the heart of the labyrinth."

"So you think that...extremely large clump of them are circling around the heart of the labyrinth? Wouldn't they be terrified to go near it, considering that an evil sorcerer is imprisoned there?" Hansrai questioned.

Arella shook her head. "Do you not know *anything*? Pixies are attracted to power, energy."

"Oh," Jared muttered, before slapping at the pixie that was pestering him. "I remember now."

Hansrai crossed his arms and looked agitated. "Since you're so smart, how about you tell me how long it will take to get there."

"It depends on how well we can travel through the labyrinth," she answered, shrugging.

"Not long, I hope," Jared groaned. "We lost our packs..."

Arella glanced at him. "I lost my sword, so stop complaining."

Hansrai shook his head. "That's not good. You need your sword if we are to fight Seuderak."

"He is an evil sorcerer that is most likely very furious after being trapped here for who knows how long," Arella said, starting to make her way down the sharp incline to the slope. "I don't think it will matter having a sword or not."

"Well at least give me time to look for it," Hansrai said, turning back to the tunnels entrance.

Jared nodded and started to follow, when a loud roar sounded down the tunnel. The young king and bandit groaned.

"Not the cave trolls *again*," Jared moaned.

"Hurry!" Hansrai exclaimed as Jared turned to look at him. Jared nodded and they both rushed after Arella, climbing carefully but quickly down the incline; racing to reach the bottom. Halfway down, they heard the trolls on the rock ledge above them.

"Shh," Hansrai whispered urgently. "Stop moving!"

Jared gritted his teeth and pressed himself against the rock surface. Trying not to move and make much noise proved to be extremely difficult after already climbing a rock wall. His arms were growing tired and ready to give out on him. Trembling, Jared glanced at Hansrai, who was staring up at the rock shelf above.

Jared followed his gaze and gulped. He could just barely make out at least five of the cave trolls standing near the brink of the ledge. Luckily, at the moment he was looking, they weren't looking down.

"Hansrai," Jared muttered, his voice just barely audible to himself.

The young king shot him a dangerous look, which Jared found somewhat surprising. Maybe spending so much time around his sister had taken its toll on Hansrai...

"Ugh, this is taking too long!" Arella said rather loudly. She let go with one of her hands and raised it over her head, sending a terrible force at the trolls, who had just noticed them. As she sent the force upward, it pushed her down, compelling her to let go all the way and start to fall towards the large slope beneath them.

"Arellaaa!" Jared hollered, reaching down with one hand, as if to grab her, when his other hand slipped and he too, started to fall.

His sister's eyes widened when she saw him falling and she quickly leapt into action. She spun in midair, until she was facing the ground. She closed her eyes and concentrated hard, quickly weaving two different energies together to create an invisible net that would catch her and her brother. Right as she finished, she hit it, followed by her brother.

There was a moment of silence as Jared lay on the net, his face pale.

"That was close," he said, glancing at his sister, who was already back up on her feet.

"Hurry up and get to your feet," Arella ordered, staring up at the ledge.

Jared groaned as he looked back up, to see one of the trolls attempting to climb down after them.

"Hansrai, *jump*!" Arella yelled. "Just let go!"

"I hate this," the young king yelled, before letting go and letting himself free fall. Arella gritted her teeth and moved the net below him, while also trying to keep an eye on the quickly descending troll. Once Hansrai had safely landed on the net and was back on his feet, they started running towards the entrance to the next part of the labyrinth.

"Hurry!" Arella shouted, moments before

the troll lost his gripping and fell.

Arella, Jared, and Hansrai rushed through the labyrinth and down the slope, finding it rather hard to do both at the same time. More than once Jared almost crashed into a wall; finding himself gaining speed as he ran downward.

His sister continually tried to help him along, while trying to weave their way through the maze, not paying much attention to any of the turns or trying to remember what she had seen above. All she was thinking about was keeping ahead of the trolls.

"I think we're going the wrong way!" Hansrai shouted as they rushed down one of the paths that was starting to bend to the left. Arella scowled, but kept going, knowing that they couldn't afford to backtrack while the cave trolls were behind them.

"I don't think we should be going this way!" Hansrai pressed, searching the curving passage up ahead, then glancing over his shoulder. "Something tells me we should have gone down the right passage!"

Arella scowled again. "Well something is telling me that we can't turn back now. We have to keep moving-*forward*!"

Hansrai glared at her, but didn't say anything back. He didn't see the point in arguing with her. She had her mind made up and it would be too hard to change it. They didn't have time to be in a disagreement; the cave trolls were probably not far behind.

Arella followed the passage, which made a sudden sharp turn to their right. Then came to an immediate halt when the path came to a void, the edge of the path rough and uneven, as if part of the labyrinth had been broken. About ten feet in front of her was the rest of the path, which went on several more feet, before turning right.

Hansrai and Jared came running around the corner, rushing down the slope after Arella, knocking into her and almost sending her falling into the void. Jared let out a startled cry and tried to backpedal, when he knocked into Hansrai. Grabbing the back of his sister's shirt, Jared fell on his rear end, his sister tumbling to the ground beside him.

"I told you we shouldn't have gone this way!" Hansrai yelled at Arella as he scrambled to get to his feet.

Arella growled as she started to sit up. "How was I supposed to know this would happen?"

Hansrai quickly stood, glaring at her. "We should've gone the other way!"

"Well there's no point in fighting over it!" Arella snapped as she leapt to her feet. Pointing a finger accusingly at the young king, she hissed, "We'll have to jump."

"What-"

"Well, we can't go back the way we just came," Arella said, crossing her arms and glaring death at him. If only fierce looks could kill, the young king would have been dead.

Hansrai was about to snap back at her, when he heard a familiar and unwelcoming sound coming from around the corner. The trio froze, holding the mere precious breath that kept them alive. For once, they didn't want to take in the precious oxygen, for they feared that the slightest noise would alert their presence to the cave trolls.

Chapter 33
The Face of Seuderak

"Jared, run!!" Arella screamed as the troll brought his club down on the wall, breaking the top, sending dust and debris flying everywhere. Arella couldn't see at first, but she reached for her sword just in case-

No sword.

Growling, Arella rolled her hands into fists. No sword, no weapon. At least she had magic...That is, if she had enough strength to use her powers.

"I can't run!" Jared hollered between coughs. "Hole, remember?"

"Then jump," Arella said, her eyes searching for the cave trolls. Everything was just a blur of orange and grey, but she could see a shadow a few feet in front of her to her right, where she guessed Hansrai was. From the sounds of it, she guessed that Jared was behind her. Hopefully close to the gap and not in the opposite direction.

She then spotted one of them. The troll was moving towards the shadow that Arella had guessed was Hansrai. It was moving somewhat slowly, trying to find its bearings, but its club was at the ready.

"Arella?!" Jared shouted. His voice seemed

closer than before.

The troll came to a halt when it heard Jared's voice, before starting to rush towards Arella, almost knocking its club into Hansrai, who brought his sword around to slice at the troll's leg. The troll roared as it stumbled forward, swinging its club wildly. Arella's eyes widened and she quickly took a step back, before raising her hands and then bringing them down in a quick motion. Immediately the dust blew away, allowing Arella to be able to see more clearly.

But then she wished she hadn't done it.

Gasping, Arella started to backpedal, but suddenly…there was nothing beneath her feet. She screamed as she started to fall, the troll lunging after her.

"Nooo! Arella!" Jared and Hansrai cried as they rushed to the edge, their eyes wide with disbelief as they watched the troll and young thief tumble downward into the large, dark void.

Seuderak sat on his throne, looking up suddenly as he felt a rush of power vibrate through him. There was a moment of silence, before an eerie scream echoed through the throne room. The scream was suddenly cut short, followed by a loud crashing sound.

The sorcerer waited, listening carefully, before leaning back and looking around at his strange throne room. It was an underground cave, with fires raging around the perimeter of it, screams of agony ringing through the air. Seuderak's throne was carved out of the brown and red rock of the caves, shaped to look like a skull. Where he sat was the bottom jaw, which stuck out farther than anything else of the throne, as if someone had ripped the skull forward, in a position that it should not be sitting.

For the evil sorcerer, he had his own hell.

Giving a slight nod, the sorcerer ran a finger over the armrest, which were the teeth of the skull. He was chanting something under his breath, tendrils of smoke rising from where his bloodstained fingernail had touched. As he continued to do this, he etched a curving figure, that resembled a serpent circling around a skull. The mark of Seuderak.

Upon finishing, Seuderak drove his knife-like fingernail into the middle of the engraving.

"Today...I will finish what I started," Seuderak snarled. The throne room started to tremble and the flooring around the throne cracked as a serpent tore through the rock surface and curved around the throne, just as how the serpent appeared in the evil sorcerer's mark. The scales of the serpent was the same color as the rock and it surely appeared to be made of stone, yet it moved with ease, circling around the throne, before stopping in its right position and going stiff.

"Arella," Jared whispered as he fell to his knees. He couldn't see her, nor hear her screams anymore. She was gone. Really, truly gone. How could he go on without her?

Hansrai knelt down next to him as he peered over the edge. Still unsure if he had seen the most wanted thief in all of Aselda, that no one could ever catch, just...fall. Fall off of the ledge. Fall to her death. Right in front of him...and he didn't do anything to help her. He couldn't have, could he?

"Jared, we need to get moving. There are other trolls-"

"You did it." Jared's voice was trembling. "You had a part in this."

Hansrai stared at him in shock. "I would have never killed your sister, even if-"

"You hated her! You wanted her dead...you wanted us dead," Jared growled as he looked up with bloodshot eyes.

Hansrai started to answer, when he felt his throat go dry. At one point he *had* wanted them dead...If he said no, he would be lying. But he hadn't been in his right mind at the time.

"I would have tried to help your sister," Hansrai said, looking at Jared and not backing down. "I...I just wasn't quick enough."

Jared growled and pushed Hansrai, before jumping to his feet. "I hope you die here, Hansrai." With those last words to the young king, he started walking back the way they had come.

Hansrai quickly stood, watching as the young bandit walked away. "Jared-"

The boy didn't listen as he turned the corner, starting to run as he tried to get away from Hansrai.

"This isn't how it was supposed to end," Hansrai muttered, retrieving his sword which was laying on the ground.

Arella tried to breath, but the troll kept its large hands around her throat, cutting off her intake of oxygen. Growing closer and closer to unconsciousness, Arella knew she had to do something quick. Everything becoming a blur, she slowly raised her hand in position with the troll's head and sent a heavy force knocking into his head.

The troll groaned as he released his hands from around her neck. Arella struggled to take in a breath of air, before sending another force reeling into the troll's forehead. Immediately the troll went limp, its face bruised and bleeding.

Cringing, Arella closed her eyes looking away before she saw too much and concentrated on trying to breath again. She didn't know what she would or could be able to do. She was falling and she didn't know when she might strike something. But she had to try.

Everything still a haze, Arella tried to find her bearings and gather enough energy to slow herself, but she was too weak. It was just a struggle to breath and stay awake. Closing her eyes and opening them once more, she saw a blur of colors. Colored dust that swirled as she fell through it.

What she was falling through appeared to be an eagle nebula. But it was just a cloud of "magical" dust.

As she fell, she thought that she might go on forever. There seemed to be no limit to the space surrounding the labyrinth. Maybe if she could gather enough energy she could somehow make her way back to the maze…

Where was Jared? Was he ok?

Her eyes burned with tears. If anything happened to Jared...Though she would never know. She was falling farther and farther away from him. Her brother. The only family she had left. The last thing that she cared about.

Grimacing, Arella looked below her and frowned when she saw the dark "sky" ripple, as if it were water. Her eyes widened when she felt her body hit the surface of the water and shoot into the depths, losing consciousness not long after the impact.

Jared started to slow when he came to a fork in the path, before coming to a complete halt.

Which way?

Looking down the left passage, he scowled when he saw that it curved upward, thorns growing on the walls and the ground. It didn't look like a pleasant way to go. Hoping the right passage would be better, he moved towards it, peering down the passageway. To his dismay, that part moved downward, the flooring covered in a strange black substance.

"If Arella were here, she would know what to do," Jared muttered. He grimaced as he felt a longing ache in his heart. He needed Arella...

"Why?" he questioned, falling to his knees and burying his face in his hands. "You have to come back to me...please."

Trembling, Jared started to cry. It had been hard enough when their parents had died, but his sister had been there with him. Though she had been shaken after the event that took their parents' lives, she had been strong and had comforted him. Now…he had no one.

CRACK!

Sniveling, Jared glanced over his shoulder, searching for the source of the sound. His eyes widened in alarm when he saw part of the mountainside that was farther back explode, large chunks of the terrain being tossed high into the air. Jared's eyes must have seen wrong, for at one point the rocks seemed to come together and morph into the shape of a face. Opening its large mouth, the bodiless head roared, before the rocks started to fall, creating an enormous avalanche.

Scrambling to get to his feet, Jared continued to glance over his shoulder, his heart thudding against his chest as he started to panic. Not giving a second thought as to what passage he should take, Jared rushed down the right passageway, but his pace quickly slowed as he struggled to move through the black substance. It felt as if he were walking through molasses, hardly able to lift his feet and move forward.

Jared gritted his teeth and tried to push forward, but as he traveled deeper into the mire, the harder it became to move, until he couldn't take another step forward. Searching for something-anything-that could help, Jared tried to think of a plan to get him out of this mess. However, he knew he had wasted time by just trying to move through this part of the labyrinth. The avalanche would be upon him soon and he would be killed.

Closing his eyes, Jared tried to picture his

sister one last time. As her face came into focus, he saw two other figures standing behind her. Their features were unclear, but he knew who they were. His father and mother...

A tear slowly ran down his cheek, off of his chin, and fell towards the molasses-like substance.

Jared took a deep breath and was about to recall his most precious memory, when he heard a sizzling sound. Opening his eyes, he looked down to where the tear had fallen. The dark substance was slowly fading away, tendrils of smoke rising from the spot where it was evaporating, followed by a hissing sound.

Then, suddenly, the fading of the mire seemed to intensify, before Jared could stand without any of it gluing him to one spot.

Thunk, thump!

Jared looked up as a chunk of the labyrinth flew overhead, scarcely five feet above him. Turning, Jared's eyes widened as he watched a mass of rock rushing at him, tumbling down the slope. Gritting his teeth, he crouched down and covered his head, expecting to feel chunks of earth beating down on him, but it never came. Once the rocks came within feet of hitting him, they were tossed up into the air, soaring overhead, and not harming the young bandit.

Not believing what he was seeing, Jared slowly stood. As the avalanche grew thicker, Jared felt himself being pushed forward by an invisible force, along with the one that was shielding him from the avalanche. Not knowing what was going on, Jared braced his feet on the ground and pressed his back on the force that was moving forward, trying to stop it. With all the rubble, he couldn't see anything and wouldn't be able to see if there was a ledge coming up where he would fall to his certain death. Just like Arella had…

No. Don't think about that, Jared told himself, gritting his teeth as he fought against the moving force.

Suddenly he felt himself being lifted off the ground and tossed into the air. Letting out a terrified yelp, Jared flung his arms wildly, before gritting his teeth and closing his eyes. Not long afterwards, he started to descend, then he felt his body hit a rough surface.

Groaning, Jared lay sprawled out on the wreckage of the avalanche. His body was aching all over and he felt as if he couldn't even lift himself up. Letting out another moan, Jared went still.

"Jared, we're almost there."

The young bandit stiffened when he heard his sister's voice. After she had finished the sentence, her voice echoed, seeming to bounce around in his head.

Quickly sitting up, Jared surveyed the damage around him and tried to find his sister, but she was no where to be seen. Of course, with all the debris and dirt flying in the air, he couldn't see very far ahead of him. Clumsily getting to his feet, Jared's legs wobbled, but he started to stumble forward. He heard his sister's whispers around him, calling to him.

"Arella!" he shouted, turning in circles. "Arella, where are you?!"

"Over the bridge," her voice said, repeating itself for what seemed like a thousand times, echoing down the slope.

"Bridge?" Jared muttered.

"The floating islands."

Jared tried to look ahead of him, but the dust that was drifting around him from the avalanche was making it hard to really see anything. "Which way?" he called to his sister.

"This way," came her soft whispers from behind him as a breeze started to sweep the dust away. Jared quickly shut his eyes, keeping out the dust. He scowled as the dust entered his mouth and started coughing. Wiping at his eyes and spitting out the dirt, Jared started to move towards the voice, taking slow steps at first. When he could finally see, he looked down the slope and saw the floating islands his sister had pointed out to Hansrai and him earlier.

Feeling hopeful, Jared started running. He was closer to the heart of the labyrinth than he had originally thought he had been. Maybe his sister was on the other side…

Carefully but quickly making his way down a steep part of the slope, Jared desperately hoped he would find his sister. That she wouldn't be dead.

Coming to the foot of the hill, he found himself on solid, flat ground, the edge of the larger island that he was on only about ten feet away. Taking in a shaky breath, he walked forward, until he was only a few inches away from the edge, peering down into the void below.

"Jared," drifted a soft voice from the other large island that was across the void. Jared immediately looked up and squinted his eyes. He could make out a figure standing at the edge of the other floating island. It appeared to be his sister…yet, she wore a white sleeveless dress.

Suddenly his head started pounding and it felt as if there was something being driven into the side. Grimacing, he clutched his head and groaned, before looking up, hoping his sister would still be there. He could see her, but it was very strange. At point he could only make out a hazy figure, but then suddenly she seemed to be getting closer to him, though he could still see her standing back on the large island in front of him. In moments an almost transparent image of her stood right in front of him, a slight smile on her face. A strange, twisted smile, as if she was holding a dark secret. A secret that could kill him.

Jared blinked. In the moment that his eyes closed and re-opened, the image of his sister had moved farther away from him. Her twisted smile broadened as she slowly lifted her arm. She stretched a hand out towards him, beckoning him to grab it.

Not knowing what else to do, Jared started to reach for her hand, when he caught movement to his right out of the corner of his eye. His eyes widened as he quickly turned to see what it was, completely forgetting about his sister for the time being.

He wasn't entirely sure if he was seeing right, again. The creature that stood before him almost looked like a large spider that at least stood three feet tall, but its body seemed to be made from sharp, ebony colored blades. As it moved forward and its blade-like legs scraped against each other, a small metallic sound filled the air.

The color drained from Jared's face as he took a step back, reaching for his sword-

He felt a sharp pain in his calf as another one of the strange creatures cut the back of his leg. Grabbing his knee and grimacing, Jared quickly tried to hop away, unable to grab his sword in time as a third of the blade spiders rushed up and grazed his cheek.

"Ah!" he yelped in pain, his hand moving towards his face, when the first spider rushed at him, bringing up a foreleg and slicing at his stomach several times.

Groaning, Jared fell to his knees and the spiders scattered, apparently pleased with what they had done to the young passerby. Jared trembled, doubling over and gasping for air. Everything had happened so fast, he still couldn't believe what he had seen. Somehow they had made it this far, for only his sister to be thrown off of a cliff? For him to be killed by a few spiders?

"N-not ordinary spiders," he muttered.

"You're right about that," said his sister's voice.

Stiffening, Jared slowly looked up to see Arella standing over him. Only…she was smirking at him, looking quite pleased. Jared blinked and suddenly, she was gone. Arella had been there one moment, but once he opened his eyes again, Zara Cyan stood over him.

"Weak," the assassin muttered, before turning to walk towards the floating islands. As she moved away from him, her form started to shimmer, before becoming transparent.

"What did you do with my sister?!" Jared

hollered, before grimacing and doubling over again.

He trembled and wiped away the sweat on his head with a bloody hand, knowing he probably didn't have long to live. He sniveled as a tear slipped down his cheek. *We should never have come here*, Jared thought, staring at the ground as a mixed drop of sweat and blood fell to the sand. He tried not to look at the puddle of blood that he was sitting in. *His* own blood. Suddenly his world seemed to spin, causing him to become nauseated.

Jared closed his eyes, trying to stay conscious. He'd already lost so much blood. Everything became unclear, his thoughts just a jumbled mess. After struggling for another breath, he opened his eyes, as if hoping to see his sister standing there.

A small flame flickered on the stone flooring…

Jared's eyes widened. Either he was clearly not seeing things right, he was dead, or he was somewhere completely different.

Staring hard at the flame, he watched as it grew bigger, before it started to cut across the stone, burning into it and creating a picture in the rock surface. As the flame parted to create smaller flames, he narrowed his eyes. The flames quickened, before suddenly going out.

"No," Jared gasped, looking at the symbol on the ground.

An image of a snake circling around a skull.

A groan to his left caught Jared's attention. He quickly glanced in the direction of the sound. Laying ten feet away was Hansrai, who was sprawled out on the floor and looking close to losing consciousness.

The sound of a sword being drawn from its sheath echoed at his right. Though he feared what he might see, he slowly turned his head towards the sound. His eyes widened even more when he saw his sister, laying on the ground, sopping wet. She lay motionless, her face pale.

"Arella!" The name barely left his mouth and his voice cracked before the word could even become audible.

He tried to move forward, when he saw the bloodstained blade hover over Arella's throat. Feeling his heart hammering in his chest, he slowly turned to see the wielder of the sword.

Chapter 34
The End, or Just the Beginning?

"Don't you dare touch my sister!" Jared snarled, quickly overcoming his shock.

The hooded figure quickly turned his head to glare at Jared. Though his features were unseen from the shadows cast over his face, Jared had a sensation that whatever was under that hood was not pleasant. Keeping his eyes on the unseen face, Jared tried to ignore the bloodstained cape and blade. He also didn't want to look at those skeleton-like hands anymore.

Just look at the shadows under the hood, Jared told himself, trembling as he struggled to do this.

What are you going to do to stop me?

Jared grimaced as the gravelly voice entered his thoughts. He found himself slowly lowering his gaze. Scowling, Jared told himself to stop and look at where Seuderak's face was...or at least where it should have been.

We are the chosen, Jared said in his mind, figuring that Seuderak would be tuning in on whatever he thought.

Yet you have fallen so easily? The raspy voice laughed coldly.

"We beat the assassin that you...sent...after us," Jared managed to say, trying not to double over as he kept a careful eye on the evil sorcerer. Or had they? He had seen her after the little blade spiders...Maybe Seuderak wouldn't know that. He was hoping to stall the wizard as he tried to think of a plan, but apparently Seuderak read that thought as well. Or, he was growing tired of debating with a dying teenager that had no way of escaping. Either way, in a rapid motion he turned and brought his sword up.

It all happened too quickly. Jared found himself shouting as he watched the sorcerer bring his sword down, aiming for Arella's neck. Falling forward, Jared let out one more desperate cry, before crumbling to the stone flooring.

ZING!

Jared felt the tears coming on again as he heard the sound. The first tear slipped down his grimy cheek, followed by many others. He figured he was about to die from major blood loss, or from the blade that had killed his sister.

But why wasn't he dead yet? Gritting his teeth, Jared ran a hand across the stone flooring as he tried not to groan. He had lost so much blood…he should've been dead sooner.

Don't look up, Jared told himself, trembling. He didn't want to see his sister, dead, her beautiful features stained with blood. Even if he had only moments to live.

"Jared," a soft voice seemed to whisper in his ear.

It was the assassin again, he was sure of it. She had come back to taunt him. Now trembling with rage, his fear had turned to uncontrolled anger.

With a furious cry, Jared's head shot up. He expected to see Zara standing near him, but he saw something very, very different. Something that he had not been expecting. Something that seemed to bring the hope, that only moments before had vanished, back in full force. It was like having a bright light suddenly able to guide you through the snare, where you had been lost in darkness.

And in truth, it was a light in the darkness. Physically, a real light burned brightly before him.

"Arella," Jared breathed, unsure if he was seeing it all right.

His sister still lay motionless, the sword hovering inches away from her face as a bright light appeared to form into the shape of a long shield, pushing back the tip of the blade. Seuderak, though, seemed unconcerned about this and continued to struggle with pushing his weapon down, determined to break the shield.

Then, without warning, the light dimmed and the fire surrounding the throne room died.

Jared held his breath, not daring to move a muscle as he stared into the darkness, still seeing the outline of the shield, though he knew it was not really there anymore. It was only his eyes trying to become adjusted to the sudden change.

Silence settled over the throne room, not a single noise echoing through the underground chamber. What had happened? Had Seuderak won? Had the sorcerer managed to kill his sister?

With the lights that had abruptly went out, so did his new found hope begin to fade. Every time that it seemed his sister might live, his hopes were crushed. Maybe that wasn't even Arella. Just a trick of the mind. Perhaps he was already dead. If this was the afterlife, he would be trapped here for all eternity…

All these thoughts were being tossed around in his mind as he waited in the looming darkness. What exactly he was waiting for: He did not know. He didn't know if he should try to do something, or just sit still. Of course, if he tried anything, he wouldn't be able to do much. Not with the wounds that the blade spiders had given him.

How long had he been sitting there, waiting in the nerve-racking silence? Jared shuddered as he started to move forward, dragging himself to where he thought Arella might be. When suddenly a brilliant flash lit up the throne room, followed by a terrible force that pushed Jared back towards the wall. Striking his head against the rock surface, he was knocked unconscious immediately. His arm dangled in the long crack that followed the wall, where the fire had come up from.

The source of the vivid blue and white light

came from Arella, who's form was glowing. Seuderak still stood over her, the hilt of the sword *still* in his grip, but the blade had vaporized. Small tendrils of smoke rising from where it had been moments before.

Tossing the useless grip aside, Seuderak reached down to grip Arella's throat, when the young thief's eyes suddenly opened. Keeping her eyes carefully on the face of the evil sorcerer, which loomed right over her own face, Arella brought her arm up and in an arc to hit the wizard's wrist. Seuderak moved quickly, stepping away from Arella and out of her reach.

Arella quickly leapt to her feet, her form growing brighter and brighter, until it was blinding. Then the light began to fade, until only a small portion of it was left. The little bit of light remaining formed into the shapes of wings, latching themselves onto Arella's back, who grimaced slightly.

A harsh laugh filled the chamber as Seuderak stood back to examine the young warrior.

"A Messenger of the Guardians? The irony," rasped the voice of the evil sorcerer.

Arella's eyes widened as she quickly glanced over her shoulder, to see the delicate looking wings fluttering behind her; but her attention quickly turned back to her enemy when she heard his voice enter into her thoughts. Gritting her teeth, she shook her head.

"I am not!"

The cold laughter became more intense, seeming to drill through right to her heart. Arella growled, her eyes flashing with anger. She rushed at the sorcerer, leaping into the air and twirling in quick, tight circles. As she started to come down, a sword swiftly formed out of light, the blade pointing at Seuderak's chest.

The wizard arched his back as the tip of the blade was driven into his torso, the thin bloodstained cape falling from his shoulders to reveal a figure of horror.

Arella's face twisted into a scowl as she looked upon the ugly humanoid creature before her. He looked as if he had been a victim of an acid spill; but the explanation of the wizard's form will go no further. For the image was immediately embedded into Arella's mind, to haunt her for the rest of her life. Why let that same horror stalk you?

Trying to overcome her shock, Arella trembled slightly, pulling a dagger from her belt and stabbing the wizard in the heart for good measure. Staring into the cold eyes of the sorcerer, she blocked out everything else. "Today, you will die," she hissed, slowly turning the blade of her dagger.

Ah...but I have no heart. The wizard stared into her eyes with his own. They were completely black, cold, and shimmered with something that seemed like a longing-a thirst-for blood. With eagerness to bring his enemies down. "Look into my eyes and see."

Arella immediately looked away, which was also a mistake. The sorcerer brought up his hand within inches of Arella, pushing her back with a terrible force. Arella let out a startled cry as she was flung backward, crashing into someone and then hitting the wall. The body behind her providing some protection from the impact.

Groaning, Arella started to open her eyes. The world was spinning and mashing together, or, at least, that was how she felt. She was seeing triple of everything around her. There appeared to be three or four sources of red light, growing closer and closer to her, in only a matter of moments.

Her eyes opening wide, Arella gasped as the beam headed straight for her. Whoever she had crashed into grabbed both her wrists and rolled over onto his side. Arella gritted her teeth and turned her head, closing her eyes and grimacing as she felt hot air rush over her.

Smoke filling her nostrils and entering into her lungs, Arella began to cough, her throat burning. Her body trembled as she tried to breath. Her eyes watering and stinging from the smoke, Arella felt as if she couldn't live much longer through this.

"Arella, your brother!"

It was Hansrai's voice! Arella slowly opened her eyes and looked over her shoulder. Hansrai had released her and was kneeling over her, his head turned in the direction where Jared was.

Arella quickly sat up, trying to look through the dissipating smoke. As the haze began to clear up, Arella could see her brother. Jared was still in the same position he had been in. If the crack that his arm was hanging in had been any larger, he would've completely fallen through. But that wasn't the problem.

Seuderak stood in front of his throne, his back to them. He had his cape back on and had his hands raised as he started chanting. The surface of the wall that was nearest the throne lit up with orange and red as flames started to rise again through the cracks.

Arella's attention immediately turned back to Jared. Her face went pale as she watched the lights being cast against the wall he was propped up against.

"Jared, wake up!" she screamed as she started running towards him. "Get *up*!"

As she rushed up to him, she grimaced when she saw the blood on his tunic. Sliding down into a kneeling position beside her brother, she examined the wounds quickly. *Don't die on me,* she thought as she gently grabbed his arm and shoulder, pulling him away from the crack.

Gritting her teeth, she tried to stand and lift him, but his dead weight was making it hard to do so. Letting out an exasperated sigh, she glanced back to where Seuderak was. He still stood before his throne, though his chanting had stopped.

Arella started to look for Hansrai, when she heard him shout at her, before he knocked into her, for the second time. Arella desperately held onto her brother as Hansrai pressed himself against the siblings, trying to shield them both from the fire that had suddenly come to life again.

Closing her eyes and hugging her brother, Arella gasped as a wave of extreme heat rushed over them. It was worse than when Seuderak had fired the beam at them. No, this heat came from a raging fire. Arella and her brother would have died, if it weren't for Hansrai painstakingly guarding them with his own body.

Yet, they still should have died. So why didn't they?

Arella grimaced as she heard Hansrai groan and felt his body contort. His torso and arms grew larger, the muscles bulging. His breathing became deeper as his body grew. Arella could hear his shirt ripping over the sound of the inferno they were in as Hansrai's growing arms enveloped them to keep them safe as the fire grew more intense.

A scaly surface brushed up against her and immediately, Arella opened her eyes. She found herself in darkness, her arms still protectively wrapped around her brother. Her breathing rigid, her heart thumping wildly, and beads of sweat forming on her brow. Arella didn't know what to do. She could sense that she was being tightly held by a large, reptile-like body, but other than that, she felt lost.

Jared groaned, bringing Arella out of her thoughts. Hurriedly glancing down, though she knew she wouldn't be able to see him, Arella ran her hand through her brother's hair. She needed light...

Closing her eyes and concentrating, she thought about the delicate wings that had been made from the beautiful, pure light. There was a dull pain in the top part of Arella's back. She winced, but didn't stop. She continued to concentrate, imagining the wings carefully. When the pain began to subside, she opened her eyes, only to find herself on the floor, Jared still in her arms.

Then she felt the hot breath rushing over her, a terrible stench following. Stiffening, Arella held her breath and scowled. She carefully and very, very slowly, laid Jared down. Still trying to not make any sudden movements, she reached for her knife.

Before she could turn to see what was behind her, the sorcerer suddenly turned to her, gripping a long, double bladed sword. As he looked down at her, his raspy voice slithered into her mind once more.

It will never end.

Arella scowled and started to stand, when the creature behind her leapt right over her head, charging at Seuderak. Narrowing her eyes, Arella took a quick look over the red dragon's scaly body and leather wings, before turning back to her brother. She figured the dragon could distract the sorcerer long enough for her to help Jared.

That's when a thought struck her. The dragon *was Hansrai*. Shuddering, Arella glanced over her shoulder to where the dragon was one last time. As her eyes caught sight of the large beast, it was colliding with the evil wizard, who was calmly bringing his sword up. Ready for the blade to meet with the dragon's hide.

A Drago Warrior. She went over the thought several times, not believing what she was seeing.

"Arella," Jared groaned.

Shaking her head, Arella turned her attention back to her brother. "Hold on," she muttered, holding her hands up. Her palms began glowing faintly with a pale blue color, before the light spread across her hands. Taking a deep breath, Arella lifted her hands a little farther above Jared, then brought them down quickly, pressing her fingers on the injuries.

Jared's body jolted, the skin slowly coming

together. Arella kept her hands in the same place, waiting quietly but impatiently as the gashes healed. When the last one closed, Arella cautiously lifted her hands and rested them in her lap as she watched Jared expectantly.

When he didn't move, a hint of worry flashed in her eyes, but was quickly gone. Leaning forward slightly, Arella shouted, "Jared!"

With a startled gasp, Jared's eyes snapped open and he sat up. Arella smirked and gave him a light pat on the back. "Feeling better?"

Jared looked confused at first, trying to figure out where he was. When his eyes rested on Arella, he relaxed. Then he saw the guardian wings and became even more confused. "Arella..."

Arella glanced over her shoulder to the wings. "Yeah, what of them? Come on," she said, grabbing his arm and dragging him to his feet, "Hansrai needs our help."

Jared's mouth fell open. "There's a dragon."

Arella rolled her eyes and started lugging him forward. "Drago Warrior."

"Hansrai."

"And you're..."

"Still Arella."

Jared's face went pale. "If he's a Drago Warrior and you're a...guardian-"

"Messenger; there's a difference."

"-than what am I?"

Arella let go of Jared as she summoned her light sword again. "I don't know. I do know this though: Xanthias has a lot of explaining to do if we get out of here. There's more to this than he let us know."

Jared gave a weak nod as he reached for his sword, still in a daze. "How do we stop him?"

Arella shrugged. "Fight. Kill. Win." Without waiting for a reply, she started running forward, ducking as the dragon's tail swung around. Dodging when the dragon moved suddenly to his left, Arella brought her sword up as the sorcerer, Seuderak, shot a beam of the blood red light at her. The hot light hit her blade and bounced off of it, shooting in the opposite direction and hitting the far left corner of the room.

She jumped and rolled as part of the ceiling started to collapse. Her brother ducked behind a large boulder that had already fallen, and Hansrai simply knocked the chunks of rock away. When the rain of stones ended, the three quickly faced Seuderak, who stood back in front of his throne.

The sorcerer bowed his head and raised his sword. A beam of light shot forth from the tip of the blade, hitting the ceiling and breaking through. The debris in the throne room trembled as a whirlwind enveloped Seuderak, before being tossed into the air, swirling around the wizard.

Arella's eyes widened and she quickly drove her sword into the stone flooring, holding tightly to the grip as her feet started to lift off of the ground. Jared tried to do the same, when he was caught up in the strong winds. Letting out a startled help, Jared let go of his sword as he desperately grabbed for something.

Placing his back legs firmly on the ground, Hansrai grabbed Jared as he flew by, closing his claws around the young bandit.

"He's trying to get away!" Arella hollered as she ripped her sword free of the stone and leapt forward, allowing herself to be drawn into the whirlwind. Forcing her sword forward, she pushed through and landed in front of the sorcerer, driving her blade into his torso.

"It *will* end here," she said, twisting the blade and forcing the weapon deeper into her enemy, until the tip broke the flesh of his back. The sorcerer made a choking sound, before he gripped the last part of the blade that hadn't entered into his stomach. He leaned forward, until Arella could smell his foul breath, as he thought one last, haunting sentence to her:

It never ends. It never will.

The grip of the sword began to burn, scorching Arella's hands, but she didn't let go. She kept her eyes settled on the sorcerer's, not willing to back down. Her face void of any emotions, Arella gave one final shove, driving the sword as far as it would go.

KKKAAABBBLLLAAAMMM!!

The wizard seemed to blow up right in her face, becoming an explosion of the light from Arella's sword. The young thief shut her eyes, raising her arms as if to shield her eyes from the sudden bright light. She felt her feet quickly lift off the ground as she was tossed like a rag doll. Spinning through the air, Arella tried to concentrate on slowing herself. Possibly even stopping herself completely, but she was barely able to keep herself conscious after the impact.

Finally she felt herself hit the ground and slide, before being hurtled into the wall. The air was forced out of her lungs as she crashed, which seemed to be the final straw. With a groan, Arella rolled over onto her back, her eyelids slowly closing.

"Arella!"

Jared's voice seemed distant as she tried to keep her eyes open. She heard a deep rumbling and though her vision was blurry, she could make out the ceiling as it started to collapse. The fires raged on, to the point of cracking the floor.

"ARELLA!"

She felt her eyes snap open and she quickly sat up, her form glowing slightly. She started to stand, when she felt a hand grab her arm. Stiffening, Arella quickly turned to see her brother.

A smile played at the corner of her lip as she stood, with the help of her brother. Together, the siblings rushed forward, dodging the falling stones, to where Hansrai stood, waiting, still in his dragon form. Arella seemed hesitant at first, but quickly climbed onto the back of the red dragon. She reached down, grabbed Jared's hand, and pulled him up.

Hansrai turned to look at the now large hole that the beam had created, folding his wings to cover Arella and Jared. The dragon started to move forward, cautiously but quickly, knocking chunks of the ceiling away with ease. Once he stood under the hole, he growled and leapt through, Jared and Arella letting out startled yelps as they clung to the dragon's back.

After spiraling upward, Hansrai tried to spread out his wings. Not used to being a dragon, he had trouble at first with balancing himself, but quickly caught on. Flying over that part of the labyrinth, he began searching for a way out.

POW! POW!

Arella swiftly looked over her shoulder at the sound. Above the heart of the labyrinth was what appeared to be a rapidly forming black hole. But what really caught her attention was the silver streams that shot up into the center. Her eyes widening slightly, she felt her mind began to think of what those streaks of light could mean.

It will never end.

Arella shuddered at the memory and she promptly pushed it to the side. Gently pushing her brother's shoulder and leaning over, she patted the dragon's neck to get his attention. When the dragon cocked his head listening, Arella yelled, "I think we found our way out!"

Hansrai bobbed his head up and down, as if nodding, and turned.

When Jared saw where they were going, his face went pale. "A-Arella…what is that?!"

"It's our way out," Arella answered, gripping the dragon and pushing her brother closer to the back of the creature. "Just hold on."

After only a moments hesitation, Hansrai began flying upward, heading for the center of the black hole. As they started their ascent, Arella glanced over her shoulder, her hair whipping around wildly as they started to enter the black hole. Her eyes widened when she saw the floating islands that connected to create the labyrinth morphing into a face, but before it could finish, they entered into the darkness.

Arella closed her eyes, took a deep breath,

and reopened them.   As they struggled to fly through the darkness, her eyes began glowing. She thought she spotted something moving in the portal with them, but when she looked again, it was gone. They were moving too quickly for her to be sure.

She bowed her head, trying not to think. She couldn't push the thought away.   It was haunting her. What the evil sorcerer had told her. What her fears were saying. It all continued to press into her mind until she finally gave in and thought it.

I don't think it's over.

And, dear reader, it's *not* over…

Special Thanks to....

First of all, I give all the praise to God. The one who

created me and gave me the love for writing. Without Him nothing is possible. My every little prayer now has a thank you to Him for the opportunity to write this and have it published.

Next I want to thank my family for being so supportive of me. Thanks mom for helping with the editing, thanks dad for encouraging and reminding me to keep calm when I was having trouble with writing this book, and thank you Ethan for helping out wherever you could! (And for not complaining - too much *wink* - for having to do my chores while I was busy) Connor and Dylan, my two crazy baby brothers, thank you for your excitement; especially Connor, for asking how many words I had every hour of writing. Also, mom, I loved watching your expressions every time you were left with just finishing reading a cliffhanger. Your great reactions to what you read helped me to keep going even when I felt like I wanted to just stop. Grandpa and Grandma, thank you two for all your encouragement! I love you all! You guys rock and I'm so blessed to be part of this family!!

A special thanks to my friends, especially Rachel, who was my first friend who read any of my writings. Thanks to all my other friends for any encouragement they gave me - even if they didn't know I was publishing this book. I kind of kept it a secret...

Thanks to the elves of the Underground! You guys were AWESOME...especially:

Taurehir Coltarian
JLiessa44
Starsinger
Ethaecia (Adelaide) Silver
Leilani Sunblade
Assassin
Tyler Dreamvine
Ryebrynn
Trista Vaporblade

Eruanna
And Draicon

Coming Soon....

Book 2 of the Guardian Chronicles:

Tome of Blood

Made in the USA
Lexington, KY
19 July 2012